DEATH ON THE LINE

THE MACKAY MYSTERIES: BOOK 1

CAROL AMOROSI

GU LEOR PUBLICATIONS

Death on the Line

A Gu Leor Publications book

This book is a work of fiction. Any references to real people, real places, or actual events are used fictionally by the author. Other names, characters, places, and events are of the author's imagination, and any resemblance to actual events, places, or people, living or dead, is entirely coincidental.

For information regarding permission, contact author@carolamorosi.com

Death on the Line/Carol Amorosi

ISBN: 978-1-7368372-1-4 (ebook)

ISBN: 978-1-7368372-2-1 (paperback)

Printed in the USA

First edition, 2021

Dedicated to my parents, who instilled in me the love of a good murder mystery.

My love and appreciation go out to my family, especially my husband, Dave, who always puts up with my craziness, not just during this process.

This could never have happened without my editors, Christina and Doris, and my cover designer, Emily.

I want to thank the members of the 7th Virginia Regiment for their input, especially for the entertaining discussion over beer vs. ale.

And my heartfelt thanks to my fellow authors in the Pickle Jar for their support.

CHAPTER I

SEPTEMBER 1763

"I hate boats," Angus MacKay moaned as he clutched his gut and rolled over. Truthfully, though, before they set sail two weeks ago, Angus had never been aboard a ship. But as the *Packet Hanover* set sail from London, he had felt nauseous. At the time, he thought it was nerves since he had never considered crossing the sea. His stomach had grown more queasy as they left the river and sliced through the channel.

Now, terrible storms ravaged the small craft bobbing on the broad expanse of water. The sky was so dark it was hard to distinguish night from day. Angus' stomach rose and plunged abruptly each time the tiny ship plummeted from the crest of a wave down into the valley below, only to climb steeply on the next surge. The sailor from the hammock above him tried valiantly to get him to eat.

"C'mon," the youthful voice pleaded, piercing the gloom of the berthing space. Angus merely shook his head when the sailor placed the bread crust beside him. Not willing to admit defeat, the sailor offered a small tin cup. "At least take a wee sip o' the ale. I put a bit o' water in it. T'will be good fer ye."

A gentle hand rested on his shoulder. Angus knew nothing he ate or drank would remain in his stomach. He drifted back into oblivion, sure that death was imminent, an unknown burial in the murky depths.

Several days later, Angus roused and discovered something was different, though he wasn't sure what. Lying quietly on the uncomfortable berth, he tried to reason it out. Disoriented, Angus' memory returned in fragments. He remembered he was aboard a ship sailing to the colonies. Slowly, he opened one eye, just a cautious slit. He could see other objects in the tiny cubicle. A shaft of light shone through the small porthole, illuminating five additional hammocks.

The sun was out!

The ship was no longer plunging violently but rocking gently. Angus attempted to sit up and immediately slumped back down again, overcome by a bout of dizziness. The room spun; he was weaker than he realized. He attempted again to sit, taking his time and placing his hand on the bulkhead for balance. Once upright, he remained still for a few moments, trying to regain his composure.

How long has it been?

Angus remembered being slammed up and down and vomiting—yes, he certainly remembered that part—but couldn't remember much after that. After sliding his feet gradually to the decking, he pulled himself up and stood, sucking in a deep breath.

Oh, I should not have done that.

His stomach clenched. The stench from the other men sharing the tiny compartment was vile. Fresh air was what he needed. Angus took his time moving from the berthing, slowly reaching the end of the narrow passage leading to the hatchway. He paused before climbing the ladder, one rung at a time, and stepping onto the deck. The warm sunshine beamed down on his face as he stepped through the hatch. A hint of salt hung in the air.

Steadier, Angus staggered over to the railing after stepping onto the deck. Grasping ahold, he clung to it, gulping more deep breaths to steady himself. The September air was cool. It smelled delightful, the crisp bite reminding him of his childhood summers in Scotland, a vast difference from the smoke-filled dreariness of the London he left behind. While he gazed out over the water, Angus felt better than he had in days. Or had it been weeks? He was not sure how long ago they set sail.

Shielded from the breeze now, he closed his eyes, relishing the autumn sun's warmth on his face. After a few moments, he opened them again and gazed at the horizon. It was almost level; the sea was as smooth as glass. As he stared at the line between sea and sky, he reflected on the various shades of blue and green. He never knew there were so many. Oh, it was beautiful to be alive.

Angus stood at the rail for quite a while, staring at the subtle variation of colors, from vivid green to pale blue. Scattered puffy white clouds flitted lightly across the sky. The ship rocked, its movement ever so slight, but he felt no corresponding motion in his gut. That was a good omen; maybe he would live after all, and all would be well.

"I saw ye up," said a gruff voice at his shoulder. Angus had not heard the sailor from the galley approach. "I was thinkin' mebbe ye could manage a bit o' bread."

"Aye, maybe I could," Angus replied his stomach grumbling in response.

A broad smile lit the old sailor's grizzled face as he held out a crusty roll.

As Angus turned to take the bread, movement to his left caught his eye. Mr. Mason and Mr. Dixon came through the doorway from their cabin, stepping onto the deck.

Oh, no. Not now. I can't face them yet.

Color flamed Angus' cheeks, and he turned away. *What must they think of me?* His uncle had recommended him for their assistant, and Angus longed to prove himself worthy. His fingers fiddled with the end of a rope hanging on the belaying pin in front of him.

The galley hand, noticing his distress, leaned over. "Aye, ye'll understan'. Don't ye fret. The taller one has the same ailment as yerself. He won't eat nuthin' and has the stomach upset as well." He nodded toward Jeremiah Dixon.

Mr. Dixon leaned heavily on Charles Mason as they made their way aft. Dixon's normally ruddy complexion was pale white. His face contrasted with the distinctive red frock coat peeking from under his cloak. Often pausing, the pair progressed slowly towards the stern. Jeremiah Dixon wobbled and shuffled his feet as he walked. Angus wondered at that.

Did other people suffer from seasickness too? Is it more common than I thought? Perhaps it is nothing to fret about after all. Angus wolfed down the bread hungrily. Almost choking on its dryness, he gasped, "Ale?"

"Come with me," the sailor said. He offered his hand. "The name's Jones."

"Angus," he choked out as he followed the sailor to the galley.

After washing down the dry bread with a measure of ale and enjoying a cup of stew, Angus felt almost normal. He ambled around the deck until he reached a comfortable-looking spot, where he plopped down, sprawling back against the anchor chain.

The sea lapped gently at the sides of the craft; the low waves were mesmerizing. As Angus drowsed watching the glorious sunset, his mind drifted to how he had grown from that wee, fatherless boy to boarding a ship sailing to America. He wondered at his fate.

Soft footsteps approached. "Good evenin'," a lilting Irish voice said.

Angus glanced in each direction before realizing the man was speaking to him. "Oh, good evening." He took in the rumpled figure before him, his red hair set aflame in the setting sun. Angus gestured for the stranger to join him.

After reclining against the chain, the man spoke. "I wondered whether we would see ye on the deck. The name's Liam O'Connor." He held out his hand.

Angus accepted the offered hand and shook it firmly. "Angus MacKay," he said. He remembered seeing the man come aboard with a petite wife and two wee boys.

Liam gestured down at his clothing. "Pardon my appearance; I just arose. My family spends their day on the deck while I sleep. It is pretty cramped down below; this gives them extra space to sleep at night." He frowned. Angus read the concern etched on his face.

Angus smiled. "None of us look too good these days." He gestured at the wrinkled shirt and filthy breeches he wore. He found stains on one sleeve of his frock coat he couldn't identify and was unsure he wanted to know.

"What brings ye here?" Angus asked. When passengers met, this was the most often asked question. One way to pass the time was to share their stories; time was one thing they had in plenty.

"We took our chances on making a fresh start in the colonies; though it was a tough decision, we felt it was a risk worth taking. I heard opportunities are available if people are willin' to work hard." At Angus' nod, he continued. "Things ain't good at home now. In fact, 'tis downright hard. I'm the fourth son of a small farmer, so there ain't much there fer me and my family. A couple o' my brothers joined the church, but that ain't the life fer me."

"Aye, myself likewise, though there isn't much left o' my home." Angus sighed and shrugged at Liam.

"My mam's cousins told us of a place called Maryland," Liam told him. "They set it aside for folk of the Catholic faith. I am hoping to get some land there. Sold everything I had fer it."

"Aye. I heard about that. I am on my way with Mr. Dixon and Mr. Mason," he pointed at the two men aft, "to settle a border dispute."

"Oh? Is there trouble there, then?" Liam's face fell.

"Well, the way I understand it is that King Charles granted land to the Calvert family; to establish a Catholic colony, but his son, King Charles II, granted land to the Penns, who wanted to form a Quaker colony. I guess the maps weren't accurate, and the lands overlapped—sometimes, they granted people the same plot o' land. They've been fighting over it for a long time. The tax collectors on both sides are trying to collect their due."

"Ah, well, guess I better avoid land on the border." Though Liam tried to smile, his shoulders sagged.

Angus noticed his disappointment and said, "Well, that is why we are coming." He gestured to the two men. "One is an astronomer, and the other a surveyor. A man named John Byrd created a telescope small enough to move around. It's down below in the hold. Mr. Mason will use it to track the stars so he can locate where he is on the ground. Once they do that, Mr. Dixon will follow with the measurements for the survey."

"I won't pretend I know what ye are talking about," Liam said, "but I hope ye can make it right."

Angus smiled at him. "I will be honest with ye; the surveys afore haven't worked. But this time, with the new-fangled method, everyone is hopeful."

"What will ye be doing?"

"It involves a lot o' mathematics, so I studied with Mr. Byrd for the last few months while they checked whether I could do the calculations. They are important to the accuracy of the locations." Though he was eager at first, Angus now lowered his voice. "Honestly, I'm a little nervous about all this, too."

"*That* I can understand," Liam replied. "My mam always told me if I believed in myself, all things were possible."

Angus nodded. His eyes drifted to the two men aft. Could he do that?

Angus laughed as he wobbled across the deck. They were almost halfway now. He discovered it took time to feel your sea legs firmly planted beneath you, but the nauseating seasickness was a dim memory. Angus found he enjoyed life on the ship, especially chatting with the interesting people aboard. Following the main meal at midday, Angus usually took a nap, then enjoyed the camaraderie of the men until late in the evening. Women and children spent time on the deck during the day, taking in fresh air and sunshine, which allowed them to escape the stench of their cramped quarters.

Liam told him that sickness had taken the lives of four women and six children so far, and families huddled together to stay safe. Angus watched them, so full of hope for opportunities to start a new life in America. However, as they watched other passengers fall ill, Angus saw them pray they would remain healthy and arrive safely. He often saw Liam O'Connor's family and was concerned for his new friend.

Stepping up on deck after a brief nap, Angus almost ran into a young blonde woman with two boys.

"Pardon, me, Ma'am," he said, looking down at her. He recognized Maire, Liam's wife.

She tucked a blonde curl back into her cap. "Oh, 'tis nothing." She peered up at him and smiled. "I had hoped to see ye to thank ye for befriending my Liam. It has been good for him. He worries about this voyage but tries to hide it from me."

"Ah, meeting him has been good for me as well," Angus smiled down at her. He noticed she was quite pretty when she smiled.

One of the boys tugged on her arm. She nodded at the child, then said, "I should go. Ye have a good day." Angus tipped his cap at her.

While the women ruled the day, the night belonged to the men. Angus sprawled next to Liam on the deck after a light supper. The two met regularly in the evenings to stare at the stars and discuss their dreams. Sometimes others joined them, and they played cards or sat around sharing stories. Angus noticed the stocky redhead's freckles were fading from lack of sunshine.

"You're looking somewhat pale this evening," Angus said to his friend. "Feeling alright?"

"Oh, aye," Liam replied. "Just tired o' spending time away from my wee-uns and Maire. 'Tis better this way, I suppose, but I have a mighty hankering fer sunshine." He turned and gave Angus a half-hearted smile. "Another wee lass passed on today."

"I heard," Angus replied grimly.

Footsteps shuffling along distracted them. Mr. Mason assisted Mr. Dixon as the pair inched their way toward them. Mr. Dixon was rarely on deck, he suffered significantly from the ship's motion, but the sea was quiet this evening.

"Good evening, lads," Mr. Mason greeted them, helping Mr. Dixon to a seat.

"Evening." The men shifted to make room.

"Angus here has been telling me ye are going to draw a border between the colonies using the stars. How do ye do that?" Liam was curious.

"Oh, we do it all o' the time at sea," said a sailor checking the rigging nearby. "Any cap'n worth his salt can sail by the stars." He grinned at the men.

"It is a similar process," agreed Mr. Mason.

Jeremiah Dixon sat a little straighter, always ready with an attention-grabbing story. "In different places on earth, you still view the same stars. The ones here are the same ones we studied in England before we set sail, and they will help us identify where we are. Even in the olden times, people viewed the same stars we see tonight. They envisioned pictures in them depicting their heroes and legends."

Angus stared at the millions of stars above, but all he saw were pinpoints of light. No pictures. "Where?"

Sensing he had an interested, although captive audience, Mr. Dixon smiled and sat for a moment. Other men joined them and plopped down beside the group, eager to hear the story. "Well," he said, "we study figures, such as Taurus the Bull, or Gemini, the twins, visible in the night sky. There is also Ursa Major and Ursa Minor, the Great and Small Bears."

The sailor spoke up. "I know them. We sail by 'em. The North Star is part of the Small Bear." The lad stood straighter, seemingly pleased with his knowledge.

"Bears? A bull?" asked Angus. Somewhat skeptical, Angus turned to Liam, who grinned back at him.

"Aye," said Mr. Dixon. "Observe, to the north. Ye will notice stars forming a dipper shape or a bowl with a handle. That one is the larger."

As he spoke, he indicated the proper direction, and each man's gaze followed his hand.

"Oh, aye," replied several of the men.

Angus merely nodded, not seeing anything.

"If you draw a line from the stars of the bowl, ye'll see a star brighter than the others. That is Polaris or the North Star," Mr. Dixon continued.

The young sailor, showing off a bit, pointed in excitement as he ensured the others saw it, too.

"Polaris forms the end of the handle of the smaller dipper. They are part of the Ursa Major and Ursa Minor constellations," Dixon explained, "since they look like bears."

"Well," said Angus, shaking his head. "I suppose I can see those dippers, like a cup with a handle." He leaned closer to Liam and whispered, "but bears? Twins? I cannae see those."

Liam merely smiled but didn't say anything. Angus' smile faded.

"Well, to be honest, we don't see actual images," Mr. Mason said with a scoff. "The figures are merely a method to identify which star is which and its proximity to the others. For example, Orion's dogs are near Orion himself, and it is easy to identify the stars in his belt for reference."

Angus stared blankly overhead, quiet now, not wanting to admit he could not see the figures. He was afraid of disappointing these men who had taken a chance on him.

"Oh, my favorite!" exclaimed Mr. Dixon. "Orion is the mythical mighty hunter, the son of Poseidon, the God of the Sea. He was considered a handsome and strong warrior. Look toward the horizon. Do ye notice three stars in a line? Those stars form his belt. Below are the stars that mark his knees and the cluster that forms his sword. He is carrying his shield and his unbreakable club. Though in some cultures, he carries animal skins instead. He fell in love with Merope..."

He pointed at the stars in the sky as he continued his story, his audience enraptured.

Fascinated by stories of this mighty hunter, Angus daydreamed that he was the hunter. He carried a great bow and a quiver of arrows from his shoulder, a sword at his waist. He pictured himself hunting through forests of towering trees, aiming his bow, and bringing down the largest deer in the woods with a single arrow. He brought the food home to his beautiful wife and children. Angus sighed deeply before noticing that Dixon had finished the story, and the men were saying goodnight.

Storms and rough seas returned for the next two days. While they were not as fierce as the initial storms, they still left Angus' stomach rebelling. He could keep little down except small sips of ale.

Angus ignored the soft knock at the compartment door. When he did not receive an answer, Liam poked his head in, peering into the semi-darkness.

"Angus, ye in here?"

"Aye," Angus grunted back.

"I think ye oughta come up on deck. The storm has passed, and the air is fresh now. Jones says ye ought to be on deck staring at the horizon, not hiding away below."

Angus grunted in reply from his berth, desiring only to remain where he was and be left alone.

"Oh, alright..." he sighed when Liam would not leave him in peace.

On deck, however, he found the fresh air following the storm did help. Angus inhaled deeply. *Jones was right,* Angus thought, holding the railing and staring at the horizon; he felt the ship's movement far less out here, and his stomach settled.

A sudden thump nearby startled him. A sailor squatted where he landed, grinning at Angus.

"End o' my shift up there. Be too dark soon." The man pointed up in explanation.

Angus realized the sailor leaped down from the rigging after being on watch in the crow's nest far above. Angus nodded in amazement.

"Would ye care to go up sometime?" the sailor asked. "The view is grand."

Angus' stomach rolled at the thought as he gazed up at the seemingly endless wooden mast. While the ship rocked slightly at the deck level, the movement was dizzying, magnified over its height. He felt light-headed just looking at it and paled at the thought.

He shook his head. "Thank ye, but nay. I am fine here."

He quickly returned to staring at the horizon, trying to recapture his previous calm. The vessel altered course to adjust for the change in the wind direction, and a spray of water caught Angus squarely in the face. He spat out the salt, wiping his mouth. *Yuck.*

The weeks wore on, and routine provided the rhythm of life aboard the ship. A few more passengers died. Food supplies grew low because of the weeks lost from that initial storm. Often, Angus found himself on deck, staring at the sky if the weather permitted.

When the sea was calm, and he felt up to it, Mr. Dixon regaled them with stories about his adventures with Mr. Mason to places with strange-sounding names.

The ship abruptly rocked in the small waves, and Angus glanced at Mr. Dixon.

"Ah, lad, that is nothing," Mr. Dixon held the glance and sat up straighter.

"Why, it was only two years ago, on our way to Sumatra, that the French attacked the ship Charles and I were aboard. Now that was exciting."

The men leaned closer, waiting for more. Angus looked at Mr. Mason, sitting alone at a distance, writing at his small travel desk. Angus watched his lips curl into a smile.

"We were on our way to a Royal Observatory project tracking the transit of Venus. As our ship, the wee *HMS Seahorse,* sailed south, a French ship appeared on the horizon. They pulled along broadside and fired their cannons. Our brave captain shot back. Both ships were heavily damaged, but neither of them sank. We made our way back to the port for repairs. But the delay required us to take our readings from the Cape of Good Hope instead."

Caught up in the story, Angus glanced again at Mr. Mason and watched him shake his head and chuckle as he wrote in his journal. Angus was in awe of these men.

On other nights, the men played games of cards, a precious item aboard the ship. Sailors shared them in the evening when they were off duty.

"Ah, at last, I won a trick," shouted Liam.

"Must be cheatin'," one man teased and nudged him in the ribs. Liam punched him on the shoulder as he dealt another hand of Whist.

It was November now. Each day was colder, and the card games and storytelling had moved to a small space below deck. Angus left the men and reclined on the upper deck, propped against the anchor chain. As he pulled his greatcoat tighter about himself, he stared at those same three stars. Orion's belt became easier to find, but the rest of the figure remained elusive. Determined and lying still, he closed one eye and peered at the sky. Then he tried closing the other eye instead and searching again.

"Ah, ye daft wee eejit," he muttered. His dialect often came out when he was frustrated. "If ye cannae see it with both eyes, what makes ye believe ye can with one?" In exasperation, he gave up and headed to his berth.

Two nights later, following a supper of a thin broth and dried biscuits, Angus wandered alone on deck. Supper was meager, though his shrinking stomach felt satisfied, nonetheless. He pulled the rope that now kept his breeches up a little tighter and straightened his greatcoat about him. Tonight was their last night at sea. They would reach the river the next day.

Unlike Jeremiah Dixon, Mr. Mason was much more reserved. Angus held him in high regard. Though chilly, the evening was clear, and Angus hoped to see Mr. Mason on deck with his journal and writing desk.

Tonight was the night he would speak to him. His palms sweated despite the cold. The man's exploits fascinated him, and Angus dreamed of getting to know him better. *How do I start the conversation? Perhaps a comment on the weather...*

His eye caught movement aft, and Angus turned, breaking the spell. Sneaking furtively along in the dark was a short, stocky crewman peering first one way and then another. Angus watched a taller, slender sailor approach the crewman briskly from the starboard side. The wind blew his cape about him. Pausing and scanning the deck, the two men met. Angus remained where he was in the shadows. Curious, he watched. Glancing first forward, then aft, the taller man bent to speak to the other crewman, withdrawing a package hidden beneath his cape and handing it to him. The sailor, in turn, pulled a small box from beneath his cloak and handed it over in exchange for the package. The sailors parted as furtively as they met.

As the men separated, Mr. Mason stepped through the doorway onto the deck. Disappointment flooded Angus, who was unsure precisely what he had witnessed. How could he explain it to someone else? Was it necessary to report? Or just private business between two men?

Doubt set in as Mr. Mason approached. "Good evening," Mr. Mason said and passed by on his journey toward the stern.

"Good evening, Sir," Angus replied. Hanging his head, Angus hurried forward and stood at the rail.

His mind reeled. *What were those men up to? They obviously did not wish to be seen. Or am I making too much of it?*

It was much colder tonight. Angus pulled his greatcoat tighter as he gazed at the dark clouds gathering on the western horizon. He hoped they would arrive before that storm.

CHAPTER 2

Later, Angus couldn't shake the nagging doubt that he hadn't said anything. And to top it off, biting rain hit his face as Angus stepped out on the deck. But he barely noticed. The heavily forested shoreline was all he saw, and he crossed himself as he offered a prayer of thanks for their arrival. The raging storm reached them as the vessel sailed up the Delaware River. Angus was pleased to find the boat remained relatively level in the river, unlike at sea. However, the wind was bitterly cold. Lightning flashed overhead, followed instantaneously by violent claps of thunder that rocked the ship's hull as it made its way along. He returned below deck, worried about lightning striking the mast.

He stared through the porthole at the unchanging scenery, watching mile after mile of soaring trees along the shoreline, which seemed to stretch forever. Over time, peering through the rain, he noticed occasional log or stone cabins set in small clearings. Further along, the view opened to small clusters of structures and muddy-looking roads before awarding him his first glimpse of a moderately sized port. Smiling at the sight before him, he took a deep breath of relief. Finally, he had made it to America.

Soon, the *Packet Hanover* arrived at a bustling, dirty-looking wharf. Angus stood in the hatchway, looking out.

"We're in Marcus Hook," a passing sailor told him. "We can't go no further. Larger sea vessels can't get up the river. We'll off-load here."

The rain slacked off, and Angus hurried onto the deck, anxious to see the new world. Huddled from the wind, he watched the sailors secure the ship along the wharf. The cold air was like ice hitting his face, but its smell was crisp and refreshing. It was like the brisk winters of his youth in Scotland and far better than London's smoke-filled air that had recently filled his lungs. He noticed a cluster of warehouses set back from the wharf, and beyond them were numerous tiny houses. A community had grown up around the port.

Mr. Mason and Mr. Dixon had expected the commissioners from Philadelphia to meet the ship, but no one came. Mr. Dixon briskly strode across to Angus.

"We've spoken to the captain. It looks like we are on our own here. He told us where we could lease horses to get to Philadelphia. We'll need to go there to inform the commissioners of our arrival." He patted Angus on the shoulder. "I'm sorry, ye will need to remain. The harbormaster will assist ye in storing the goods."

The pair left Angus with their cargo and hurried off to find the commissioners. Angus' shoulders sagged as he watched them depart. In their absence, he would arrange for transporting the delicate instruments, which were still wrapped in bedding and stored in crates in the hold.

The storm picked up as he watched the other passengers disembark and find transport to the city twenty miles away. It was raining in earnest now; the large drops drummed on the wooden deck. Angus scurried below.

The O'Connors were among the last to go down the gangway. With a lump in his throat, Angus shook hands with Liam and gave his wife,

Maire, a brief hug. He didn't know if he would ever see them again, but he hoped so.

"All the best, my friend," he said to Liam as they shook hands. Liam tried to smile.

Stormy weather raged, and they shoved off to anchor in the river to ensure the vessel would not be thrust against the pier. Angus was trapped, able to see land but forced to remain aboard the ship. He couldn't wait to get to Philadelphia and see the city.

"My favorite is Christ Church," said Smith, a sailor, as he dealt the next hand of Whist that evening after supper. "That steeple reaches up to heaven."

"Nay, it has to be the government building. I never saw so many red bricks in one place in my life," argued Jones.

Angus eagerly looked forward to seeing these sites and grew weary of being cooped up onboard. However, he made good use of the time by writing a letter to his aunt and uncle in London, informing them of his safe arrival. Before Angus sealed it, he scribbled a quick note to his cousin, Rose, about the interesting people he met. When he finished, he delivered the letter to Captain Falconer for his return voyage.

He paced the deck in the cold, misty rain on the third day, feeling like a caged animal. This feeling worsened as he noticed the O'Connor family on shore, climbing into a wagon. He waved goodbye, his eyes following them until they disappeared.

When Angus awoke the following day, there were glimpses of blue sky outside the porthole. *The storm has passed!* Scrambling up on deck, he saw the crew heaving up the heavy anchor. Small boats had attached lines to pull the ship to the pier to unload their cargo.

Standing at the rail provided a splendid view of the harbor where men scurried about unloading other ships and moving cargo to and from warehouses. Angus spied two of the most intriguing-looking men near the harbor wall. Both were lean and rather tall, but instead of the great coat and breeches he was used to seeing gentlemen wear, these two wore what resembled huge pelts. *What kind of animal is that?* Animal skin covered their legs below the furs, quite different from Angus' breeches, with footwear of similar material. But their most striking features were their partially shaved heads, which sported a long, black braid that curled across each man's shoulder. Neither man wore a cap. Their skin reminded him of burnished copper.

These must be Indians, Angus thought.

Angus had heard tales of the native people and descriptions of their appearance. African slaves were common enough in London, but these men were different. He knew some English colonists traded with the natives, finding them honest. But others believed they were dangerous heathens, citing a recent war between England and France in which tribes fought for each side. This war had only recently ended, though fighting continued in the ensuing months. Much discussion in London had been over whether it was safe for the astronomers to come. While the sailors secured the ship, Angus studied the men in fascination as they spoke together on the wharf.

The ship buzzed with activity as workers unloaded crates and barrels from the hold. Sailors from other vessels joined the bustling commotion as their cargoes of rum and sugar cane from the islands were off-loaded. The harbormaster would safely lock up the barrels of rum. The *Packet Hanover* carried crates of mail, wool and linen fabrics, tea, glass, china, and other items imported from England. Angus stared in wide-eyed amazement at the harbor's workings, wondering at the crates full of items from all over the world.

Jones paused next to him and pointed at a nearby ship. "Aye, Laddie, now there's the ship to be aboard. *The Two Brothers*. She's full o' Madeira."

Another sailor paused, saying, "Aye, but they'll have to deal with John Swift, and that is nay a man I care to deal with." Seeing the confusion on Angus' face, he added, "The Customs man. He's well known in these parts as a dangerous man to cross."

Angus smiled. "Ah, I understand."

Things eventually quieted down. After ten weeks aboard the ship, Angus was excited to escape and explore—but he had work to do first. To his dismay, he looked down at his clothing and noted his filthy and rumpled appearance. His sleeve cuffs were far from white; there was another new stain on his frock coat and streaks on his hose beneath his dirty breeches. Well, there was no hope for it; he buttoned his greatcoat, which hid most of the stains, and proceeded down the gangway.

"Thank goodness for cold weather," he mused as he stepped onto solid ground.

His first steps on land jarred his bones. It was disconcerting how the world remained solid and unyielding. *I waddle like a drunk, staggering about after too much wine.* As he watched the people on the wharf, he was relieved to realize he didn't look any rougher than anyone else—and everyone coming off the ships was staggering about as they adjusted to solid ground. With a deep breath, he straightened his shoulders and headed to the harbormaster's office.

"Aye, Laddie, ye can store yer equipment in the small warehouse out back a few nights. It'll cost ye one pound six shillings." Angus had no choice but to accept. Luckily, Mr. Dixon had given him funds to cover these expenses.

"Thank ye, sir," he took the receipt, "can ye recommend somewhere to stay and a carter to transport the crates to Philadelphia?"

"Aye. If ye take the second street yonder, the locals call it Discord Lane. Ye can find both. I recommend Will and Sons for cartin' yer goods."

"Discord Lane? An odd name," Angus said.

The man smiled. "Ah, it dates from when Blackbeard, the pirate, sailed into the harbor, avoiding the Customs man upriver."

Angus shivered, remembering the stories of Blackbeard the sailors sometimes told in the evening. Angus hadn't believed them to be true at the time. Now he wondered.

He thanked the man and headed toward Discord Lane.

Angus rode in the wagon a week after arriving as their instruments, baggage, and supplies were brought to Philadelphia. He located a warehouse near the smaller waterfront in the city where he could store the crates. While Mr. Mason and Mr. Dixon stayed at the *George and Dragon Inn*, Angus found cheaper lodging in a seedy guesthouse nearby, close to their belongings. A week after their arrival, he was finally free to explore.

To Angus' surprise, Philadelphia was not significantly different from towns in England, though it was smaller than London. He saw townsfolk dressed similarly to Londoners, though their clothing was somewhat outdated and not so elegant. Angus noticed only a few striped gowns on the women here. They were all the rage in London, with stripes going in every direction. And the frock coats the men wore here reached mid-thigh, whereas, in England, they had grown shorter. He felt a bit better now about his attire as he exited his lodgings, heading into town.

Dodging puddles, Angus strolled along the cobblestone streets past two- and three-story brick row houses and shops with Georgian arches over their doorways, their windows lined in rigid symmetry. *These are like the ones in London.* However, they were more stylish than he remembered in Scotland, where there were many old, gray buildings and few new ones. The most significant difference, he noted, was that everything here was quite new. No old buildings squatted squarely between the recent constructions here—no ghosts of the past.

Leading away from the waterfront were markets heading toward High Street; however, not much was available in November. Angus imagined it would be a busy place with plenty of fruit and vegetables available during the spring and summer. He imagined the loud vendors hawking their wares. With the river nearby, there would be fish as well. He couldn't wait to see what would be on offer then. Today, only a handful of women in drab-colored cloaks huddled out of the wind in the dreary stalls in the center, selling woolen goods. In the distance, he spied impressive-looking buildings and tall church steeples. He was surprised. *I understood this was Quaker territory.*

A few blocks in, the steeple of Christ Church became visible, towering above everything around it. Smith was right; it was tall! About two hundred feet, Angus guessed. He stood for a moment, impressed, studying the church. Aside from the steeple, the brick building was imposing, with its classical Georgian symmetry and arched windows.

Turning to continue his tour, he recognized a familiar face emerge from a building further down the lane. It was Liam, his shoulders hunched, his head hanging. Angus hurried to catch up to his friend.

"Liam!" he called out. "Wait."

Liam turned and waved, a large smile lighting up his face. "Well met. I see you escaped from prison." He joked and held out his hand.

"Aye, 'tis good to be free," Angus replied, clasping his friend's hand. "What is the news with ye?"

"Och, worse than I reckoned. We hoped to reach Maryland, but it will cost more than I expected. I'm looking fer work but not havin' much luck." Liam hung his head and then shrugged it off, looking up at Angus.

"Ye'll find something, I'm sure," Angus said hopefully. "Maire good? The boys?"

"Aye, Mrs. Smith, a friend of Jones, has put us up in her home near the markets. Her sons are grown, and she has a spare room. She is spoilin' my boys."

"Ye aren't far from me then. I'm near the warehouses along the waterfront at Mrs. Frisk's establishment. I'll be there for a few days, as far as I know. Stop by if ye can."

With that, the friends parted. Angus hoped to see him again soon. Seeing more spires off to his left, Angus turned down Fifth Street toward a large red brick building with a domed tower. The imposing structure had two side buildings connected by arcades. *This must be the government building Jones mentioned*. Mr. Mason and Mr. Dixon were meeting the commissioners there. It certainly looked official.

The church bell rang as he thought of the men in their meeting. It was three o'clock. He ought to return and stay near the equipment, he realized. Passing the building, he turned down Cypress towards the waterfront.

Along the way, he passed St. Mary's Catholic Church, which was currently under construction. The whole city had a newness about it everywhere he looked. A team of horses pulling a heavy wagon approached.

"Move out o' the way!" the driver hollered at Angus, who realized he stood in its path.

"Sorry!" Angus dove out of the way. The team hit a puddle as they thundered along. A spray of water hit Angus, knocking off his tricorn hat. At least his heavy greatcoat took the brunt of the shower of muddy water.

He shook himself off, scooped up his hat, and proceeded along the road, marveling how much cleaner it was than London. He took a nice deep breath of the crisp, clean air.

His stomach rumbled. Angus felt in his pocket and found a few shillings. Ahead stood a small tavern near the corner, which looked cleaner than the ones he noticed near his lodgings. The equipment could wait a bit longer, so he approached the tavern.

A huge man wearing a dirty white apron stormed through the door, half-dragging a drunk outside. "Get out," growled the tavernkeeper, "and stay out. I have told ye afore ye ain't welcome here. Do yer drinkin' somewhere else."

As he approached the tavern, the two natives Angus noticed in the port rounded the corner. The proprietor threw the drunk to the ground.

"Ye don't know who yer dealin' with; this ain't done yet," the drunk screamed at the owner as he fell at the natives' feet.

In a drunken rage, the man rose, swinging his fists as he staggered to his feet and noticed the natives for the first time.

"It is *yer* damn fault," he growled at them, then roared off down the street.

The natives shrugged at each other, then continued past the large crowd gathering in front of the tavern.

Angus watched in amazement. The two natives simply walked away. They had done nothing, yet they took the man's accusations in stride. Angus remained until they were out of sight, realizing that America may look like home, but it was very different.

Still hungry, Angus entered *The Rose* tavern, found a table near the large hearth, and warmed his hands by the fire. He could smell stale beer inside the smoke-filled room, but wafting above rose the enticing aroma of fresh-baked bread. The smell was irresistible. After the chilly day, he felt cozy and warm in the quiet tavern. Angus slipped his coat from his shoulders and hung it to dry on a peg near the fire. It was well after the two o'clock main meal. Only a few white-haired men remained at one table, sipping their beer, while two grizzled older men played cards in the corner.

The tavernkeeper, the man in the apron outside, brought over a steaming bowl of stew, some crusty fresh bread, and a pint of beer. The tantalizing aroma swirling up with the steam reached Angus' nose. The food smelled so much better than the meager slop he had so recently enjoyed. He blew on the spoon, yet still, he winced as the hot liquid burned his lip.

Curious, Angus asked, "What was that about? Outside?"

"Ah, ye mean Gil?" the tavernkeeper asked. "He comes here from Lancaster sometimes, looking fer work. Nuthin' but a drunkard. He takes after his old man who worked at the courthouse afore drink got the better o' him. Big chip on his shoulder that young 'un. He blames everyone else for his troubles, especially the Indians."

"Aye, I know the type," agreed Angus. He grew up with relatives like that after his father was killed. His father was a Scot who married an English woman during the Scottish rebellion. When his father died in the battle at Culloden, his family moved around amongst Scottish and

English family members. Whenever there was trouble, the family blamed Angus. With his mixed blood, he was an easy target.

The stout tavernkeeper suggested he have some lovely bread pudding, and with the cinnamon aroma floating under his nose, how could he refuse? *If I keep eating like this, I won't need that rope for my breeches.*

He was nice and warm, and with a full stomach, Angus decided it was time to return to his lodgings. He paid the man and pulled on his greatcoat as he stepped onto the street. Soon Angus spied the government building's dome. Realizing he had walked in the wrong direction, he turned around.

Angus was nearing the warehouse when a shuffling to his right caught his attention. Down a dim alleyway lurked a man hidden in the shadows. Crossing the alley, Angus noticed the man was missing his left arm. The sight of him caused a prickling sensation in the hair on his neck. Angus' senses were now on full alert.

His gran used to talk about the Highlander's ability to sense something was amiss. Angus took a step, shaking his head—when he observed a second man approach the first. He immediately recognized him as the taller of the sailors he witnessed secretly exchanging packages on the ship.

Angus paused, pretending to admire the shop window on the corner as the taller man handed a box to the first man. The men leaned furtively toward each other, speaking quietly before slipping off down the alley, going their separate ways.

The hair on Angus' arms tingled, and a sense of foreboding filled him. He was convinced that he should have mentioned that exchange to Captain Falconer before they arrived. Though, admittedly, he was still unsure exactly what he had seen or whether it was any of his business. He emerged into the warehouse district, trying to put the situation behind him.

Wary, Angus remained near the warehouse for the next two days. He was unsure what had occurred between those men, but he sensed a need to keep a close eye on the instruments. Each day, he checked their cargo and only ventured out to eat at *The Anchor*, a seedy tavern near the small harbor. Their beer was excellent, even if the food was not. It was greasy, and the stench of unwashed bodies from the warehouse workers was overwhelming. Still, the window provided a safe lookout, and Angus was close enough to react if he noticed anything amiss.

It had been a week since he reached the city when Angus received word from Charles Mason that they would meet him at the warehouse the following morning to unpack the equipment and check it for any damage.

As he approached *The Anchor*, he saw Liam passing by and invited him to join him. Liam hesitated.

"Ye look right starved. Let me buy us a bowl of stew and a pint," Angus offered, understanding his friend's situation.

"Thank ye, I'd enjoy the company," Liam gratefully accepted. While they ate, they regaled each other with their latest adventures. Ultimately, Angus asked Liam's opinion on what he had seen between the two men.

"Seems a bit shady to me," Liam said, nodding in agreement after Angus described the events. He took a swig of his beer.

"Aye, to me as well. Something was not quite right," responded Angus.

"But it may not be anythin' to do with yer work," Liam added. "Could be anythin'. I know there was mail aboard as well as items from England. Might be doin' some smugglin'. I hear that is common."

"True enough." Angus let the subject drop. "What is new with ye?"

Liam shrugged. "I worked unloading a small ship yesterday but not much else. I am hopin' on another tomorrow."

Angus hoped things would work out for his friend. They finished their meal and went their separate ways.

"Stop by for a visit," Angus called out as they parted, vowing to keep in touch. Angus returned to his room, having already checked on the equipment.

As promised, Mr. Mason and Mr. Dixon arrived early the following day. The three men spent the next few days unloading the delicate cargo, inspecting each piece thoroughly for damage. Once they determined everything was in working order, arrangements were made for their transport, with the fragile zenith sector packed in bedding while they loaded the other items onto horse-drawn carts.

"Well, after much discussion, they agreed the mandated southernmost point of the city is the north wall of a house on the corner of Second Street and Cedar, known as the Plumstead-Huddle house," Mr. Mason informed Angus as they loaded the wagon.

"We will start our observations from that point, provided the Maryland commissioners agree when we meet with them next week," added Mr. Dixon.

Angus nodded. The location details did not matter to him; he was anxious to leave the waterfront and start working. They would hire local people along the way as the project progressed. Before leaving, Angus asked Mr. Mason's permission to hire Liam as a laborer, which was willingly granted.

On the move again, they traveled the short distance to the Plumstead-Huddle house, a large three-story structure filling the lot. After much debate, Mr. Mason declared they would construct their observatory on the empty lot across the street, as there was no space on the property.

Mr. Mason and Mr. Dixon left for their meeting with the Marylanders and returned a few days later after receiving their approval of the site's location. John Loxley, the carpenter, arrived and immediately began working, with Angus and Liam assisting him.

The observatory was completed by mid-December, though the weather had frequently delayed construction. A terrible snowstorm reached the town the day they finished, preventing them from starting their observations for an additional two nights. Angus found small tasks to help Mr. Dixon. Liam returned to the warehouse district to pick up work as he could.

"Don't worry, lad," Mr. Dixon told him. "We'll need your help again." Liam grinned.

When the snowstorm finally ceased, the astronomers unpacked and calibrated the instruments. On the 16th, they finally began their work, taking readings on their relative relationship to the individual stars.

The terms of the grant specified the border to be the fortieth parallel. Their work would be an ongoing effort to compute that latitude's exact position based on observations of the stars. This required several nights of viewing to average the margin of error—which was Angus' responsibility. Being the starting point, accuracy in defining the location was of the utmost importance.

The observatory, with its wooden walls and canvas roof, provided little in the way of comfort. During their nightly observations, tracking the stars, they were kept warm with the aid of a small brazier. Soon, the three men fell into a companionable routine.

"I'll fetch some wood from the lean-to," Angus said. He stepped out into the bitter cold and quickly grabbed an armful of the fatwood to keep them warm.

Mr. Mason was on his back on blankets on the ground beneath the lens of the new zenith sector. This was a telescope mounted on a base that pointed vertically at the sky. The astronomer would track each star using the reticule, or crosshairs, in the lens. A candle or spirit lamp was used to illuminate the reticule.

Angus took turns writing down the readings and holding the candle for Mr. Dixon while he adjusted the leveling screws. Mr. Mason recently explained they were testing the accuracy of the new six-foot lens on the sector.

Finished with their observations in the wee hours of the morning, Angus handed Mr. Mason his hat as he and Mr. Dixon stepped outside. The two men usually slept late in the home of a nearby proprietor. Angus slept inside the observatory to watch the equipment and save the money he was earning.

"Thank ye, good work tonight." Taking his hat, Mr. Mason smiled at Angus as he left. Once the men were outside, Angus did a little twirl, grinning from ear to ear. He was growing more comfortable in Mr. Mason's presence. This compliment was the icing on the cake.

After several consecutive late nights, the astronomers slept later than usual the following morning. Mr. Dixon arrived carrying a jug wrapped in fabric containing bitter, hot coffee.

"Charles will be along directly. I know ye prefer tea, but this is what I could get." He smiled at Angus and offered him a ceramic mug. "Once we pinpoint this location, the next phase will be to move fifteen miles south," Mr. Dixon explained while they calibrated their equipment. "At that point, the commissioners are providing local tribesmen as guides. The Indians are familiar with the territory and will be helpful to us."

Three men overheard this as they passed by, heading down Cedar Street. They stopped and stared at the observatory.

"I certainly wouldn't trust them," one snarled, slurring his words.

Mr. Dixon straightened and turned toward them. "And why not?"

"Them lazy Indians will cheat ye blind."

Puzzled, Angus stepped toward the men. He recognized one of them as the drunk he'd seen thrown out of *The Rose*. "Then why would the commissioners recommend them?"

"I dunno, they're lazy, worthless heathens." With his pals at his side nodding in agreement, the man stepped up to Angus. "They'd much rather kill ye than work with ye."

"I don't believe that," Angus replied. He remembered the men he saw and how they ignored the drunk's accusations.

"Well, ye'll have to learn for yerself then, won't ye? They rob ye and kill ye. Then they scalp ye. I bet they'd love them curly red locks of yours." Angus stood his ground at first.

Then the man reached up and ran his finger in a slitting gesture across Angus' forehead. When Angus gulped and stepped back, the man smiled. He grabbed the hat from his friend's head, revealing a scar on the man's forehead as he pretended to scalp him, running his finger along his hair and dragging it back to the nape of his neck.

Angus swallowed. As the men staggered down the road, laughing at their antics, Angus subconsciously reached up and tucked his hair, which was tied back with a ribbon, under his cap.

"Don't pay them any mind, Lad," Mr. Dixon told him. "They are just drunks."

Angus smiled but noticed Mr. Dixon's face had paled at the men's actions.

An hour later, as they returned their instruments to the observatory, a man running by stopped and stood gasping. The men offered him a seat.

"Have ye heard the news?" he asked, collecting himself. "Six days ago, a group of men from Paxton Township in Lancaster County raided the Conestoga Nation's village and burned it to the ground. Six tribe members were killed and scalped, and others kidnapped—fortunately, most residents were not there." Stranded by the same snowstorm plaguing the astronomers, the natives had not returned home but fled to friends for safety, only to find devastation on their return.

Upon hearing this news, Angus trembled. While he was still upset at the men's actions earlier that morning, he tried not to take them seriously. Hearing this was another matter, however. He began to wonder if, perhaps, he should not have come. Maybe America was not as safe as they told them.

"I do not understand how people can hate one another that way," Mr. Dixon said to Angus.

But Angus only gulped in reply. He had experienced it firsthand.

CHAPTER 3

The man who brought the terrible news of the attack on the tribe caught his breath before he continued, his voice trembling, "I hear tell women were taken, but I'm not sure 'bout that." His story told, he leaned against a tree and stared at the ground. The man's voice had grown hoarse from telling his gruesome tale. His hand trembled as he wiped his brow.

Angus felt a sharp pain in the pit of his stomach as he collapsed onto the large crate behind him. The sky was a dull, leaden gray, matching his mood.

Memories of that cave above their home in the hills near Inverness flooded back—the piercing screams and acrid smoke from those days long ago. The cave was chilly, dark, and damp, though the sun shone brightly on that April day. Many clan members fled to the hills, but not everyone escaped in time.

Crouched in the dank depths with his mother, Gran, and wee sister, six-year-old Angus heard the screams of the people below ringing in his ears. His sister, Fiona, cried in his mother's arms as she tried to soothe her. While he did not understand the events happening below, Angus tried to be brave. He bit down on his quivering lip.

Sitting in Philadelphia, Angus was transported to that hillside again. He felt the dampness anew and heard the screams, which continued no matter how deeply he had retreated into the cave. Angus covered his ears with his hands, trying to block the sound. He smelled the smoke, but today, he was safe in Philadelphia, and the smoke swirling around him wafted from the surrounding chimneys.

And there were no screams.

Slowly, Angus lowered his hands from his ears while the messenger resumed his story.

"The Conestoga have lived here forever," he explained to the newcomers. "They are part of the Susquehannock confederation. Some even turned Christian. They were never the enemy."

Neither were we, thought Angus. He clasped his hands to stop their shaking.

Angus' mind was awash with doubts; he wondered why he thought coming here would make a difference. What made him think he could prove himself worthy in such an endeavor? He wanted to go home.

Liam arrived in time to hear the tale. Angus gasped, and Liam turned to him with a puzzled expression. He kneeled on the hard ground beside him.

"Are ye alright, Angus?" Liam whispered as he lay a hand on his arm. Mr. Dixon watched, then edged closer and gestured for Liam to take Angus away. He slipped him some coins. Liam took them and nodded.

"I think we should go sit somewhere warm. It's *my* turn to buy *ye* a pint," Liam told his friend. There was no response.

Angus seemed very far away while Liam helped him to his feet. They walked together to the tavern a few doors down the lane. Liam stamped his feet as he entered so as not to track in the snow. As if in a trance, Angus mechanically followed suit, stomping his feet with no awareness of his actions. It was not yet mealtime, so tables were available near the fire, where Liam helped Angus out of his heavy greatcoat and into a chair. Angus was still shivering. Liam gestured to the tavernkeeper for two pints of cider and removed his cloak before sitting next to his friend. He waited silently, sipping his drink until Angus was ready to speak. The tavern was so quiet Liam could hear the ticking of the oversized clock above them on the mantle.

Frozen in place, unable to speak, the number of people he would disappoint if he left dawned on Angus. What would Mr. Mason and Mr. Dixon, the men he so admired, think of him? He envisioned the look on his uncle's face after putting his reputation on the line in recommending Angus for the position. And what of himself? Could he accept another failure?

Eventually, Angus roused and reached for the cider, taking a big swig. "Thank ye," he said and took another sip.

Liam nodded.

"I was but six, ye ken," Angus began slowly. "At that age, the idea of fighting for a king sounded heroic. My pa and others fought for our freedom and our way of life. But later, word trickled in that the Army slaughtered our brave men on the moor at Culloden."

He paused a moment. "I didna understand then what it was all about, only that the men in the red coats hated us. I didna ken why." Angus' dialect crept back into the proper speech he had practiced so hard. He paused, taking a deep pull on the cider, and wiped his mouth with the back of his hand.

"No word of my pa reached us at first. Three days later, the soldiers came through the clan lands with a vengeance, imprisoning any clan members they found, slaughtering any resistance, and raping the women before taking some of them away. Word reached us ahead of the troops, allowing us a chance to escape."

Liam blanched at the story he was hearing. Caught up in his memories, Angus struggled to get the words out.

"We hid in the caves in the cliffs above; mere sheep tracks were the only way up those hills... Mam, Gran, my sister Fiona, and some cousins. The soldiers were unfamiliar with the area and probably decided the vertical hills were too steep. They didna search up there. Saved many lives on account o' that."

When Angus paused again, Liam reached across and rested his hand on his arm. "I canna imagine..."

"They rounded up all the men, even the elders. They stole our possessions and herded up our beasts. But the worst, the worst, was the women... their screams still ring in my ears."

"I'm trying to understand," Liam spoke after a few moments. "I'm also a Catholic, as ye ken. Folk nearby were persecuted and often left to starve. We were forced off our land but faced nothing like this." He gazed sympathetically at his friend in silence, letting him finish his tale.

"My mam herself was English. I didna understand at the time why much of the clan hated us. And I didn't learn until years later that some clansmen were fighting with the English soldiers. So it wasna just Mam they hated, but my pa too, our way of life. The other lads called me names. They wouldna let me go hunting with them. I was always in trouble."

He looked down sheepishly, "I suppose I brought some on myself. When I was ten, wee Fiona, my sister, died of a fever. My mam was never the same again and just wasted away."

He swallowed the cider, saying softly, "I wanted to fight, to be a hero. My pa's last words to me were, 'be a hero and take care of your mother.' I failed as the man o' the family."

"Ye were a child! None of that was your fault, Angus," said Liam. He paused in thought. "But I guess ye understand what happened to the Conestoga yesterday. Mrs. Smith told Maire and me about those folks in Paxton the other day. A preacher named Elder is riling up folks and sending letters to the governor. I don't think anyone expected something like this, though I guess ye'd understand it better than most."

He leaned toward Angus before he continued. "But ye a failure? Nay, it looks like ye turned out well to me. I won't even pretend to understand that work ye do but look what Mr. Mason and Mr. Dixon are doin'. And ye are a part of it."

"Aye, I suppose. One good thing came out of it." Angus smiled wryly. "I hid out with the monks who took pity on me. They taught me to read and write and do figures. I loved the figuring. It came so easily to me and was something my cousins couldna do. I felt special."

"Well, that's grand. And look where it got ye today."

And with that realization, Angus knew he would stay to face his fears and prove himself. He crossed his fingers that all would be well.

Angus and Liam remained in front of the warm fire, sipping their ciders. After a while, Angus rose.

Liam studied him, "yer color's returned to normal."

Angus looked down and noticed his hands were no longer trembling.

"Thank ye, Liam. Ye are a true friend, but I must get back. I have work to do."

Liam settled up with the tavernkeeper and bundled against the cold; they headed out into the dreary afternoon.

That evening the clouds dissipated, and Angus stared at the night sky. Inside the observatory, Mr. Mason and Mr. Dixon took their observations through the zenith sector's long cylindrical tube. The weather was clear; the stars shining brightly overhead were easily visible, even to the naked eye. Angus tugged his greatcoat tighter and shrugged. Tonight, he found Orion's belt easily. Though the hunter remained elusive, he felt more grounded in that minor achievement. He stared at the three twinkling stars until late at night.

Days passed, and life fell into a routine. Sundays were a day of rest, and Angus tried to spend time with Liam and his family after attending mass. On other days, he threw himself into his work on calculations, running errands, or other tasks as required. Mr. Mason and Mr. Dixon tracked the stars whenever the sky was clear.

This survey was the first test for the newly designed zenith sector, which they would use to observe the stars directly overhead as they passed through the peak of their arc across the night sky. Before this, the sheer size of the telescope prevented its usage outside of large observatories. John Byrd, in London, had recently developed this model, which could be transported easily. Angus knew a little about the equipment. Mr. Byrd was a friend of his uncle, and Angus had helped in his shop in London. With this being its trial run, everyone was eager to see the results "the stargazers," as the locals called them, would achieve.

After Mr. Mason, the lead astronomer, finished his observations, Mr. Dixon, a brilliant mathematician, checked the raw data, then Angus compiled it, looking for further discrepancies. He threw himself into the calculations required to minimize the margin of error. Surrounded by numbers, he was distracted from the real world's troubles. He had mathematical problems to solve instead.

Angus blew on his numb fingers as he rose from the table a few days later. He stretched his back and headed to re-stoke the small brazier in the corner. Concentrating on the numbers, he had let the fire die. The woodpile inside was low, so Angus stepped outside to grab more from under the lean-to. The frigid air burned his lungs.

Someone was standing at the corner, but he slipped into the late afternoon shadows when Angus emerged. But the stranger was not quick enough. Angus recognized him as the one-armed man. He had noticed him lurking in the shadows before, and the hair on the back of his neck rose each time.

Ten days after the first attack on the Conestoga, Angus was sitting on a wooden chair at a makeshift table, surrounded by papers covered with calculations. He ran his fingers through his auburn hair and was startled when Liam burst into the observatory, slamming the door open.

"What's with ye?" Angus asked. "At least ye could close the door. Ye are letting in the cold air."

He rose to close the door. It was then he glimpsed Liam's face. His ordinarily ruddy complexion was pale white. Angus stopped in his tracks.

"What is it?"

Liam reached back and closed the door, taking a moment to catch his breath. "Ye have not heard? There was another attack yesterday. I wanted to see whether ye were alright."

"Oh?" Angus slowly sank back down on the chair, his knees weak.

"The women and some o' the elders took shelter in the jail in Lancaster Town after the previous raid. With their village destroyed, the people thought they'd be safer there. Yesterday, thirty men with rifles, tomahawks, and scalping knives rode through the town. They busted down the jail door and killed several Conestoga inside." Liam stuttered as he tried to deliver the news. "Fourteen dead. The elders were shot and scalped."

"In the town? And no one did anything?" Angus saw Liam's hand shaking and realized his own were trembling. He felt as if someone had punched him in the gut.

"Aye, but what could townsfolk do against heavily armed men?" Liam asked. "They say that Reverend Elder encouraged them."

"My God," muttered Angus. His voice shook with emotion. He swallowed. After Liam left, his mind refused to allow him the peace he usually found in the numbers.

Despite his misgivings, Angus chose to remain and help the astronomers complete their observations. He had nowhere to go. Once compiled and accepted, the pair would proceed with the next phase. Methodical as ever, Mr. Mason wanted to confirm the final accuracy himself, leaving Angus little to do for the time being.

On January 2nd, the astronomers proclaimed that the proper latitude of Philadelphia's southernmost point was 39° 56′ 29.1″, close to the fortieth parallel. Mr. Mason and Mr. Dixon did their final checks and sent word to the commissioners requesting a meeting. Meanwhile, Angus sorted the paperwork and placed it in the leather pouch where

Mr. Mason kept his journal. Paper was difficult to obtain, and getting it would be challenging once outside the city. Angus saved every scrap.

Once again, when the astronomers returned from their meeting, they tasked Angus with the travel preparations for leaving Philadelphia. He was curious about where they would go next but did not have to wait long to find out.

"The next phase is identifying the point fifteen miles south of this location. But if we measure it from here, fifteen miles south is across the river in New Jersey. So, we plan to find a point at the same parallel thirty miles or so straight west. Then we can measure fifteen miles south from there," Mr. Dixon explained. The pair would leave soon to scout a potential site to the west.

"We'll help ye pack the instruments, as we won't be taking all of that with us now," said Mr. Mason.

"Aye, sir," Angus replied.

"We'll return in a few days."

Angus helped load the instruments in their crates. Wrapped in old blankets, they placed each delicate piece into a wooden container. Mr. Mason packed the zenith sector himself in a special sail cloth wrapping, which he put on a horse chair with springs resting on a feather bed. Mr. Dixon grabbed a transit, a navigator's quadrant, and other small instruments for their journey. They would use these to identify a suitable location before moving west for more precise readings.

"In our absence, I'd like ye to store the rest of the equipment next door. There is a cellar beneath the house. I've arranged for ye to stay there," Mr. Mason said, handing him the key. "John Loxley will be back soon to help ye dismantle the observatory and have it ready to move. We'll send word when we start back so ye can also load the observatory onto a wagon."

Seeing Angus about to say something, Mr. Mason smiled. "Aye. Ye can hire Liam to help."

Angus grinned and hurried off to tell his friend the good news.

Two days before their departure, Mr. Dixon burst into the small wooden structure, clad in the bright red frock coat he always wore. The blast of cold air interrupted Angus as he packed the items in the observatory. Mr. Dixon grinned at him. Angus arched an eyebrow in return.

"Present for you, Angus." His grin widened as he handed him a bundle wrapped in brown paper and tied with string.

"For me?" Angus was unsure what to expect. Tearing open the packaging carefully to preserve the precious paper, he peeked inside. It looked like fabric. Opening it, he discovered odd-looking items of clothing made of coarse, scratchy material.

"Don't worry. We'll all be dressed like this. It is more appropriate in the wilderness than a waistcoat and breeches." Dixon headed back outside and left Angus pondering the items. He fingered the rough material. *Itchy.* He supposed he could get used to them.

Angus discarded his usual white shirt, breeches, waistcoat, and frock coat. After fumbling with the various pieces, he emerged from the observatory clad in his new attire. A red-checked heavy linen work shirt thankfully protected his skin against the scratchy osnaburg hunting frock. Full-length woolen trousers covered his legs, with soft buckskin gaiters wrapped around his calves and held in place by leather garters. There were also stiff leather boots, a belt, gloves, a scarf, a red knitted cap, and a heavy woolen cloak. Angus surveyed what he could see of himself. He wasn't exactly impressed, but at least he would be warm.

That Friday, he helped Mr. Mason and Mr. Dixon's preparations to leave early the following morning. As he worked, Mr. Dixon arrived at the observatory with two natives.

"Angus, I would like you to meet Running Bear and Gray Wolf. They will be our guides on this trek. These men will also accompany us when we move to the next site. Charles and I will return soon." Mr. Dixon gestured to each man as he spoke his name.

Angus held out his hand in greeting. The pair were dressed in buckskin and wrapped in what looked like striped woolen blankets. Beneath their outer garments, he could see linen hunting frocks, not unlike the one he now wore. Their heads were bare even in the chilling wind blowing down the street. Angus recognized them as the same men he had seen before. Up close now, he saw a tattoo on one man's face consisting of a series of dots fanning across his cheek, much like the tail of a comet.

"Hello. A pleasure to meet you," Angus stuck out his hand and wondered if they would understand. He did not know what was appropriate.

"Running Bear, and this is my brother Gray Wolf," the one who took his hand replied, gesturing at the man with the tattoo.

Angus was astonished at the man's perfect English.

"We are traders. We've worked with Europeans all our lives," the man smiled. He was accustomed to this reaction.

Angus looked back and forth between the two men.

Running Bear smiled. "Aye. We're twins, but I am the eldest." Over his shoulder, with a smirk on his face, his brother mouthed the words as his brother spoke. He winked at Angus, who chuckled.

"Maybe ye can teach me some of your language," Angus said. "I'd be keen to learn."

"Maybe we could work on that as we travel," Gray Wolf answered. He smiled at Angus as he shook his hand.

This journey was undoubtedly shaping up to be an adventure. Angus eagerly looked forward to the trip.

Within a week, the surveyors returned, having found a potential spot thirty miles to the west at a place called Harlan's farm. The observatory was packed, and the equipment was ready to move. Everyone was excited about the next phase of the survey. Why, then, did Angus feel a premonition of doom ahead?

CHAPTER 4

On the 12th of January, the party set off. Excitement filled the air as they loaded the final items on the wagon. Angus was excited about this adventure and tried to shake off the sensation of impending doom still haunting him. He would stand by his decision to remain.

In the days leading up to it, Mr. Mason hired Will & Sons Carters to haul the equipment, a cook, a carpenter, and two laborers—to Angus' delight, one was Liam.

A wide grin split Liam's face as he approached Angus that morning with Maire and the boys at his side. "I don't know how to thank ye. I am not sure how we would have fared otherwise." Maire nodded in agreement.

"Ye proved ye are a hard worker, and we need those on this project," Dixon said.

"That is true," added Angus, grinning. "And I sure will enjoy the company."

"Oh, aye. Me too. Not to mention earning a few shillings as well," Liam winked at Angus.

Mr. Dixon smiled at Liam as he passed by. He completed a final check, ensuring everything was stowed correctly and nothing was forgotten. Angus knew Charles Mason had already done this twice.

Dixon turned to his partner. "Ye are alright with this?"

Mr. Mason nodded. "I thought about what ye said. Liam is a hard worker and has promised his family will not get in the way. And traveling in the company of others is safer. It is the right thing to do." He spoke softly, but Angus overheard him.

The O'Connor family would accompany the party to the west. Later, when the survey moved south to mark the Maryland border, they arranged to travel with them again, joining the larger party for safety. Liam would keep working for them until they arrived in Maryland. The rest of the hired crew would return to Philadelphia until their services were required.

"Up ye go," Angus said as he tossed a giggling Patrick onto the seat next to Will, the wagon master. The blonde three-year-old's blue eyes stared up at the large man holding the reins.

"Me too! Me too!" Michael, a freckle-faced redhead, jumped up and down, laughing. Angus swept the five-year-old off the ground into the air before placing the squealing child beside his brother. Maire gasped as her son flew up into the air but relaxed when he landed safely on the bench. Liam shook his head and grinned at Maire.

"It's good to see ye smile again," Liam told Angus, who shrugged.

Running Bear and Gray Wolf, now clad for the journey in heavy furs covering their hunting frocks, were amongst the party. Beneath their pelts, buckskin leggings wrapped their legs. Angus saw Maire succumb to the temptation to touch the fur as she quietly slipped up behind Gray Wolf. But she did not move quietly enough. Both men noticed.

"Go ahead, Ma'am," Running Bear said, startling her. Angus snickered when Maire jumped. It must have surprised her, as it did him, to hear them speak English.

"It is a bear pelt," Running Bear said, "and quite warm and soft."

"What is a bear?" piped up Michael from the seat above. Patrick, not to be outdone by his older brother, echoed, "bear."

"It is a large animal in the woods," replied Gray Wolf. "It is huge and strong." He spread his arms wide and growled at the boys, sending them into peals of laughter. "We usually hunt smaller game such as rabbits or deer, but sometimes we catch a bear. We are always thankful when we are blessed with one."

Running Bear explained to the young boys, "The meat feeds our people. The fat has many uses, such as cooking or making candles. This fur keeps me warm in the winter." He indicated his garments and leaned closer to let the boys feel their softness. Michael and Patrick stroked the thick fur with youthful excitement.

"I want to hunt one," exclaimed Michael. Liam exchanged a glance with Maire, uncertain about that. Maire tentatively stroked the soft fur. She had met them earlier, but Angus knew she remained tentative around the natives.

Watching the emotions play out on Maire's face, Angus remembered hearing Mrs. Smith's horrible stories when he visited the family at their lodgings. She told tales of heathens running wild, living in mud huts, and scalping people.

"I just can't reconcile Mrs. Smith's stories with these men," Maire admitted to Angus. "They are so helpful and polite. Besides, they speak English better than most people I know."

Angus smiled down at her. And after helping Maire into the cart, Liam and Angus mounted their horses and joined the others. Proceeding down South Street and turning along the river, there was suddenly a commotion in front of them. A dirty-looking man staggered down the road, shaking his fist.

"Ye tell that bastard Cresap he is a Pennsylvanian now," he shouted, slurring his words. The wagons could not pass the man as he staggered drunkenly, despite the early hour.

"What is going on?" asked Angus, recognizing the man as the drunk who had threatened him. Angus still shivered at the thought of being scalped.

"I'll explain it to ye when we are on the road again," the wagon master, Will, said in a low voice. He edged his wagon over, jumped down, and gently guided the man from the roadway. Will remained with him as the party moved past before climbing back up on his seat and following them. Angus slowed and let the others pass. Glancing over his shoulder as he went by the drunk, he saw him waving his fist at them. He staggered, shouting vehemently, but Angus could not hear him above the noise of the wagons.

As he rode, Angus admired the scenery unfolding before him and managed to forget the drunk. The luxurious townhouses gave way to smaller homes as they made their way along the river. Soon, there were merely scattered clearings and small homesteads. This stretch of road consisted of tiny stones packed in the dirt, unlike the town's cobblestone streets. The forest loomed dark in the distance. Clear of Philadelphia, Angus maneuvered his horse next to Will and matched pace with the wagon. There had been no rain lately, and the road was dry and hard-packed. The cooler air here chilled his face.

"So, what was that about?" he asked, eventually. "That drunk man? The Cresaps?"

The wagon master smiled. "There has long been a feud between the Cresaps o' Maryland and the Jacksons o' Pennsylvania. I suppose Gil Jackson, that young drunk back there, is hopin' ye will find in their favor with this line ye are drawin'. He'd like nothin' more than to see Cresap lose."

"Ah, a border dispute then?" Angus was familiar with those.

"Aye. But it runs deep around here. A long time back, mebbe eighty years or more, one king gave land to the Penns that the king afore him had given to Lord Baltimore. There has been fightin' over it ever since." He glanced at the young man beside him. "I am sure ye will be in the midst of it soon."

"Aye, they warned us in London. But that's why we're here, to sort it out."

Will continued, "Thomas Cresap moved west into what was then the wilderness. That's when the feud with the Jacksons started. They claim he was a representative of the Governor of Maryland and was there to keep the Penns out o' his land. Back then, Cresap ran a ferry across the river, and one day two Pennsylvanians, claiming they needed to cross, threw him off his own boat into the river when they reached the middle. Cresap filed charges with the Lancaster sheriff, but nothing came of it. That's when the trouble began."

"I suppose I can understand that," Angus said in wonder at these events.

"Cresap attacked anyone from Pennsylvania who came on his land, be it the sheriff or the tax man. He even fortified his house."

Angus was fascinated with the tale.

"Old man Cresap is a character," Will continued. "I heard stories how he and his followers holed up in his cabin and fired on the sheriff's men, refusin' to come out. The sheriff lit a shed on fire to smoke 'em out, but the wind blew up, and it caught the roof o' the house alight. They all ran out shootin'. Cresap's wife shot a deputy in the kneecap. Cresap was captured and put in jail for a year."

"His wife? Shot a man?" said Angus in disbelief.

"Sure enough." Will was taking great delight in his story. "That border is nothin' but trouble. Gil's pa couldn't seem to keep a job, as he was always drunk. He and Gil blamed it on the Marylanders taking their work from 'em. There has been a feud between them and the Cresaps ever since. No surprise that Gil wants that to be Pennsylvanian land when ye finish." He chuckled.

"And I guess that explains why I keep seeing Gil everywhere I go. He is watching that border." Angus had wondered about why Gil kept showing up.

Angus glanced into the wagon where Will made a space for Maire to ride nestled amongst bags of grain. Her young sons were curled up with her, all three sleeping peacefully. Angus thought about this story as he rode beside the wagon.

Fortunately, their first day on the road was a delightful day for traveling. At midday, the caravan stopped to rest, water the horses, and eat bread, hard-boiled eggs, and cheese, not wanting to waste time building a fire. If they maintained their current pace, they would arrive late in the afternoon the following day. Angus had not been on a horse for long periods in quite some time, and his stiff muscles groaned as he dismounted. He stretched his legs a bit, pacing in a circle, before joining the others for the meal.

Angus sat on a sun-warmed rock as he ate and gazed at the stream, watching the water trickle through the ice lining the edges. A hawk watched them from the highest branches of a nearby tree. The boys were too excited to sit still, so Liam took his sons to the water's edge and threw small pebbles across the ice. When he finished eating, Angus joined them.

"Mine went the longest," exclaimed Michael, jumping up and down. Angus deliberately fumbled a stone. It barely went two feet across the surface. "Aye, ye won."

Gray Wolf joined the fun, scooping up a giggling Patrick; he pretended to throw the child across the ice.

"Onskat, tiggene, axe," he counted as he swung the child toward the ice. The young boy squealed. His brother attempted to repeat the native words for one, two, and three. Soon, Mr. Dixon joined them, teaching Michael how to throw his pebbles further across the ice.

Angus returned to the wagon and helped Maire clear their picnic. The excited group spent a leisurely hour before everyone remounted, and the journey continued.

The terrain was level, and the ride was easy. Mr. Mason demanded they not move with great speed for fear of the delicate instruments being jostled.

Toward late afternoon, they reached the town of Chester, where they put up for the night at Esquire Worth's lodgings. They combed the horses and fed them fresh oats while Fielding, the cook Mr. Mason had hired, fired up the brick oven on the property. It was not long before they dined on the rabbits Fielding had trapped during the midday respite, served with the fried potatoes he brought with him. The tantalizing aroma of the food drew everyone around the fire.

While it was a substantial structure, only Mr. Mason and Mr. Dixon slept in the lodging house. The remaining travelers felt the cost too dear. They curled up in the fresh straw and slept comfortably in the stables. The lengthy ride and full bellies caught up with everyone, and as darkness fell early, no one objected to retiring to the stable with the setting sun.

That uneasy feeling remained with Angus, though he still could not figure out why. Regardless, he fell asleep shortly after the others. The group faced another long day in the saddle before reaching Harlan's farm.

"Rise and shine!"

Mr. Dixon's cheerful voice was met with loud groans from those rudely awakened by his intrusion. Angus rolled from under his blanket, surprised at the stiffness in his back and legs.

"Good grief," he muttered. "Like an old man." And they still had half a day's ride ahead.

He stood, groaning at the effort, and grabbed his blanket. Stepping out of the stall he shared with Will, he noticed the natives were already gone. Usually a light sleeper, Angus was astonished he had not heard them. Slowly, heads appeared from the other stalls along the row. Maire reached to remove the straw from Liam's fiery red locks as Michael, the spitting image of his father, peered out beside him. With a grunt, Will stood and stepped out beside Angus.

"Ye have straw in yer hair as well, Laddie," he muttered, "I used to have fine auburn curls like yours." His own balding pate retained only a few strands of gray.

Outside, the natives had the horses already saddled. Unlike the others, they seemed wide awake and alert. Mr. Mason checked the horse chair's trappings, ensuring the zenith sector was secure and well-wrapped. Angus helped Will and his sons hitch the wagons.

Mrs. Worth, the mistress of the house, provided mugs of steaming hot coffee and fresh warm biscuits with butter to break their fast before returning to the road. Angus quickly gobbled down three delicious biscuits, licking the melted butter from his fingers. He slurped the strong, black coffee. The rich aroma filled his senses.

"My thanks, ma'am. This coffee is excellent," he smiled happily. Tea had always been his preference back home, but Will had warned him it was harder to obtain these days.

"Why, you're welcome. I roast the beans myself," Mrs. Worth replied. "I'm well known for having the best coffee... Though I will never reveal my secret."

Will grunted at her. Angus watched as Gray Wolf snuck three biscuits into his pouch.

Over the native's shoulder, Angus saw the most striking-looking woman leave the house, stepping onto the porch. She wore buckskin leggings with a bright yellow woolen tunic that reached nearly to her knees. The woman laughed at something Mr. Worth said, and Angus was enchanted by the sound. She shook her head, the early morning sunlight glistening in the silky blackness of her waist-length hair.

The woman pulled on a heavy woolen cloak and stood on her toes to hug Mr. Worth before crossing to hug Mrs. Worth.

"I'll see ye again soon," the woman told her in the same perfect English the other natives spoke. She then hurried to join the two brothers and stood braiding her long hair as she spoke with them in their tongue.

"Stop ogling and get a move on, Laddie," teased Mr. Dixon. Angus blushed bright red and mounted his horse, grimacing as his leg muscles objected to another day in the saddle.

It was another sunny morning; if the weather held, they would arrive at Harlan's farm in the afternoon. The surveyors determined it to be about thirty-one miles west of Philadelphia's southernmost point and agreed it would be ideal to begin the fifteen-mile survey south as soon as possible.

On arrival at the farm, they would confirm their precise location using the stars, as they had done in Philadelphia.

Just before midday, Angus sidled his horse up alongside the natives. Running Bear grinned and replied to the silent query. "Meet our wee sister, Little Hawk. She'll ride with us now and then as our paths cross."

"I knew ye'd be passing through, and I have some salve for Sarah Harlan." Little Hawk smiled at Angus and held out her hand. "Good day, nice to meet ye."

"Are ye all named for animals?" Angus blurted out. He quickly blushed at his rudeness.

"Aye, many are, though also plants and objects of the earth."

Gray Wolf added, "We are not named at birth, or christened as ye call it. By the time we have lived through two cycles of the seasons and are young children, our natural characters have shown themselves. We are given our names in a ceremony. These we loosely translate into English for business, as our tongue is difficult for most settlers."

Angus was fascinated with this idea. "I see. So a person named after a bear is strong, something like that?"

"There are many powerful animals," replied Running Bear. "A bear is protective and courageous besides being strong. Wearing a bear claw is a good omen for protection and good health." He displayed the claw hanging around his neck. A cross hung beside it.

This was something Angus understood. His gran was a great believer in such charms. "And the wolf?"

"Wolves again are strong. But they show fierce loyalty and intelligence. They are also known for intuition and showing compassion."

"So," Angus said, looking at their sister, "what about the hawk?"

"A hawk," she said, "has wisdom and the power of observation. It is an intuitive animal, able to see the big picture."

That made sense, too. Angus knew intuitive women in his youth who also had second sight. Nodding at her, Angus said, "Well, my name's Angus. But I don't imagine it means anything." He smiled at this, and the others laughed.

That day, they rested midday on the peaceful banks of a babbling brook. Sunlight was not yet shining through the trees, and ice rimmed the water's edge, making it icy cold to drink. Angus filled his canteen for later, hoping the water would warm up, hanging next to his body. Birds twittered about overhead as he stretched out on a sun-warmed stone nearby. He drowsed for a spell and found himself somewhat disappointed to move on from the tranquil spot. Fascinated with learning more about the natives, Angus joined them again when they returned to the road.

"Have your people always lived here?" Angus asked.

"Aye. Today, the Susquehannock are part of a loose confederation of Iroquois living along the river, including our friends, the Conestoga." Running Bear answered. He grew quiet. Angus realized they must have known members of that tribe.

"In the past, our people lived on the land from Maryland up into New York." He picked up his story after a bit. "When the Europeans arrived, we decided to work together. We thought that made sense, but not all tribes agreed. That belief sets us apart from the rest of the Iroquois who are related to us. But our numbers were weakened by a sickness we could not fight, and we no longer have the large numbers we once maintained. Today, we live in peace in small clusters in our former lands along the Susquehanna River in Pennsylvania and Maryland."

Angus thought long and hard about this as they rode. These people, also forced out of their ancestral lands, were perhaps not altogether different from himself.

Gray Wolf picked up the conversation. "We tend to stay in one place today, unlike our ancestors who roamed the area. The earth provides what we need. Living on the river allows us to travel and gives us plenty of fish to eat. Who needs more than that?"

"Leave it to you to bring the conversation back to food," Little Hawk teased her brother. "One difference, though, our line comes through the mother, not the father, unlike the white man," she added proudly. "Families live together in longhouses centered on the clan mother."

"Ah, now that is different," replied Angus.

"Aye, but at least ye always know who the mother is," Gray Wolf retorted. He glanced at Angus with a wry grin and winked.

"So what do the men do?" Angus was curious.

"With our father being from a different clan, Running Bear is now the eldest male in our line after the death of Gran's brother. So he represents the clan at gatherings and is the one who meets the Europeans for business. They are less accepting of women making the decisions."

"And this lazy one here just hunts and has fun." Running Bear grinned at his brother.

Gray Wolf laughed, "aye, but at least we eat!" Little Hawk rolled her eyes.

It was a pleasant afternoon, and they arrived at Harlan's farm late in the day. John Harlan, a stocky, muscular man, brought his entire family out to greet them.

"Welcome, welcome," the jovial farmer greeted the party. "This is my wife, Sarah. And our middle son, Stephen. Our two eldest are married now and have their own homes. Our only daughter, Abigail, and our youngest, Thomas." He pointed at each in turn.

Sarah Harlan was a tall woman with blonde hair peeking out from her cap. Abigail, entering her teens, was tall and slim, the image of her mother. Thomas, a short lad for his age, had unruly blonde hair hanging to his shoulders. Stephen, also blonde, was a copy of his father.

Mr. Mason, in turn, introduced the other members of their party. He and Mr. Dixon had met the Harlans when they scouted the area the previous week.

John Harlan continued, "I hope ye will be comfortable here fer your work. That border has caused nothing but trouble. 'Tis a wonderful thing ye are doing; I hope ye can resolve it."

The surroundings provided a beautiful setting, with the sturdy stone house and barns in the middle of neatly cleared lands. The verdant forests stretched beyond as far as Angus could see. The air was full of the sound of birds, including the clucking of Sarah's chickens plucking bits of grain on the ground. Breathing in the fresh air, Angus wrinkled his nose at a whiff of manure coming from Sarah's garden.

"Thank ye for your hospitality, Mrs. Harlan," said Angus, joining in with the others.

"Ah, lad," she answered as she extended her hand in welcome. "We are not so formal here. Please, call me Sarah." She gripped his hand firmly in hers.

John led them around back, where they unhitched the horses. Sarah placed some biscuits and lemonade on the table, inviting them to some refreshments before unpacking and getting settled.

"Well, now that ye are here, we must keep on to the trading post," Gray Wolf said as he filled his pouch with biscuits. Little Hawk scolded him for being so rude. After saying goodbye, the trio promised to return soon and mounted their horses.

The rest unloaded the wagons and set up the temporary tent where the equipment would live until Mr. Mason selected the location for the observatory.

"I will fry anythin' ye catch," the cook told them. He was hired to cook for the smaller party not to burden the Harlan family. Mr. Mason kept a detailed accounting of their expenses for reimbursement by the commissioners. The wagon masters would depart in the morning. John Loxley, the carpenter, would come when it was time to erect the observatory.

Dusk settled on the farm, and at last, Angus relaxed, at peace in the surroundings. He was among friends in a picturesque place. Life was good.

This was not to last, however. Angus looked up just as the party headed toward the stream to catch some fish. The one-armed man sat astride his large, black horse just down the road. Once again, the hairs on the back of Angus' neck stood on end.

CHAPTER 5

On Saturday night, Mr. Mason and Mr. Dixon took their initial readings outside the temporary tent. Mr. Mason did not want to assemble the structure until he confirmed the location was accurate. Though Sunday was a day of rest, Angus spent the morning hunched over the calculations. Once he finished, Angus joined the others, fishing for dinner in the babbling stream running along the property.

"I saw the one-armed man yesterday," Angus leaned over and said softly to Liam.

"Here?" Liam jerked his line.

Angus nodded as Liam expertly landed the fish.

"Who is he?"

"I think he is spying on our survey," Angus said, his jaw set.

"Should ye say something?"

"What? I've seen a man with one arm?" Angus shrugged.

After the children were in bed that evening, the adults sat around the warm fire, sipping ale. Clouds rolled in early, ensuring the stars would not be visible that night.

"How did you get involved in this?" Fielding asked Angus while settling in by the fire.

"My mam's brother is a member of the Royal Society in Greenwich, where they study astronomy," Angus replied. "He recommended me for the position when he learned of my skill with numbers."

"Numbers is somethin' I never learned," Fielding responded, "although I can do enough sums for my work."

"Aye, me too," Liam added, "I learned to count enough shillings to pay for things, but it seems there are never enough." He grinned, and the men agreed. "And I barely learned to read and write, though God knows the monks tried. I had no interest in it then, and as I grew older, they needed me at home." Liam shook his head ruefully at this.

"For me, the monastery was a place to escape," Angus said, "Learning was something I could do well, and I was happy there. My uncle has put a lot o' faith in my abilities, and I don't want to disappoint him."

"How does this work?" asked Will, shifting in his chair.

"Mr. Mason tracks the stars through the telescope as they appear on one horizon, and he follows them across to the other," Angus began. "While he does this, Mr. Dixon adjusts the leveling screws, and they note the middle point of the arc on their zenith sector. That is the piece with the long tube. If the middle point is forty degrees, we are at the fortieth parallel on the earth. And that parallel is the bit in the land grant causing all the trouble."

As the others looked confused, Angus tried to explain. He picked up a stick and drew a triangle in the dirt. "If I know some angles and sides, I can figure out the rest." Eventually, he realized he had lost them entirely and shrugged. "Aye. Simply put, it is a method of figuring out where we are on the earth."

Fielding picked up the stick and completed a circle from the triangle Angus had drawn. "Now that is a measurement I can understand," he claimed, pointing at the triangle. "A nice wedge o' pie." He patted his ample stomach. Laughter erupted from the others.

The laughter died down, and the men relaxed in silence around the fire. They sipped the strong, dark ale, each man involved in his thoughts.

John Harlan was primarily a farmer, but he had a small forge for making the necessary hand tools, and Angus and the O'Connor family slept there. Eventually, Liam rose and stretched.

"I oughta go join the missus," he said. "G'night."

I guess I ruined that conversation. Angus yawned but waited to give Liam some time with Maire before entering. He would move to the observatory once it was set up to give them more space alone.

Monday morning dawned bright and clear, and shortly after breaking their fast, the crew from Philadelphia were on their way home. The Harlans' children, fourteen-year-old Abigail and thirteen-year-old Thomas, played games with Liam's young sons. Angus emerged from his work in the tent and spied Abigail as she suddenly straightened her dress and smiled at him. Unsure what to make of this, he smiled back. When he turned, he saw Maire, her petticoat hitched up in the waistband of her apron, helping Sarah with the washing.

She looked up and smiled, rolling up her sleeve, "I want to earn my keep here," she said to Angus in a manner that accepted no argument. "While I am about it, do ye have any washing?" Angus nodded and hurried to grab his dirty garments.

The sky remained clear that night; the stars shone brightly as the two astronomers crouched next to the tent, following their path across the heavens through the sector's lens.

While they worked, Angus tried to find Orion. *Aye, there's his belt.* He found those three stars quickly now. A cold breeze blew, and he pulled his greatcoat tighter about him as he gazed intently at the night sky. Below the stars of the belt, two brighter stars appeared. He'd not noticed them before. Angus gasped—they must be the hunter's knees! He struggled as he tried to remember the name of the brighter one. *Ah, yes, Rigel.*

"We will review these again, lad, but if my preliminary calculations are correct tonight, we are on the proper parallel." Mr. Dixon told Angus as he straightened. "We'll send for the carpenter to erect the observatory soon, providing all is well with these numbers. We will look for an appropriate spot tomorrow."

"Aye, Sir, I will look at those figures now if ye'd like."

"If ye'd not mind, or it can wait until morning," he replied. "And call me Jeremiah. Sir was what they called my father. Ye know I am not so formal."

"Yes, Sir, uh, I mean Jeremiah," Angus stammered, "I have time, and I am still awake. I'll look at them now."

Dawn was far off yet. Mr. Mason carried the zenith sector back inside as Angus squatted and gathered the papers Dixon carelessly left strewn on the ground. When Angus entered the tent, Mr. Mason looked up. Seeing Angus straightening the stack of paper, Mr. Mason rolled his eyes and shrugged at Angus. He replaced the cover on the sector and squatted to help Angus sort through the scattered bits of paper Mr. Dixon left behind.

"We tracked Beta Aurigae again tonight to add to Capella and Castor," Mr. Mason informed him, naming the stars. "Those readings should be sufficient to determine we are near the southernmost point of Philadelphia—or at least close enough to set up the observatory and leave this freezing tent."

"Very good, Sir." Angus was learning the stars' names, though he doubted he could locate them in the night sky.

Mr. Mason was much more proper than his partner, and he still made Angus a bit nervous, but he enjoyed the moments he spent with him. He was in awe of him and his accomplishments. *He is only about ten years older than I am.*

Except for one night, the sky was clear that week, and the astronomers easily took their readings. Angus alternated between burying himself in the figures and working with Liam and John Loxley to erect the observatory during the daylight hours. Mr. Mason reviewed the data and decided on a location nine yards south of the tent. This seemingly minor distance added 0.3 seconds to all the northern stars they observed from the tent's position.

Finally, on the 23rd of January, the zenith sector was relocated from the tent to the completed observatory. After finishing the calculations, Angus crawled into bed in the wee hours before dawn. The evening before, he had grabbed his bedroll and blankets from the forge despite Liam's objections. Since Angus came and went at such odd hours, he was sure he was intruding on the family—whether or not Liam would admit it.

He learned a great deal and enjoyed the work immensely, often staying late with the astronomers. As he added wood to the tiny brazier in the structure, Angus had to admit that the forge was warmer, but he was comfortable enough despite the canvas roof.

"Stop!" a young voice squealed outside the observatory.

"I'm gonna get ye," shouted another from the other side.

Angus rolled over and shivered as he crawled from his bedroll. It was freezing. Sunlight shone high on the canvas roof of the wooden building. The brazier was no longer lit. He almost fell asleep staring at the figures. Angus hadn't undressed, merely slipped his coat from his shoulders and added his cloak to the blanket on his bedroll. He pulled the warm greatcoat on as he fought to open the door. It stuck on something and wouldn't budge. Throwing his weight into it, he opened it just enough to squeeze his head out and was met with a blinding white scene outside. There was a foot of snow on the ground!

Had it been snowing when he went to bed? He could not remember. Angus checked the roof of the structure; thankfully, everything seemed fine. The roof's steep pitch had caused an avalanche piling snow around the door. The five children scampered about in the depths, all engaged in a snowball fight. All the boys ganged up on Abigail, but she quickly escaped them. Stuck between outgrowing her childhood and becoming a woman, Abigail still enjoyed playing games in the snow.

Angus' first thought was to curl back up in his bed where it was warm, but though he was almost twenty-four, he couldn't resist a good snowball fight.

"Hey, help me with the door," he called after finally getting the children's attention.

"Sure," called Stephen, Harlan's sixteen-year-old son, as he ran over to free the door, then turned away.

He screamed as Angus took full advantage and fired a snowball, striking the lad square in the back.

"Take that!" Stephen, who already had a snowball in hand, rapidly fired back, catching Angus in the shoulder.

"What?" Angus grunted, suddenly hit from behind.

As he turned, he saw Liam duck behind the observatory. Angus gestured silently to Stephen, and the two cornered Liam, pelting him from both sides. The younger children cheered them on with peals of laughter.

When they were tired of the game, the children helped roll large balls of snow. They collected some stones from the field for eyes and begged a carrot from Fielding's stores for a nose. Sarah contributed a bright red scarf, and John Harlan added an old, knitted cap. By that afternoon, a gallant snowman guarded the house.

Days later, Angus heard a commotion outside and rose from his work to check what was happening. A horse pulling a small cart was approaching the house. The Harlan farm sat on a busy post road near a mill and, therefore, was a meeting point. Carts, wagons, and men on horseback coming up the lane were regular occurrences. Mail meant news, and the deliverer was always welcome. As the rider drew closer, Angus recognized John Loxley returning from his run to Philadelphia and went to greet him.

"Hail, the house!" Loxley's booming voice rang out as he approached. He dismounted and was greeted by hugs and handshakes from all.

Seeing Mr. Dixon approaching, the carpenter said, "I brought yer levels for the survey with me since I was heading out this way. I figured ye might be needin' them soon enough."

"Well, thank ye," replied Mr. Mason, stepping from the house behind Dixon. "I believe we will be finished with our observations here soon. We had a few flying clouds of late that rendered some readings a bit dubious, but I hope to clear that up soon."

"Come in, come in, warm yerself a spell," Sarah greeted him warmly. "I've got some stew left from dinner. Sit yerself down and let us hear the news." Eager to help, Maire rushed to the cupboard for a bowl and a spoon.

"Recent reports reached Philadelphia about some trouble with several o' the tribes as settlers push further west," he said, inching his feet closer to the fire and slurping his soup between sentences. "Not with our Indian friends, o' course, but I hear o' trouble with some o' the ones further west that fought with the French. They ain't happy with the British gainin' more land and burned three homesteads in as many weeks in the wilderness. That Reverend Elder is in the midst of it all, o' course."

That was not good news. John Harlan shifted uneasily in his seat.

"I am sorry to hear this," John said as he mulled it over. "My father's father and his family afore him set up on this property when they left England. I understand folk's reasons for comin' here, but without money, their only choice is to make a living on the land. Though to be fair, the Indians were here afore 'em, and those treaties keep gettin' broken. They're honest, hardworking folk, and I also understand their point o' view."

He glanced at his wife, and Sarah patted his shoulder affectionately.

"It's scary for folk like us, who are coming to start a new life," said Liam.

Maire, standing behind him, leaned down and kissed the top of his head.

"Well, for some better news, I hear tell Johnny Baker's young daughter got married and has her first babe on the way," Loxley added.

"Lizzie Baker! And her but a year older than me!" exclaimed Abigail huffing as she flopped down heavily on a bench. Loxley shared the rest of the gossip he had picked up along the way, knowing he held the family's rapt attention. Abigail pouted.

The natives rode up the lane a few days later. The brothers' service as guides was not required while the astronomers observed the stars. They resumed their trapping and trading in the meantime. Like many others, they used the farm as a gathering point, passing through regularly. They, too, brought news of the uprisings.

"We saw Loxley at the Fleming trading post, so I guess ye heard three more homesteads were burned." Running Bear approached the men on the porch after taking care of his horse. His voice was grim, and Angus noted his frown as he turned to face them.

"Aye," John answered. "Looks like the Fightin' Parson is rallying his boys again."

"The governor ought to do somethin' about that man," Sarah said, hands on her hips.

"Aye, he should." Gray Wolf hustled over to join them. "But I suspect he agrees with him." The brothers exchanged a troubled glance.

The astronomers had finished their observations, and there was little work for Angus. Mr. Mason and Mr. Dixon conferred over their final readings, validating they were at the proper parallel to begin the survey.

Angus rose to help Running Bear unload their pack horses, removing deer skins, beaver pelts, and willow baskets containing smaller items. In one box, he found abalone shells with gleaming pearly coloring and intricately decorated clothing. They planned to leave for a trading post near Lancaster the next day to do business.

Running Bear straightened and approached Angus. "Would you care to join us? We will only be gone a short time, perhaps a few days."

Angus was intrigued by the idea and asked permission. Mr. Mason and Mr. Dixon were heading to Philadelphia to meet with the commissioners to present their findings, so Angus had free time.

"Aye, lad, we can spare ye. Though I must admit, I'm jealous; it sounds interesting," Jeremiah admitted. "Sure wish I could go, too."

As he left, Dixon suddenly turned back. "Don't forget there's an eclipse in three days. On Saturday. Ye won't want to miss that." Angus agreed.

Thus, the following morning Angus mounted and rode out with the three siblings and three heavily laden pack horses.

"What are the furs for?" Angus asked.

"We trade with Old George out at the post. He takes our furs and deerskins in exchange for tobacco, metal pots, and other items we need. Sometimes we trade for woolen fabrics and such as well." Gray Wolf answered. "I hear beaver hats are very popular in London." He grinned broadly and winked at Angus.

"Aye, ye see them everywhere."

By evening, they came to a village unlike anything Angus had seen. Several men met them inside, greeting the natives but warily staring at Angus. He assumed these men had been on guard outside of the gate.

Inside the twelve-foot high palisade wall stood several structures of varying sizes surrounding a sizable fire pit in the center. The buildings were rectangular, with curved ends and arched roofs running down their length. Their construction appeared to be of woven branches and tree bark. The main structure, located in the middle and centered on the massive fire pit, looked more extensive than the others. All of them had hide-covered doors on the ends. In front of the larger buildings were tall poles carved with animals. From the gate, Angus saw bear, wolf, hawk, and turtle. There was a raven in front of the largest.

"This is our village, the home of our mother's family. Everyone here is kin to us; we will sleep here tonight," said Little Hawk. She put a hand on his arm. "Relax, most of us speak English."

Angus was fascinated by the structures. After dismounting, he stepped closer to study their construction. "So, these are long-houses," he said to Little Hawk. "They are not quite as I pictured them." She smiled.

Reaching out, Angus touched the exterior and was surprised to find it was made of bark strips stretched across a series of saplings cut, positioned in the ground, and laced together by branches placed horizontally for stability. It was an ingenious method of construction and very different from the stone houses back home.

A buzz of activity hummed through the village as everyone finished the day's tasks. Little Hawk introduced him to several people as she showed him through the settlement. A man straightened, putting down the knife he was sharpening, and watched. As they passed, a woman removing brightly colored clothing from the line peered out at him. Angus counted ten longhouses, many over eighty feet long and twenty wide. There were also smaller shacks around the perimeter where people stored their tools.

As they returned to the central building, an older woman with thick, silver hair streaming past her shoulders waited for them.

"Soars with Ravens, I'd like ye to meet our friend, Angus." Little Hawk said to the older woman. "Angus, this is my grandmother, our matriarch, Soars with Ravens."

"Pleased to meet ye," Angus extended his hand. Now the poles of animal figures made sense. This was the longhouse of the Raven clan.

Soars with Ravens took his hand. "Welcome." She invited him inside, where they joined the others at the fire pit.

"The members of our clan all descend from the same ancestors," Running Bear explained as he joined them inside. "We live here with our mother's family now, but Gray Wolf and I will leave when we marry and join our wives' families."

"As the eldest daughter, our mother will inherit this clan when our grandmother goes to the Great Spirit." Gray Wolf joined them, a piece of meat in his hand. "And as her only daughter, Little Hawk will continue the line."

Angus' cheeks flamed as the matriarch gestured to the seat of honor beside her near the fire. Shyness overcame him. While the surroundings were very different, Angus wondered if this was how his father had felt when he met a clan chieftain.

Once seated, Angus studied the interior. He looked down a long central aisle.

"Compartments line both sides," Little Hawk explained. "These belong to individual families. The family units on either side share the fire pits you see down the center."

Angus nodded. His eye followed the smoke up to the roof above each, where he noticed small holes above each fire.

Noting his gaze, Soars with Ravens explained, "We can close those with a small flap when there is snow or rain. The height of the roof prevents it from becoming too smoky inside."

Though many spoke in their native language among each other, the natives spoke English in deference to their guest. Unlike the colonists who chattered constantly, Angus noted the natives were people of few words.

"The white man builds his house as though he will be here forever," said Soars with Ravens as she watched him study the composition of the structure. "Eventually, he will turn to dust, as we will. The village meets our needs on the earth in this life."

Angus stopped studying the space and turned to look at her. Sensing his interest, she continued, "we do not share your idea of ownership of the land."

Angus thought this over; he had much to consider if he was to understand these people.

An older woman, whom Angus realized was blind, was assisted inside and led to the seat beside him. Little Hawk introduced her as her grandmother's younger sister, Clever Otter, who lived in the next longhouse with her children and their families. Angus had seen the carving of the playful otter in front of the adjacent structure. In a way, they reminded Angus of the symbols important to the clans, each with its traditions. Though he had not asked, Little Hawk explained that otters symbolize grace, empathy, and never-ending curiosity.

Angus rose politely as the older woman was seated. She was petite, her gray hair in a single braid down her back. Angus was struck with the image of his gran, who wore her hair the same way.

Clever Otter stared at him so intently that Angus forgot she was blind. Eventually, she stretched out her arm, taking Angus' hand. Her grip was firm. He sat still and waited.

"Ye have been through much in yer life," she began. Her voice sounded surprisingly strong. "And ye have further troubles ahead. But ye will come through it all. Be true to yerself." She let go of his hand, breaking the spell.

Angus sat stunned as images of his gran doing the same thing filled his mind.

The foursome mounted and left early in the morning. On the ride, Angus was pensive as he mulled over his visit. He found the natives intelligent, polite, and generous. They shared their food, fire, and a place to sleep in an empty compartment. While he was in Philadelphia, he heard people call them savages. Folk claimed they were lazy and never tried to better themselves, shunning what they considered a better lifestyle. Angus could not reconcile those stories with what he had seen.

He was saddle sore by midday when suddenly Running Bear halted in front of him. Angus was startled until he caught the whiff of smoke. It had a distinctive stale smell, not the fresh aroma of a hearth fire. They dismounted and walked the horses slowly toward the wisps they could now see curling above the trees. Gray Wolf hobbled the horses while Angus and the others entered a modest farmstead.

Before them lay the charred remains of a wooden cabin and a barn. Smoke curled upward, spiraling above the center of the remains, though the fire appeared to be out. All that remained standing was the stone chimney and the stone steps where the door once stood. The rest lay in smoldering ashes. Only one end of the barn was burned. The other end was slightly charred around the edges but still stood. An empty paddock spread out behind it.

Not seeing anyone, Angus hoped the people who lived here had escaped. He recognized the same concern on his friends' faces.

CHAPTER 6

Angus picked up a broken arrow lying near his foot as Little Hawk approached. "What did you find?" She studied it a moment, then, pointing at the fletching, she said, "I don't recognize that pattern. It is not ours... nor any tribe I know." She gestured to her brothers.

As Little Hawk and her brothers examined the arrow's fletching, Angus wandered off toward the burned cabin and barn. *Was anyone home? Did they take the family?* The smell of smoke filled his nostrils. Angus felt dizzy and collapsed to his knees on the ground near the ruined homestead. A wave of emotion flooded through him as the memories came surging back.

A young Angus was hiding from the other boys in the small clearing behind the barn when he spotted men in red coats setting fire to the shed. The men were now heading toward the house with their blazing torches held aloft. A few crossed towards the stables—*the horses!*—Angus flew toward the back of the stables, his wee legs pumping hard.

As it whirled about him, the acrid smoke burned his lungs. He reached the back door of the L-shaped structure; no one had seen him. They were busy setting the house alight. Angus wasn't sure where his family was; all he knew was he needed to save the horses. He opened the door and saw the building filling with smoke. One end was already in flames. The scorching heat made its way toward him, burning his face. The horses, sensing a chance to escape through the open door, hurtled toward him and outside to freedom, knocking him to the ground as they fled. Tears filled his eyes, nearly blinding him, and ran down his cheeks. He could scarcely breathe. Unable to see and coughing from the thick smoke filling his lungs, he crawled toward the door and collapsed on the ground a few yards away.

"Angus, wake up," his mother shook him, trying desperately to get a response when she found him lying half-hidden behind the rabbit hutches.

"Mam... the horses..." he gasped out. "Are they safe?"

Little Hawk kneeled next to him. She shook him gently and repeated his name. "Angus? Angus! What horses?"

Jolted back to the present, his face was pale white, and his shoulders trembled under her hand. It took him several moments to realize this was not his mother, this was not Scotland, and he was no longer that frightened child. He rose unsteadily to his feet, staring at the charred remains of the home. That was not his house and barn smoldering before him.

"Ye have been through this afore?" asked Running Bear, watching his friend as he slowly came around and realized where he was.

"Aye," Angus replied, shaking his head to clear it. After taking a deep breath, he continued. "The soldiers burned the house where we were staying when I was a lad." He paused and took another deep breath. "But I saved the horses." He smiled meekly at them.

Gray Wolf swallowed and looked at their horses peacefully, munching the grass at the edge of the clearing. Little Hawk rested her hand on Angus' arm, comforting him. Angus reached and took the broken arrow from her, his eyes questioning.

"We don't know who did this," she replied to his unspoken question as they took in the scene.

They examined the area. Angus discovered several more arrows scattered randomly, each with that same fletching he found on the first one. "What were they shooting at?" he wondered aloud. There were no bodies in the rubble nor any blood on the ground. "Was anyone here?"

"Aye, 'tis strange indeed," muttered Gray Wolf, looking around. "Either no one was home, or they were taken. And where are the beasts? Did they take them too? This is O'Donnell's place. He owns a couple of cows and a pair of donkeys. Where are they?"

"So ye know them?" Angus asked.

Little Hawk nodded, "aye. We do."

"Over here," shouted her brother from the small ridge behind the house. The others ran to him and saw the animals grazing contentedly on the hillside.

"Now, that is odd indeed."

Gray Wolf looked puzzled, gazing down at the peaceful scene below where the animals munched the meadow grass. "Why burn the home but leave the animals?"

"This does not look like any raid I've seen," admitted Running Bear.

The others nodded their agreement. "Some tribes befriended the European settlers, but just as many didn't. After the recent war, uprisings increased amongst tribes that fought with the French. They pride themselves on collecting scalps but usually leave the bodies behind and take the animals." Gray Wolf explained to Angus.

Little Hawk picked at her braid as she surveyed the scene. "That is true, Brother. And what will we do with the animals? I don't want to leave them."

"Is there anyone nearby we could lead them to?" asked Angus.

Just as she was about to answer, they heard a stick snap. All four turned as one toward the sound. Three grubby men approached them. Angus recognized the one in the middle as the drunk he saw in Philadelphia, the man they called Gil, who warned them about the Indians. The men flanking him were the ones with Gil that day in Philadelphia. One was short and stocky with dark hair, the other a bit taller with greasy blonde hair, a strand of which hung in his eyes.

"Come back t' admire yer work?" Gil slurred his words. He snarled.

"This was not of our doing. We just now came upon it," replied Gray Wolf.

"Well, o' course ye'd being sayin' that," Gil looked to each side at his friends, who nodded in agreement.

"I was with them. I can attest to it," Angus said, noting the aggressive stance the men assumed. He took several steps to join Gray Wolf, facing the men.

"Well, then ye should learn to pick yer friends better," Gil snarled. Pleased with himself, he smoothed down his greasy hair. "It's good that Miz O'Donnell's ma took sick, and they were away."

Angus sighed in relief. So no one was harmed.

"Ye can see it was Indians, don't say I didn't warn ye." Gil snarled at Angus, pointing to the arrow in his hand. "Ye'll have to answer Sheriff Brown. I know he'll have questions fer ye."

Angus shoved the arrow into his pouch.

Running Bear took a step towards Gil. "Ye know us better than that, Gil Jackson. Now, go back home. Leave us. We'll take care of things here."

Gray Wolf stepped beside his older brother and crossed his arms over his chest. Gray Wolf was tall and muscular, towering above Gil and his friends. "We will take the animals to Joe Schmidt's farm and then get word to the O'Donnells."

Gil and his friends closed ranks and faced the others. Then Gil backed down. "Whatever. We're gonna go fer the sheriff." He looked at his friends, "c'mon, lads." He staggered a bit as he stormed off.

As Gil's friends turned to follow him, both cast a surreptitious glance at Angus. One peered over his shoulder a second time as they disappeared from view.

"C'mon, Simon," Gil called over his shoulder.

The two natives kept their aggressive posture until the men were out of sight.

"Does he live out here?" Angus asked. "I saw him several times in Philadelphia."

Then Little Hawk snickered, and the three of them burst out laughing. Angus was puzzled at this response.

"Aye, he does, just up the way, when he's not getting drunk in the city. But if they plan to fetch the sheriff, the town is in the opposite direction," Little Hawk sputtered. "Gil's whisky still is the only thing that way." She turned to Angus to explain, "it is well known hereabouts, but he thinks no one knows about it."

"I think his feet have worn such a path they naturally turn that way," joked Gray Wolf.

"Or he's already forgotten where he was headed," Running Bear said with a smile.

"We'll pass the Schmidt place on our way to the trading post," Gray Wolf informed Angus. "I have some rope we can use to lead the animals. Joe Schmidt is a good person; he will take care of them until the O'Donnells return."

The Schmidt homestead was usually a short ride. The cows followed docilely behind, but the donkeys stubbornly planted their feet, unwilling to leave the sweet grass. In the end, they dismounted and led them to the homestead on foot. Two sheepdogs bounded happily up the lane to greet the riders as they turned down the path. When they neared the house, a giant blond man stepped out of a large stone barn. Nestled in his muscular arms was a young lamb. He immediately recognized the siblings, and a huge smile filled his bearded face.

"Good day," he cried out. "Let me put this one back with his ma." He stepped into the barn while the riders dismounted and tethered their horses. They led the O'Donnell's animals toward the barn door; even the donkeys didn't resist now. They smelled the sweet hay inside.

The lamb situated, Joe returned to them.

"Those look like the O'Donnell's beasts," Joe said in surprise.

"Aye, they are. We bring sad news, Joe," said Running Bear as he waited outside the barn. "And I am hoping ye can be of help."

"Aye, of course," he replied, looking puzzled. "How can I be of service?"

Running Bear explained what they had discovered, while Joe shook his head sadly. "Can ye keep their beasts until they return?"

"Gil Jackson told us Miz O'Donnell's ma was poorly, and the family wasn't there."

"Gil Jackson? What was he doin' there?" He scanned the barn in thought. "Yes, yes, of course, I will help. I heard the O'Donnells were away. Let's put them in the paddock for now, then c'mon up to the house."

Angus studied the stout stone house, much more solid than some of the wooden cabins they passed on their way. Joe followed Angus' gaze, explaining, "My family has lived on this site for three generations. My name is Joe Schmidt." He wiped his hand on his leg before extending it to Angus.

He shook his hand heartily. "Angus MacKay, pleased to meet ye." Angus wasn't often forced to look up at a man's face. As they strolled toward the door, Angus noticed the man walking with a limp.

When they entered the kitchen, a tall native woman straightened up from the pot she was stirring. Angus was surprised that she nearly reached his own height. Her dark eyes spied the natives over his shoulder. Her face lit up in a smile as she threw open her arms and embraced Little Hawk.

"My wife, Hannah," Joe introduced her to Angus and smiled at the surprised look on his face. "Though amongst her tribe, they know her as Long Willow."

"Angus MacKay, Ma'am," he stammered.

The Schmidts were used to this reaction when meeting newcomers. "While ye rarely see white men marryin' Indian women elsewhere, it is not uncommon in these parts," Joe explained. "Though there is folk less acceptin' of it."

"Well, pleased to meet ye both. How did ye meet?"

"In truth, she saved my life. I had a young horse on my rig. A snake slithered across the path, scaring the horse and upending the cart, which landed on my leg. I thought I was a goner, but she came along with her sister foragin' for medicines. They got me to the house. I took a fever, but they saved my leg and cured it. I fell in love on the spot." He crossed and gave his wife a big hug.

The warmth from the substantial fireplace gave the house a cozy, comfortable feel. The conversation soon returned to recent events. Guests always meant news.

"Rumors are going around about raids just north o' here," Joe said. "What do ye hear?"

"Three homesteads burned in as many weeks. Now four." Running Bear answered.

"They say the reverend is behind them or at least encouraging the men doin' his dirty work," Gray Wolf added. "And I don't doubt it. Based on what we saw at the O'Donnell's, it didn't look like any tribe I recognize."

"Even though they are crossing treaty boundaries?" Joe looked back and forth among the natives.

Gray Wolf looked at his brother. Neither of them knew for sure.

Little Hawk and Hannah cleared the dishes from the stew and fresh bread as they listened. Hannah served an apple pie made from the last of the dried apples following dinner. All too soon, the travelers were back on their way, their mission accomplished.

"We should still reach the post later today," Gray Wolf informed Angus.

The foursome rode up to the trading post in the early evening, following a quick ride from the Schmidt homestead. Frontier folk traveled from miles around to barter for necessary items, and a modest community had grown up surrounding the post.

"There are rooms available above the tavern, but they are costly," Gray Wolf told Angus. "And I am concerned about leaving the merchandise unattended. It used to be safe here," he added, looking at Angus. "Since the war, things have been different. I am uncomfortable now when there are those present I don't recognize."

"I suppose we ought to sleep here with the pelts," Running Bear decided and arranged for three stalls in the stables where they could stay with their horses. They would sleep comfortably through the night, and fresh straw was plentiful.

"Ye go eat. I'll stay with the animals and feed them," Gray Wolf offered. "Just be sure ye bring something back with ye. I'm half-starved."

Angus laughed; by now, even he was aware of Gray Wolf's ravenous appetite. He followed Running Bear and Little Hawk to the tavern. Here at the trading post, Europeans and natives of various origins did business together. Amazed, Angus listened to the mixture of languages. While he never learned any, he recognized two men speaking French and heard Spanish further along. There were several languages he did not recognize. Two men with jet-black skin hovered just inside the doorway, seemingly unsure whether they should enter. Spying an Indian they knew, they slipped into the corner to join him.

It was dim inside the smoke-filled room. A dozen large tables with bench seating down each side filled most of the space. A large wooden bar with stools lined one wall, with antlers hung above it. An additional room had been added through an arch on one side.

The weather was pleasant, so the trading post was busy, and the tavern was bustling. The room was warm, though the stench wafting from the crowd was nearly unbearable. Little Hawk wrinkled her nose in disgust as they entered. They grabbed hunks of bread from the baskets placed before them once they found space at a table.

The frazzled tavern wench, her dark hair curling out from under her cap, soon brought plates of roast pork with potatoes and mugs of beer. She set these in front of them and wiped her hands on her dirty apron. Grabbing a basket with more rolls from the main table, she slid it toward Angus as she hurried off to another table. Despite their surroundings, the food was good, the meat tender and full of flavor.

A commotion off to one side caught their attention as they finished. On a bench stood a scrawny older man arguing with a much taller one.

"Well, we shall see, won't we?" he spat in the other man's face as he jabbed his chest with his finger. "Ye are standing in Maryland right now, and the surveyors from London will show ye I am correct."

"We shall see about that, Cresap," exclaimed the taller man in a deep voice. "We shall see. If they are worth their salt, though, they know this here is Pennsylvania. Besides, why do ye believe they will do a better job than the others afore 'em?"

The two men continued bickering in the same vein as Angus slunk lower in his seat and chewed his fingernail. He recognized the name from his chats with Will and shifted uncomfortably; though he was exceedingly curious to see this man, Cresap, he was worried they might realize who he was.

"It is alright, my friend," Little Hawk said quietly, as though reading his thoughts, "we will not say who ye are. Besides, I cannot abide the stench in here much longer, anyway. Eat up, and let's go."

After quickly eating, Little Hawk grabbed bread and meat for Gray Wolf, and the men followed her out the door, much to Angus' relief.

Gathered together in the stable later, the friends told Gray Wolf what they'd overheard and determined the best course of action was to rise early, take care of their business, and be back on the road to Harlan's farm as soon as possible. They faced an exceedingly lengthy ride, but it was possible to cover the distance in one day if they returned in a straight line and bypassed the village.

The sun was clearing the horizon when they rose the following morning, and the natives hurried off to meet the proprietor. Angus was delighted to explore the trading post. What began as a modest log structure now had an addition attached, with a lean-to propped alongside to add even more covered space to display the goods. Construction was started on another addition along the length of the main building, and paddocks of cattle, sheep, and horses completed at each end.

While the natives traded their pelts and baskets for the items they needed, Angus wandered amongst the stalls. A person could get anything they wanted here. Barrels of grains stood in the doorway, and inside the main room were piles of beads and shiny silver adornments. They caught his eye, and he paused, admiring the beadwork stitched to the pouches lying on a table before heading into another room where he found fabric goods and men's clothing. A further room held household items, large washtubs, wool blankets, and iron pots—but the rifle drew Angus' eye. It was almost as tall as he was, and the wooden stock was polished to a deep, mellow sheen.

"That's a Pennsylvania long rifle," the man behind the counter said to him. "Ye'll not find nothin' more accurate than that. Beats a musket any day."

Angus was gazing longingly at the piece when Little Hawk came to retrieve him. He followed her outside, where the others waited with the laden pack animals and their horses. They had finished their trading, and it was time to return. After mounting his horse, Angus suddenly felt the hairs on the back of his neck standing on end. He edged his horse sideways and watched as a one-armed man emerged from the building where Angus had just been admiring the rifle.

Unable to shake his concerns about that man, Angus rode in silence. He wondered about the confrontation he witnessed with the man Cresap. The local folk seemed to place great importance on their survey, and the consequences of their results might be more severe than they initially thought. He decided it might be good to mention his concerns to Mr. Dixon when he returned.

Their ride back was quiet, and they were surprised to see everyone in the garden when they arrived at the Harlan's that night. An eerie gray-green dimness filled the air. Angus had utterly forgotten about the lunar eclipse Jeremiah mentioned before they departed.

John Harlan heard their approach and motioned for them to come and join them. The children were sitting around Mr. Mason, listening in rapt attention. The adults behind them listened intently as well. Mr. Dixon was standing beside Mason, dangling three different-sized balls attached to strings from his fingers.

"As ye know, the moon revolves around the Earth, and the Earth revolves around the sun," Mr. Mason patiently explained. Everyone nodded. He indicated each ball, saying, "sometimes, the three fall in a line."

Jeremiah fumbled as he attempted to line them up; Angus grabbed a ball to help.

"When they are in a line, the Earth blocks the sun's light from falling on the moon," Mr. Mason told them. The light from the fire fell across the ball, representing the moon. The shadow, caused by the earth, moved across the ball as Dixon swung the others into position. "It creates a shadow, which is what we see tonight. Notice the shadow moves across the moon."

Mr. Mason pointed to the balls first, then to the sky. He stared in amazement. "The edge of the sun's shadow on the moon is the best defined I have ever seen. The air is so clear it is remarkably distinct from the penumbral shade."

Oohs and ahh's rang out from the children as they stared overhead. Even the adults looking on were impressed. Angus noticed everyone was outside except Maire, though her children were there.

He asked Liam, who replied, "ah, she is with child now. She should not be outside during this."

"Congratulations!" Angus clapped his friend on the back. He was happy for him, though his logical brain did not understand her absence at first. However, he recalled his gran had said the same thing when he was a child. She believed pregnant women should not be out during an eclipse. Gran also placed their food in the underground cellars, locked the animals in the barns, and latched the doors securely. They could not eat or drink anything until the threat passed.

Angus gave up on these folktales long ago. Now, understanding the science of it, he often scoffed at the unfounded fears of others. Yet, despite that, his logical mind readily accepted phenomena such as second sight, and Angus passionately believed in the ability to sense or be aware of things about to happen. He had often witnessed it often enough with his gran and also his mother before her untimely death.

As he watched the earth's shadow pass across the surface of the moon, the words of the native seer returned, unbidden, teasing at the back of his mind, making him restless.

The long-silenced words of another seer came to mind.

"Ye shall see," the old crone had chanted. "Ye shall see. A dire outcome will strike this village. Even the manor will not be spared."

A chill ran up his spine as he stood in the garden thirteen years later.

CHAPTER 7

Sleep remained elusive that night as Angus' thoughts drifted to memories of his young sister, Fiona. A fever came through the village when he and his sister were young and eventually struck the manor house. Despite the skilled nursing of his mother and Gran, six-year-old Fiona did not survive.

Their mother sent Angus off for the healer when her condition worsened, but he had not returned with her in time to save Fiona. He failed to save his sister.

Two weeks prior, a seer had predicted a dire outcome would strike the manor. Angus knew this yet, could not prevent it. His mother never recovered from this latest blow and passed away soon after, leaving Angus and Gran alone.

He could undoubtedly shake off Maire's beliefs about the eclipse tonight, but he firmly believed in premonitions since that day. He understood how strong Maire's beliefs were to her. He sat up on the mat, feeling a bit hypocritical of his own point of view.

As he curled back under the blanket, Angus could not ignore that feeling of impending doom. It had hung over him like a cloud since encountering the seer in the longhouse. He snuggled deeper into the bedroll.

What further troubles lie ahead? Be true to yourself. What did she mean?

His reactions to seeing the one-armed man again merely added to his unease. Though his English friends and the monks at the monastery laughed at him for his beliefs, Angus recognized the respect he saw in these native people for the seers in their tribe. They believed.

Eventually, Angus drifted off into a restless sleep.

He woke to the sounds of activity outside the observatory. Men were moving about, and horses were stamping their hooves—then he heard men's voices. Pulling himself fully awake, Angus remembered the workers were arriving today. These must be the axmen.

Their first task was clearing the heavily wooded forest, heading south from their present location. In defining the tasks to be accomplished with the survey, the commissioners had agreed that the Maryland border would start fifteen miles south of Philadelphia. Mr. Mason and Mr. Dixon determined the starting point was at Harlan's farm. Ever the perfectionist, Mr. Mason completed more observations to triple-check the data and satisfy himself.

At the same time, the men started to clear a visto, a wide path through the woods that would enable them to do the survey. Joel Bailey, a local surveyor, would oversee these men and keep them on track. Jeremiah Dixon and his team would follow once the men cleared the pathway through the heavy forest. They would perform a more official measurement of the fifteen miles with his equipment.

Angus rolled out of his makeshift bed and dressed before stepping into the morning light, afraid of missing anything. The weather was crisp and cold. As he squinted at the brightness, he noticed Liam with the other men and joined him. His footsteps crunched in the frosty grass beneath his boots.

"Mornin'," Liam blew on his gloved hands as he greeted him. "Ye look a right mess. There is coffee yonder." He nodded toward the barn.

Angus smiled as he ran his fingers through his unruly hair. "Aye, thank ye. I didn't sleep well, and coffee would not go amiss just now."

"I am leaving with the first team helping Mr. Bailey. But I will be back to join the rest of ye when the official survey starts," Liam explained.

"Well, good for ye," Angus answered. "I will look after Maire and your sons while ye are working. Ye needn't worry about them."

"Thank ye, I appreciate that."

The nagging feeling he experienced during the night remained with him that morning as he grabbed a mug of hot coffee. The five men hired to clear the trees listened to Mr. Dixon's instructions. Angus hung back, listening as he allowed the coffee to cool.

"Mr. Bailey here will work ahead of ye to keep the path on track as ye head south," Mr. Dixon explained. "If we keep the cleared area wide enough, it will allow us to follow ye for a more detailed measurement. Does anyone have any questions?"

The men glanced around and shook their heads. It was a simple enough task. Besides the surveyor and the axmen, a wagon carrying basic supplies would accompany them. As they worked, the men would fend for themselves, fishing or snaring rabbits.

When Dixon finished speaking, Angus looked uneasily at the others standing around, glancing at each, then suddenly returning to the face of a short, stocky, dark-haired man. There was something familiar about him.

"Do ye know that man?" He asked Sarah as she passed.

"Well, I know George, the tall blonde one. He lives up the way a piece. Is that the one ye mean?" She glanced again at the men, "The rest are from Philadelphia, I reckon."

"Nay, I know *him,* the one second from the left. Something familiar about that man, but I can't place him." He nodded toward the man as he spoke.

Sarah looked again and shook her head. "Aye. That happens to me sometimes too. Ye, for example, remind me of somebody, but I can't recollect who it is."

"Me?" Angus shivered.

"Well, I suppose ye just have similar features to someone I have seen afore."

Sarah headed back toward the house, stopping to chat with her husband. John Harlan helped ensure the men were well provided for before. They would start by cutting down trees on the edge of his property. Mr. Mason and Mr. Dixon, accompanied by Mr. Bailey, emerged from the observatory, and receiving their final words of advice, the team left.

Mr. Mason and Mr. Dixon returned to the observatory to organize their notes before presenting their findings to the commissioners, updating them on their progress.

Angus waylaid Jeremiah on his way toward the observatory. "Do ye have a moment?"

Dixon looked around. "Uh, sure. What's on yer mind?"

"While I was away with the Indians, I heard Thomas Cresap arguing with another man about whether we are doing a good job. They disagreed over where the line really was. And well, it seemed important that ye know about it."

Jeremiah nodded. "Aye, one side or the other is bound to be disappointed. But don't ye worry about that. Charles and I are the ones making the decisions based on the science."

"Also, there's a one-armed man following me around. I see him everywhere. He was even at the trading post."

Mr. Dixon paused as if considering this news. "Probably a coincidence," he said in a tone that left Angus doubting he believed it. Dixon left to join Mr. Mason in the observatory.

With little to do now, Angus assisted John Harlan and spent the morning helping him repair a fence around the field where he kept a few cattle. The men chatted as they worked.

"How long have ye lived here?" asked Angus.

"All my life, my grandfather came from Durham as a young man," he replied. "He started the farm, and me and pa added to it over the years. My two older boys, Phineas and Jesse, have each taken a piece to farm for themselves as they married. I suppose Stephen will want to marry soon, but I'm not in a hurry to see him go." He sighed.

Having something to do and John's excellent company, Angus soon relaxed, and the uneasiness melted away. His spirits were much lighter by the time they returned to the house.

The next several days were warmer and brought more rain than snow. Finally satisfied with their results, Mr. Mason and Mr. Dixon departed for New Castle. With both men agreeing they were on the right parallel, in line with Philadelphia, they placed a marble marker where the zenith sector sat, marking where they had taken their readings. Mr. Mason packed that instrument himself, while Angus packed the rest. Soon, John

Loxley returned, and he and Angus dismantled the observatory. While surveying their way south, they would store the equipment in a room in John and Sarah's house. The dismantled observatory and other items would be stacked in the barn. Fielding, the cook, was away gathering supplies for their journey. Will and his son would arrive again soon. Angus was eager to see them again, especially now that Liam was gone. He missed all his new friends, but the preparations kept him busy.

He sorted the items to go in the wagons in the subsequent phase. They would not be doing any stargazing until they located that next point. This phase would be a simple matter of surveying the distance. There was Jeremiah's transit, of course. Along with it were bits of red and yellow cloth—so it would be easier for the men to see Dixon as he gestured. Behind them, the chain crew would measure the distance along the path. It seemed straightforward to Angus.

Angus checked to ensure the pouch with the stobs, or small wooden markers, was packed. While unsure of what role he would play in this next phase, he eagerly looked forward to doing something. Angus laid out the first chain and counted one hundred links or twenty-two yards, which he calculated equaled eighty chains per mile. He ensured the other chain also contained one hundred links.

A few days later, the surveyors returned from their meetings in high spirits. Precisely locating the point had taken longer than the commissioners expected. Still, Mr. Mason and Mr. Dixon had assured them that the next phase would move quicker, and they hoped to have the Maryland border point located soon. Itching to see how the visto cutting progressed, Jeremiah invited Angus to ride along to check the men's progress.

"They have done a good job," Jeremiah said. He pointed out the trees along the broad avenue as they rode. "I have never seen such an abundance of oak, beech, poplar, and hickory."

"Aye, I would agree," replied Angus. "Oh, and look at the firs, too." Jeremiah considered the young man with surprise. Blushing, Angus continued, "I have had an interest in botany since I first saw Linnaeus' book at the monastery. As a lad, I was fascinated studying the pictures of the plants and birds."

"Goodness, Lad, ye are well read," Dixon said, chuckling to himself. He glanced again at Angus riding next to him. "Ye just reminded me of myself when I was younger."

Angus grinned, thinking how much Dixon had accomplished since then.

Soon they reached the workers and dismounted. Dixon ambled off to join Mr. Bailey while Angus hurried to find Liam and let his friend know Maire and their boys were well. While they chatted, Angus observed the one he had seen before, hanging back a bit. He remembered his own awe of Mr. Mason and Mr. Dixon and understood the man's shy hesitancy.

When Dixon determined all was satisfactory, he and Angus sauntered toward their horses to return to the farm. Suddenly, the short, dark-haired man stepped toward Mr. Dixon. He paused, considering whether to approach, and took another step, determined now.

"Do ye have a question, Lad?" Dixon asked.

Glancing at the surveyor and then quickly away, the man removed his hat and played with it, running the brim through his hands. Stuttering a bit, he said, "Well, uh, no, Sir. Umm, my name is Rupert, uh, Rupert

Jones. I was but wantin' to thank ye for the work." He shifted his feet as if he wanted to say something else as he peered at Angus. Then he shook his head and merely said, "Thank ye, Sir." With a lingering glance at Angus, he hurried to rejoin the others.

"Well, that was nice," said Jeremiah.

Angus didn't reply, as he had recognized the man when he removed his hat. Angus saw the scar on his forehead and remembered him being with Gil in Philadelphia and again at the burned homestead. *What is he doing here? He must have thought I'd recognized him.* An icy shiver of unease ran up his spine.

"When we get back, I need to speak with Charles. Joel Bailey told me there have been fights between his men and the locals over the border." Jeremiah looked concerned.

"Sir," he said. Dixon scowled at him. "I mean Jeremiah. There may be more. That man back there, Rupert, he was one of the ones in Philadelphia that warned us that day about working with the Indians."

Jeremiah looked over his shoulder toward the men. "Maybe he needed work." Though brushing it off at the time, Dixon was quiet on the ride back to the farm.

Was the man spying on them? Angus wondered.

By April 2nd, the team was ready to move. Will arrived with his son, Young Will, and two more wagons. Under Angus' direction, the men loaded food, supplies, and tents into these, along with the surveying gear. Throwing himself into the work, Angus temporarily forgot about the axman in the woods.

Bright and early the following morning, Mr. Dixon took command of the expedition. The survey began with a reading taken from the stone they placed before they broke down the observatory.

"Ye know the locals have a name for this rock," John informed them. "They've named it the Stargazer's Stone." The men smiled, taking great delight in this news.

"I want to participate in this portion, if I may," Mr. Mason requested, approaching Mr. Dixon. "Ye know I have no professional experience as a surveyor, but I understand the process. And it is something I've long desired to try."

Dixon agreed and handed him the rod. Moving away, following Jeremiah's directions, Mr. Mason used the spirit level to ensure the rod was vertical and turned to watch for his partner's signals. Dixon directed using colored bits of cloth, and Mr. Mason moved the rod to the right or left as indicated until it was aligned correctly. He pushed a stob into the ground to mark the spot, and Jeremiah moved the transit to the mark and repeated the process.

"Well, I hoped to get further today," Jeremiah said to the men as they ate their meal of crusty bread and hard-boiled eggs. Washing it down with cider, he wiped his chin and said, "Now that we know this process will work, maybe we should take some measurements."

Angus was excited as they walked back to the farm. He wanted to be on the chains that measured the distance. Like Mr. Mason, he, too, was eager to join.

"Do ye understand what to do?" Mr. Mason asked him when they arrived.

"Aye," Angus replied, explaining the process to his satisfaction.

As the team left the farm, Angus waved at Sarah Harlan, who was watching them. She was elbows deep in the laundry as the men moved out of sight.

The initial process was straightforward as the land was flat. However, they soon reached a downward slope, requiring Mr. Loxley's levels. His longer ones, at twenty-two feet, proved too cumbersome to use, so they switched to the shorter ones, which were a more manageable sixteen feet. On their first day, they measured 95 chains—or just over a mile.

April 3rd brought heavy rains, and the men could not work. However, it was not without its pleasant moments, as later in the day, Liam arrived, dripping wet. He and Angus happily greeted each other.

"I am free to come help ye," he said, patting his friend on the back. "We are nearly finished cutting, and they have plenty o' men to finish the rest."

Angus was pleased to see him and invited him into the tent. The men squeezed inside were playing cards. There was not much else to do.

Thankfully, the next day brought glorious weather. Though they had to stop once to free a wagon stuck in the mud, the men covered roughly five miles. First, they traversed the Wilmington road, and further along, they crossed the main road between Philadelphia and Nottingham. Much of their time was spent moving along the visto through thick woods, though occasionally, they encountered a farmstead. They spent one night companionably in the barn of a young farmer who listened enthusiastically to the details of what they were doing.

Days blurred together. Survey, measure, count... survey, measure, count... They measured 160 chains on the fifth, after which they spent the night at the farm of Joseph Freads.

"Ye are most welcome here," Joseph and his wife greeted the men. "We've been expectin' ye since the axmen came through. We want to offer ye a feast of roast venison."

"Why thank ye kindly," Mr. Mason accepted for them all.

Dixon was eager to check the accuracy of the chain and sent Angus to count the links when they arrived. After settling in, the hungry team enjoyed the excellent food and the pleasant weather. After dinner, they sat around the fire in jovial camaraderie.

Joseph and his wife had many questions about their work, and the men demonstrated the process. After a long day and much good ale, this humorous affair ended with Dixon taking a bow. Though enjoying themselves immensely, the team knew they had an early start in the morning, and eventually, the men curled up and drifted off to sleep.

Angus had checked the chains and placed them in the wagon when he heard an angry shout. Racing to the barn, Angus found Will alone with the draft horse. The harness hung on the wall the previous day was nowhere in sight. The men searched in vain.

"Why would someone steal that? It was old but softer for the horse," Will said. "I have spare parts for wheels, but who carries a spare harness? It was my favorite." He gritted his teeth.

"I have an old one that might do," Joseph offered. "Ye can return it later when ye can. I don't use it these days."

Mr. Mason thanked him profusely. He and Mr. Dixon were noticeably upset. Dixon shook his head at Angus when he started to speak, now was not the time for Angus' concerns about sabotage on the survey.

Angus knew Mr. Dixon was unhappy with the headway so far. Their efforts were slower than he was accustomed to in England. Many things impeded their progress; soggy ground in which the wagons bogged down, waterways they had to ford, not to mention the briars and heavy undergrowth that entangled the chains. But the work continued, and they proceeded with another 161 chains the following day. These last two days, they traversed rougher terrain where the going was slow.

The men knew they were getting close now. Early in the afternoon on April 12th, they reached the farm of Alexander Bryan. Adding in the difference in relation to Philadelphia, this brought them to 15 miles, 2 two chains, and 93 links. Satisfied, Dixon called a halt to the survey.

The party received a warm welcome from the Bryans as the men unloaded the wagons and set up their camp. Alexander Bryan, recognizing Mr. Mason and Mr. Dixon as gentlemen, offered them a tiny bedroom in the house while the others happily set up tents and claimed a corner of the barn. In the morning, they would return to Harlan's farm for the rest of the equipment. As before, they would observe the stars here to confirm their location.

Later that evening, Angus strolled away from the others and crossed the valley into the clearing. On starry nights such as this, he often searched for the hunter, Orion. The visto was expansive, but it was not wide enough for him to view the stars above the treetops opposite. Angus could easily see in the darkness as the moon approached full again.

He stepped closer to the edge of the cleared area, backing up as he stared at the sky. One more step and he could see above the trees. Angus stepped slowly backward, gazing over the treetops opposite... when his foot struck something solid, and down he tumbled backward.

With a thump, Angus bounced off something solid that gave a little as it broke his fall. He landed hard beside it. Uninjured, Angus saw he was sitting next to someone and apologized to the man for falling on him. However, he gasped as he saw blood on his hand. An arrow protruded from the man's chest. His fall had broken it.

Angus stared at the man's face in horror as he realized it was Rupert Jones, the axman.

CHAPTER 8

Angus crawled a few feet away from the body. On his hands and knees, he vomited violently. A feeling of dread churned in the pit of his stomach; he did not realize he had cried out until Liam came running.

"Angus?" he shouted. "Where are ye? Are ye alright?"

Liam peered to either side in the moonlight as he drew closer up the path. He slowed as he approached, making his way through the clearing.

"Here," Angus choked out as he sat back on his haunches as his friend drew near.

Liam observed the scene. His eyes widened at the sight of the man sprawled before Angus. He stayed well away from the body but peered at it, his sunburnt face growing pale in the moonlight.

"What happened?"

"I dinna ken. I just found him." He looked around in case the killer was nearby.

"Why... it is Rupert, the axman!" Liam exclaimed as he looked closer. He spotted the broken shaft of an arrow clenched in Angus' hand and looked around. "Surely, it was not Indians? Have ye seen any about?"

"Nay, I haven't. But I am sure the local Indians did not do this." Angus stared at the arrow, having recognized it from the homestead. "And I ken who he is. I met him when I came with Mr. Dixon to check on the tree clearing."

He thought back, wondering anew whether Rupert had wanted to speak to him that day and why. He paused, unsure how much to reveal. Angus feared telling anyone about meeting the dead man at the burned homestead might look suspicious. But this was Liam.

"I also saw him afore," Angus admitted. He was at the O'Donnell homestead."

"The one they burned? Indians did that." As Liam spoke, a shadow of doubt crossed Angus' face. "Didn't they?"

"I am not so sure," Angus remembered Running Bear's doubts about the arrows. He gathered his thoughts. "I don't believe it was, and I doubt they killed this man either." He felt he had every reason to trust the native. Like the Harlans and the people at the trading post, he knew frontier folk thought highly of the brothers.

"I had it in mind Gil was behind burning that homestead." He waved the arrow. "But not after this. This man was Gil's friend." Angus told Liam about finding the same fletchings there.

Liam helped Angus to his feet. Before attempting a few tentative steps, Angus stood still a moment, steadying his weak knees.

"We should go for help," Liam told him, "Mr. Bryan will know where to find the local sheriff, and we can let him deal with this."

Angus agreed, releasing his hold on Liam's shoulder. The pair retreated toward the camp. A short distance away, Angus paused, his mind awash with images. He stared at the arrow in his hand and relived the night he spent with the Susquehannock in their longhouse. Angus remembered the people he had met. Though he only stayed with them one night, Angus thought it was one of the few places he had felt accepted since childhood.

"Nay! I just canna accept the Indians we've met could have done something like this," he said imploringly to Liam. How could he explain it so his friend would understand? "It's just not right... the pieces don't fit."

"Maybe them other Indians?" Liam offered. "I hear not all of them are so friendly."

The broken shaft slipped from Angus' hand when he shrugged. He looked helplessly at Liam and bent down to retrieve the arrow.

"Ye go. I shall remain here and watch over the body. I can't just leave him here."

"Are ye sure ye will be alright?" Liam asked before leaving. At Angus' nod, he made his way back down the clearing, glancing over his shoulder several times until Angus could no longer see his friend in the gathering darkness.

Angus slowly crossed back to the body and bent over it in the dim light. *It doesn't look like he was killed recently.* Angus knew little about dead people though he hunted animals in his youth. There was no stiffness to it, and the muscles had grown limp. The skin was shrinking, pulling tighter across the bones. And it was cold to the touch. At a guess, he'd say it had been at least a day since Rupert was killed.

After studying the scene for several minutes, Angus stepped away and sat nearby on a large, flat rock. As he spun the shaft in his hands, he noticed a small piece of cloth stuck to it. That had not been there when he first picked up the arrow; maybe it clung to the dried blood when he dropped it. It was slightly torn, and he caught a whiff of gunpowder. He held it up. It was a rifle patch.

"Probably someone hunting," he mused to himself and stuck the oily scrap into his pouch. They had snared rabbits and hunted other small animals to supplement the food the cook had prepared. But several of the men did carry hunting rifles.

"Rifles." Angus pulled the oily scrap back out of his pouch and stared at it. "I wonder."

He rose and returned to the body. The only wound he could see was the hole from the arrow, the broken end of which was lodged in the dead man's chest. Though the arrowhead was buried deep, the end of the broken shaft moved easily in his hand. He returned to the rock.

Angus fretted about the survey and the rest of the team. So far, there were only minor incidents. But he was concerned about the effect of this on their progress. Murder was the last thing they needed. And Rupert Jones was a member of their team.

After what felt like an eternity, Angus heard voices and rose to his feet. *Thank God.* A pair of lanterns came toward him through the trees. Moments later, Jeremiah Dixon appeared with Liam. Other men followed but remained in the shadows. Angus did not recognize them—they must be local men.

"Charles rode off with Mr. Bryan for the sheriff," Dixon said to Angus. "He felt someone should represent the project."

Mr. Dixon moved toward the body and shone the lantern he carried over the man. There was blood on his hunting shirt surrounding the hole in his chest. He looked curiously at Angus, who held up the arrow.

"Ah," was all Mr. Dixon said.

"I am sorry, Sir," Angus hung his head. "This will hold everything up."

"Not yer fault, lad," Mr. Dixon replied, "unless ye did it, which I very much doubt." He grinned, but the attempt at humor was lost on Angus. Dixon moved the lantern nearer to the body as he examined it.

"Do ye recognize him?" Angus asked. Dixon paused and looked again.

"Why he's the one who came and spoke with me in the clearing." He studied the man's face again, "the one ye thought was spying on us."

"Aye." Angus nodded.

Dixon indicated the arrow. "And ye think this was Indians? Was that man right?"

"No, sir," Angus interjected. "There is something odd about this fletching." When Jeremiah raised an eyebrow at this, Angus told him about the events at the burned homestead. "Running Bear and Gray Wolf were suspicious about this fletching; they didn't recognize it."

Mr. Dixon turned to Liam. "Was Jones with ye when ye finished the clearing?"

"I wasn't there at the end, Sir. I was released to join ye."

Then, moving to Angus, Dixon continued, "come, let's return to the camp. Mr. Bryan's men will keep watch until the sheriff arrives."

Mr. Dixon waved to the locals who would stay. "If all goes well, we will head to Harlan's farm tomorrow as planned. Going back should be easier."

"Don't fret, lad." Mr. Dixon clasped Angus on the shoulder as they turned toward Bryan's farm to wait for the sheriff.

When they arrived back at the camp, Angus sat by the fire, staring into the flames, unaware of his surroundings. Mrs. Bryan took pity on him and offered him some port to drink to steady his nerves. The empty tin cup sat balanced on his knee.

"Ye should eat something, Lad," Fielding, the cook, tried again

"Nay, thank ye," Angus replied once more.

The evening grew late, but nobody wanted to go to bed until Mr. Mason returned with Mr. Bryan and the sheriff. Curiosity bubbled through the camp, though they were wary of saying much in front of Angus. Each man was filing away stories to share on his return home. Murder was big news.

Much later, they heard horses coming up the road. Will stood and placed a hand gently on Angus' shoulder. "They are here, Lad."

However, as he turned his head, Angus noticed the two men returning alone. "The *sheriff,"* Mr. Bryan spat out the term, his voice dripping sarcasm, "decided he cannot see in the dark. Therefore, he will arrive in the morning and look around then. He preferred to remain in the tavern with his whisky." His voice dripped scorn.

"What about the body?" asked Angus. He rose, much steadier on his feet now. "We can't just leave it lying there," he protested.

"I suppose we should," answered Mr. Mason. "I imagine the sheriff would prefer to see it where it lies. Though we don't need any animals finding it."

"Aye," replied Will. "Sir, my son and I can stand watch while ye get some sleep if ye like. I know ye plan fer an early start in the morning, but we can stay with the wagons and follow after a few hours of sleep. We will catch up to ye later in the day."

George, the third carter, spoke up, "shall I stay with Young Will so ye can take a wagon with ye when ye start on your way? Ye will need one fer the equipment."

"A good plan," said Mr. Mason. "And Angus, ye should remain as well. I think the sheriff may want to hear what ye found. Young Will, ye go up with George to relieve the men. We will see ye in the morning. Everyone else, try to get some sleep. We will start early."

Thanking Mr. Bryan for his help, Mr. Mason followed him into the house where he and Jeremiah would spend the night. The rest of the men ambled toward the barn.

Angus lagged behind, strolling to the barn with Liam. He sighed, and Liam gave him a slight smile. "It will be alright. Just tell the sheriff what ye found. Ye will catch up with us shortly."

Angus certainly hoped so.

Angus tossed all night, only getting a few hours of sleep. His thoughts alternated between wishing he hadn't come and wanting to see this put right. *But what can I do? I shouldn't have come. Did Rupert wish to say something that day? How can I help with this? Or can I?*

In the wee hours of the morning, he rolled over and sat groggily in the straw in the corner, trying to clear his head. Except for the snores of the sleeping men, it was quiet. Rising, Angus sent a silent prayer that this had all been a dream. But as he rose to his feet, he knew it had not.

The plan that day was to confirm the survey and check the measurements on their way back to Harlan's for the instruments. This would ensure their initial length was correct. They had made slow progress heading south; however, knowing what they faced, Mr. Dixon hoped the return journey would be quicker. Most likely, they would only recheck the trickier areas that had caused them problems.

The men were all called to a meeting in the morning. After contemplating the amount of work they had, Mr. Mason decided his team needed two carts.

"We'll empty that wagon and go straight back to Harlan's for the equipment. I will ride to the farm with three men in the other wagon," he said. "We'll leave one cart here with the remaining workers to check a few measurements on their way. We'll meet up at Harlan's to finish loading the wagons." Mr. Dixon agreed this was a workable plan.

Young Will looked sheepishly at the group that morning as they heard the change of plans. "Afraid I fell asleep on the watch and left Georgie here on his own. I reckon I can manage the second cart well enough today." His father glared at him. Young Will shuffled his toe in the dirt.

George looked at him and smiled. "Aye. And ye snore somethin' fierce too like to wake the dead." He gave Will a playful jab in the arm. Young Will blushed hearing this—as did George when he realized what he said.

Liam approached Angus. "I will be workin' with Mr. Dixon today. I wish I could stay with ye, but he'd like me to work with Andrew since we worked together on the chain comin' down."

Unhappy at hearing this, Angus replied, "I understand. That makes sense. I hope the sheriff shows up soon, and I will be on my way shortly after ye. With horses, George and I will surely catch up to ye afore long."

Liam smiled as Mrs. Bryan stepped out of the house with a huge plate of fresh hot biscuits and sliced ham. Her daughters followed with strong, black coffee and freshly churned butter for the biscuits. The tantalizing aroma tempted Angus, who had eaten little since the previous afternoon.

He followed the men to the make-shift table, eagerly wolfing down two flaky biscuits laden with thick slabs of ham and dripping with melted butter. Angus followed this with strong coffee in a large clay mug. Afterward, he felt fully ready to meet the sheriff and put this all behind him.

Angus sipped another cup of coffee as he watched the wagons pull away, feeling somewhat lonely. He and George meandered around the property. Eventually, Angus took the path toward the body to examine it by daylight.

Two local men sat in the clearing. As he approached, Angus studied the area a moment before greeting them. Nothing looked any different by daylight than the night before, except he noticed the smell emanating from the body when he drew near.

"Mornin'. Everything alright?"

They nodded, one man saying, "yep, been pretty quiet. I didn't see any animals yet, but the hawks are circling." He pointed up at the sky.

Angus glanced upward at the spiraling birds overhead before returning his gaze to the dead body. Next, Angus studied the arrow lying where he placed it after showing it to Mr. Dixon. Now he pulled one he found at the homestead from his pouch and compared the two. As he thought, they were identical.

One of the local men watched him. His friend was picking at his shoe when the first man nudged him and nodded toward Angus. Angus saw them, placed the arrow back in his pouch, and slowly left for the house.

It was afternoon before the sheriff finally showed up, bringing one deputy and a small horse-drawn cart. Sliding off his horse with a grunt, the sheriff strutted toward Alexander Bryan.

"Well, let's get this done. I gotta be getting' back soon. Important things to do. I'm a busy man." The sheriff was almost as wide as tall, with red cheeks and a bulbous nose poking out above his full beard. His thumbs in his belt, he strutted around importantly. "Now, where is this body?"

"I will show ye. It is up the way a piece," Bryan answered. He indicated to Angus, "the lad here found him."

The sheriff looked at Angus. "Well, I suppose ye might as well come along too."

His relief at finally seeing the sheriff arrive quickly melted at this exchange.

Sheriff Brown, and the others, followed Angus along the visto to where the body lay. The two local men were still there. One reached to shoo away the flies with this hat when they approached.

"I fell over the body here," explained Angus.

"Fell? What were ye doing up here?" the sheriff asked suspiciously, peering up at him. "Were ye drunk?"

Angus looked sheepish. "No. I was looking at the stars."

"Ye were what?" The sheriff said in disbelief. Angus felt a moment of panic. He wondered how he could explain it.

Mr. Bryan came to Angus' aid and explained that the men were conducting this survey, using the stars to navigate. Angus gave him a look of relief.

"Humph," responded the sheriff. "Nonsense. Met one o' ye last night. All prim and proper, rich type, not sure I believe in all that educated stuff."

Angus wanted this all to end as he reached down, picked up the arrow, and handed it to the sheriff. As he explained how he had knocked it over when he fell, the sheriff cut him off abruptly.

"No need for explanations. It is obvious that them Indians are stirring up trouble again."

"I don't agree," Angus began, about to explain there was something unusual about this arrow. Running Bear was sure this did not belong to anyone local.

But the sheriff again cut him off. "Maybe ye oughta come along too, hmm? I assume ye know more than ye are telling."

"That's ridiculous, Sheriff. I can vouch for him," Alexander said.

The sheriff backed down, giving Angus a look of disbelief.

Are ye sure no one heard anything?" He asked.

The men shook their heads. "I figure it has been a couple of days since the murder, and we were up north then," Angus explained. "Through this section, we were working near the opposite tree line. We wouldn't have seen him in this tall grass."

Mr. Bryan, who living nearby, mentioned men were hunting in the woods, and they heard rifles. However, the locals were often hunting, so that was normal. "Besides, a bow makes no noise."

The sheriff glared at him.

"Ah, well, I've seen what need, might as well load him up and move along," said the sheriff. "No sense wasting time. Georgie, help John put that body in the cart." George grimaced but did as he was ordered.

As the sheriff passed him, Angus detected the potent smell of stale alcohol. He spied the top of a flask sticking out of the man's pouch. Although he wanted to say more, Angus realized it would get him nowhere. He watched them load Rupert's body in silence.

This was a mess, but at that moment, Angus knew he would stay in the colonies. He needed to solve the man's death. It was only fitting.

CHAPTER 9

Joseph Freads removed his woolen cap as he entered *The Crown* tavern. Earlier that morning, he labored on his farm, felling trees to clear more land. While he ate his midday meal, his wife insisted the package to her sister in Virginia must go to the post right now. She had heard the post rider was expected to pass through the following day. Thus, Joseph found himself at the crossroads of the Nottingham Road. With the package delivered, he wanted a wee drink before returning home.

"A pint o' yer best," he called out to the tavern-keeper, Nathaniel. Both men knew he only served one type of beer, but this was Joseph's standard greeting.

"Aye, coming up," Nathaniel replied. "What is new with ye?" He asked Joseph as he pulled on the tap. Though the tavern was busy, he always managed to chat with his regular customers.

"Those London surveyors stayed with us a few nights back, some locals with 'em. That created a bit of excitement. That one called Dixon is alright, but the other sat most o' the evening at his little travel desk writin' in his journal." He paused when Nathaniel slid the beer across to him and took a pull on his mug. "Nice bunch o' folks, but I was sorry that someone stole one o' Will's harnesses while they slept. Felt bad about that, so I loaned 'em one o' mine."

"Really?" Nathaniel asked. "Why would someone do that?"

"Don't know." Joseph shrugged and took another swig. "I'm interested to see whether they'll do any better figuring out that border than the others who tried."

"Aye. More settlers are arrivin' every day out here, it seems," Nathaniel reflected.

Joseph, settled onto his stool, was ready to expand on the topic, but a patron at the far end of the counter, called out for a pint. Nathaniel left to serve him.

Joseph sipped quietly, enjoying the few moments of peace and solitude with his drink. Warm and cozy in his corner, he knew he couldn't stay long if he wished to be home by dark. However, he would delay his departure as long as possible, enjoying it while he could.

As he sipped, he tried his best to ignore the commotion emanating from the main room behind him. The room was crowded. The voices, which were only a murmur when he sat down, grew louder. He was curious, but they sounded angry, and he didn't want to become involved. Others joined the crowd, which grew increasingly rowdy. Hunched over his beer, he heard a voice ring out above the others.

"That bloody sheriff ain't doin' nothin'," said the man. "My friend was killed by them Indians, and I think them surveyors are hidin' the truth."

A few of the men agreed. One man encouraged him, yelling, "ye tell it, Gil."

Curious, Joseph spun around to listen. He had heard about the death of Rupert Jones. Working his audience now, Gil hopped onto the stone hearth and continued his rant in a louder voice.

"I saw that younger surveyor with Runnin' Bear at the O'Donnell's homestead when they burned it. He had an arrow in his hand. And

Jacob," he nodded to a man nearby, "heard the sheriff say they shot Rupert with an arrow."

"Aye, I did," Jacob agreed, enjoying his moment of fame.

Several of the men looked at Jacob and turned to each other.

" I oughta go tell the sheriff who I saw at the homestead." Gil continued his story. "He'll listen to me. Those folks are involved. I know it." A hushed silence filled the room.

Gil paused, allowing that to sink in before continuing, "My friend, Rupert, ye all know Rupert." Several men nodded. "Well, he took some work with them to earn a bit fer his family. Now he is dead." He strutted to the end of the hearth and spun back toward the crowd. A few men whispered among themselves. He had their attention.

Joseph sat quietly, reflecting on the men who stayed in his home. They seemed like good folk to him. Joseph shook his head and sipped as he recalled that night around the fire. The men appreciated the venison he prepared for them. They were polite and gracious. This didn't fit at all.

"Well, all o' ye know who uses bows and arrows around here. They shot Rupert while he worked with those survey men." He paused, ensuring the men were still listening. "Who do they think they are coming from London and making important decisions for us? I saw that red-haired one with those Indians. He's involved." Again, he paused. "Ye know, he was there when Rupert was found." Several men gasped while a few shuffled their feet and stared at the ground. But some continued to encourage him.

Joseph was pretty sure Gil was wrong. His opinion was reinforced when he glanced behind Gil at Simon Tanner, Gil's sidekick. As Gil continued his rant, Joseph noticed a look of puzzlement spread across Simon's face. Joseph watched Simon lean across and whisper something to Gil, only to receive a stern glare in return. Then Gil snarled and grabbed his arm, saying something to Simon that Joseph could not hear. As Joseph observed the scene, Gil clenched his fist and turned his back on Simon. Soon after, Joseph watched Simon slink further into the crowd. He noticed Simon shake his head in disbelief and slip out the side door.

"Hmm... Simon knows something," murmured Joseph.

"What did ye say?" asked Nathaniel, returning to his end of the counter. He splashed a little extra beer into Joseph's mug.

"Aww, 'twas nothing, just mumbling to myself." Joseph considered for a moment, then turned to speak to Nathaniel. "That tale he's tellin', though, doesn't ring true with the men I met. That redhead Gil mentioned must be the one called Angus, a nice young lad. And I know Running Bear and his family. Ye know them too, Nathaniel; those Indians had no part in this. Just don't seem right to me."

"Ah, I don't know. Their friend was just killed. Simon's probably more upset than ye know. Gil, too, most likely," he replied. "And he still holds a grudge against the Indians, just like his pa."

"Aye, I hear word he's been meeting with Reverend Elder," Joseph said.

"Oh, I wouldn't make too much o' that," Nathaniel shrugged. "That man loves his pulpit. It'll be a good thing when this is all settled."

After a moment, Joseph paid for his beer and bid Nathaniel farewell. When he opened the door, it was raining in earnest; the storm looming on the horizon all day caught up with him. It would be a long, wet ride home. He pulled his oilskin cloak from his saddlebag, glad he kept it there, and mounted his horse to begin the dreary ride home.

Meanwhile, further south, the rain poured down all day, turning the visto into a pool of soggy ground. While Mason originally planned to head straight back, his wagon got stuck in the mud. Once free, he remained with Dixon's team.

"Alright, men, one more good push oughta get her free." Will directed the men as they pushed and shoved to free the wagon from the wet muck. And on the count of three, the wagon rolled free at last.

"I guess we ought to give up doing any work on this trip," Dixon said to Mr. Mason as he slogged out of the mud. "Though I hate to give it up altogether, maybe we can check some sections further north and cover this stretch later when we come back through."

Mason nodded in agreement. The workmen could not confirm the measurements in this weather; this was the third time a wagon got stuck in the mud. "Ye might as well quit and come to Harlan's with us. We can load the wagons for the return trip. If the weather changes, we shall see what ye can do, then."

The pouring rain started at Bryan's farm shortly after the sheriff departed. Angus secretly hoped that the man was caught out in the deluge. Mrs. Bryan prepared tea, though Angus was itching to catch up with the others—despite her hospitality.

Alexander joined them inside, shaking off his cloak in the doorway. "Ach, 'tis a miserable day, boys. Ye ought to stay the night." Angus rose to his feet, objecting, but Alexander interjected, "Now, now. I know ye want to return to work, I understand. But I am sure they are not getting anything done in this weather, anyhow. They are probably holed up somewhere out of the storm. It looks much worse to the north."

Removing his boots, he approached the table and smiled at his wife. "Nuthin' like a good cuppa tea on a dreary day."

"Aye. Lad, ye best sit yerself down. Ye are wearing a path in my rug," said Mrs. Bryan genially as she smiled at him. She placed cups of tea on the table in the warm, dry kitchen and motioned for him to sit. "Ye too, George."

The steam swirled under his mustache as Mr. Bryan added, "ye two can take the room Mr. Mason and Mr. Dixon used for the night. No one uses it now with the boys grown. It will be more comfortable for ye than the barn."

Angus backed down and returned to his seat at the long table. He sipped his tea, realizing that argument would be impolite and most likely useless. They would leave in the morning instead. He hated to admit it, but Mr. Bryan was right.

Angus woke early the following morning to soft rain. Dim light slipped through the crack in the curtains, shining on George, still asleep in the other bed. Having decided to stay, Angus slept deeply for the first time since arriving in the colonies. Now, he launched himself from the comfortable bed, waking the other man as he did.

"Time to rise and shine," he sang out cheerily.

George grunted, pulling the covers back over his head. Angus grabbed the blanket, pulled it off, and started dressing. With a sigh, George gave up his warm bed and followed suit. As he dressed, he looked out of the window.

"Still raining, but lighter," he said. "Probably pass on by soon."

"Aye," said Angus. "Let's head out."

Mrs. Bryan was downstairs in the kitchen with the coffee ready, though it was still early. Rashers of bacon sizzled in the skillet over hot coals. The scene he beheld was homey, the smells so delicious that, for a moment, Angus was reluctant to leave.

But leave, they did. By the time the pair finished eating, the light rain had stopped, and laden with food for their trip, George and Angus set off on horseback. The men could quickly complete the fifteen-mile trip with good horses and clear weather. Though the storms made the paths through the woods challenging, Angus chose to follow them anyway. The road was easier and faster, but he hoped to catch up to the others by following the visto.

"Look. Here, as well." George pointed to deeper ruts, evidence another wagon had been stuck in the mud. "The storm was much worse here."

"That's the third time. If the storms were that bad, I doubt they did any work."

"Mebbe, they just gave up and went straight to Harlan's," George mused.

The day began overcast with low-hanging clouds, though the sun soon broke through. George and Angus made good progress despite the mud and reached Harlan's farm late that afternoon.

When they arrived, the sight of Young Will and Liam standing naked and shivering in large wooden tubs greeted them. Their clothing lay in a pile on the ground nearby.

"What happened?" Angus asked as he dismounted. He wrinkled his nose, trying to identify the awful smell wafting toward them.

The others, standing nearby, laughed hysterically.

Will, tears streaming down his cheeks, turned to Angus. Choking with laughter, he attempted to speak. "My son and Liam... ducked into the woods for a piss... and ran into a polecat."

"The locals call it a skunk. This animal ejects its piss, which has a terrible stench. It'll suffocate whatever is within range," Jeremiah told them, wiping his eyes. "We arrived about an hour back... but they couldn't wait."

Angus took a deep breath and regretted it immediately. The odor was potent even from where he stood several yards away.

Sarah Harlan bustled out of the house with a scarf tied around her face and handed each of the men sliced onions. "Onions, that's what ye need for the stench. Do a proper job washing with these, and after, ye can wash with this lye soap," she instructed. "That'll take the onion smell away."

Wrapping their clothes in an old blanket, she crossed the yard to where her daughter was stirring lye soap into the scalding water of the washtub. Steam swirled about her, curling the strands of hair escaping from her cap.

"Ye'll not come near us smelling like that!" Maire informed Liam as she kept the boys well back from their father.

The two men began rubbing themselves down with the onions, tears streaming down their cheeks—but it was better than the skunk.

Angus scooted over to make room for Liam when he joined him later, the aroma of onions still lingering on his scrubbed-red skin. They sat on the porch, listening to Mr. Mason and Mr. Dixon discuss the best way to proceed.

"Some men can remain with me to load the wagons," Mason said. "Ye take Angus and Liam, Andrew as well, and start ahead of us, checking the measurements as ye go."

"Sounds like a good idea," Mr. Dixon said. "We can load the smaller wagon, taking only what we need. We'll take Young Will, too. I imagine the measuring will be quicker than last time. We ought to reach Bryan's close behind ye."

Dixon turned and asked the younger men, "what do ye think, lads, ye up for it?"

"Oh, aye," they replied in unison.

"Will Maire and the boys ride in the wagons with ye, Sir?" Liam asked Mr. Mason.

"Of course," he replied. "That was part of our agreement in exchange for yer labor."

With that, Liam hurried to find his family and plan for their move to Bryan's farm. Since that potentially was the Maryland border, their journey would end soon. It was nearly time to purchase land and begin their new life on a small farm.

Mr. Mason and Mr. Dixon continued discussing their plans. Angus sat quietly, listening. Suddenly, dogs howled and ran around the house. Not long after, they heard men on horseback approaching slowly up the lane. Jeremiah and Angus rose and followed Mr. Mason to the front of the house just in time to view three horses arrive. Angus recognized Cresap, the man he saw in the tavern the night he was there with the Indians. Cresap was questioning whether the Londoners could correctly settle the border dispute.

Angus whispered to Dixon, "He's the man I told ye about at the trading post." Dixon nodded, glancing at Angus in understanding. The men dismounted without issuing a greeting to the members of the household.

"Ye are a bit off yer normal patch," John Harlan said to the men as they approached. John crossed his arms over his chest.

"I got no beef with ye, Harlan," Cresap replied. "Ye are rightly in Pennsylvania here. Me 'n my sons would like a word with those men, the ones doin' the survey." He pointed towards Mr. Mason and Mr. Dixon standing nearby.

"Oh?" queried Jeremiah Dixon. "Is there a problem?"

"We have seen Finlay Mack hangin' around hereabouts." He stood with his hands on his hips.

"Well, he lives just beyond here. It is free to use the road," John protested before Cresap cut him off.

"I just wanted to warn ye, Mack is spying for the Pennsylvania commissioners, and that lot is tryin' to cheat us of land that is *clearly* in Maryland." He glanced at the two young men with him, who nodded in agreement.

Angus watched the exchange and realized John Harlan had not extended the usual courtesies afforded visitors. The friction in the air was tangible.

"Ain't that what he is doing? Only he's spying for the *Maryland* commissioners?" spat out Harlan's older son, Stephen, under his breath to Angus.

Angus smiled at Stephen's comment. From what he'd heard, it was most likely true. Sarah hushed her son with a look and stepped forward.

"Now, y'all come out back and sit a spell, take a rest from yer ride," Sarah said, attempting to defuse the tension. She glared at her husband. Frontier hospitality demanded she provide for her visitors. "I made some nice lemonade and a batch o' fresh scones."

Angus followed the others to the table, listening with interest as Cresap explained how ye should not trust some folk. Mr. Mason and Mr.

Dixon listened politely, but Angus could not help noticing the smirk on Jeremiah's face.

Angus remembered the stories he had heard about Cresap and how he fought against the Pennsylvania sheriff. This land was a strange place, full of characters. *Can we trust this man? And who was Finlay Mack?*

Sarah crossed to Angus after serving the others. She offered him a glass of lemonade.

"Join me," she said and pulled him aside. "I just want to check to see whether ye were alright... ye know, with what happened and all."

Angus reassured her he was fine. "I am puzzled a wee bit by it. There is a lot I don't understand. That sheriff, for example, could not wait to get away from us."

"I know the man. He's worthless," she replied, nodding. "Remember when ye were last here? I told ye I thought ye reminded me o' someone."

"Aye, but ye could not recollect who it was," he replied.

"Well, I reckon it is Finlay Mack, the man Thomas Cresap is talking about. Ye have a likeness about ye. I can't quite place my finger on it, though there is a manner ye have... I dunno, maybe from when he was younger."

"Oh?" asked Angus. "I don't know of any kinfolk here. I never heard of anyone coming to the colonies. Except for my mam's brother in London, most of my family is dead."

"Nah, ye just remind me o' each other. It's not that ye look like him. However, ye both have a way about ye," she explained. "Well, except, ye still have both yer arms. He lost his left one in his youth."

Angus froze. Finlay Mack was the one-armed man.

CHAPTER 10

Wednesday dawned a beautiful spring day, full of promises and April sunshine, not a cloud in sight. Each day was warmer than the previous, and tiny green shoots were poking up in Sarah's garden. The chaining team left in high spirits, though Angus was sorry to bid farewell to the Harlan family. Receiving a big hug from Sarah, Angus promised to visit again.

The small survey party would begin their trip south, confirming the previous measurements for accuracy along the way. The additional workers were loading the final items and equipment into the remaining wagons, which would accompany Mr. Mason to Bryan's farm.

Angus crossed the field to the stone marker where the observatory stood and watched as Andrew held one end of the chain above the marker while Liam carefully stretched out the links. The terrain remained relatively flat for several miles, so compensation for hills was unnecessary. Angus stretched, listening to the sounds of the birds. So many sounds filled the early morning air now. The events of the evening before ran through his mind. Thomas Cresap accused Finlay Mack of causing trouble. Angus had no doubt the feeling was mutual between the two men. *But how far would either man go?* He thought about their motives as he caught up to the others. Angus paced alongside Liam.

"Onskat... tiggene... axe... raiene... wisck," he counted the Indian numbers as he paced.

"Ah, so ye picked up a bit of the Susquehannock yerself," Liam said as he stretched the chain, ensuring it did not become entangled as they entered the swath through the forest. "My boys count better in that strange tongue than in English."

Angus chuckled. "Aye, but I can't remember what comes after five! When I try, all that comes out is a sia, a seachd, a h-ochd, a naoi, a deich, the Gaelic I spoke as a child."

Liam laughed. "I understand completely. Alas, the boys are not interested when I speak the Irish." Liam shook his head sadly. "Maire and I speak it occasionally, but I learned English at the parish school. Coming to the colonies, we practice that language now."

"Twenty-two, twenty-three," Angus continued counting as Liam spoke. Suddenly he noticed Liam stooping to place a stob into the ground at his feet.

"That is one," he said to Angus.

"Hmm... I must have miscounted. There should be two more paces."

"Well, the chain is stretched nice and straight," said Liam, looking down its length.

The chain was not snagged; all sixty-six feet were nice, taut, and straight. Angus scanned the ground at their feet, searching for signs of the previous stob, yet found no marks in the soil. With the heavy rains in recent days, all evidence had disappeared.

"Ah, well, we were talking. I must not have been paying attention," Angus said. "It is no matter; the chain looks good." He made a mark in the booklet he carried in his pouch.

At Angus' signal, Andrew moved the following end of the chain to the next point and readied it to repeat the process.

"One. Two. Three." Angus counted out the steps, intending to pay better attention this time. However, after only a few paces, he and Liam chatted amiably again, sharing stories of the clerics that formed both men's educations.

"Ah, but Father Michael was the worst," Liam told Angus. "He made my friend Paddy leave school on account of him writing with his left hand. Claimed it was the devil in him. Paddy had the best handwritin' of us all. I never understood what that was about. I wasn't in school much longer after that myself."

"Twenty-two, twenty-three."

Liam stopped. Angus shook his head; once again, they came up short.

"Maybe I grew taller during the night," he joked, pulling out his notebook. "The rain has washed away the mark again."

Angus wrote a tally in his book and signaled to Andrew, who picked up the stob and joined them again.

"One more time." Angus was determined. "It is not yer problem but mine. Ye both are doing a good job with the chain. It seems I can't count today."

He gestured for Andrew to line up on the stob, and Liam headed south again. This time Angus stayed focused on counting and bit back the urge to chat.

However, once again, they stopped at twenty-three paces. Angus could not understand it. He had paced alongside the men on the initial survey. Each time he counted out twenty-five paces. Pulling the small booklet from his pouch, he flipped through the pages to double-check himself. *Yes. Twenty-five each time.* He did the calculations in his head, mumbling out loud.

"Sixty-six feet in a chain... this equals twenty-five paces. If I walk twenty-three paces, it is just over sixty feet... a loss of over five feet per chain..."

Angus shook his head as he muttered, "that would be close to a mile short across the total distance to Bryan's."

Andrew grinned at Liam. "I wish I could do that." By this time, they were used to their friend's random mutterings as he made his calculations.

"Aye, I must admit, I am in awe of his abilities," Liam agreed.

Angus hung his head and paced the additional six paces for the three runs they had made so far. As he began scanning the ground, he spied the small round hole from the previous stob.

"Here it is!" He hollered just as Jeremiah Dixon rode up on his horse.

"What is it, Lad? Is everything alright?"

"Nay, Sir. It is not." Angus shook his head. "The numbers were off, and I am trying to figure it out. The previous stob is here, but we finished measuring there after three chains." He pointed from where Andrew stood to the end where Liam stood.

Mr. Dixon dismounted. "Are ye sure that is from a stob?" He asked as he approached the spot. Angus explained what had happened as they stared at the perfectly round hole in the ground. Only a stob created a circle like that.

Confused, Angus looked at Mr. Dixon. "How did this happen? I paced it out three times. And each time, I only counted twenty-three paces."

Dixon thought for a moment. "Did ye check the chains?"

"Aye. I counted both yesterday afore I put them into the wagon."

"Well, shall we take a look?" Dixon suggested.

Liam and Andrew brought the chain to Mr. Dixon. The men counted; there were ninety-two links instead of one hundred.

"Nay!" Angus grabbed the chain from Andrew and counted the links himself. He also came up with ninety-two. "How can this be?"

He counted them twice the previous afternoon, and both chains contained one hundred links. He hung his head, the chain dangling from his fingers. Responsibility for ensuring everything was in working order fell to him, and he had not accomplished that simple task.

In that instant, he remembered how Thomas Cresap and his sons remained at Harlan's until late into the evening.

"The Cresaps, Sir," he cried out. "The Cresaps stayed late last night. Moving the line northwards by shortening the chain only benefits Maryland."

Mr. Dixon pondered this. "Aye. That is true enough, but are Thomas Cresap and his sons so bold as to cheat like this? Yet... who else was around? Who else could it have been?" Mr. Dixon considered this development. "I'll discuss it with Charles when he catches up with us later today."

Just then, a wagon rumbled up with Young Will at the reins. He always drove at great speed when he was away from his father. He raced through the cleared lands, slowing the horse when he spied Mr. Dixon.

"Whoa, careful, lad," Dixon admonished. At least the observatory equipment was in the larger wagon. Will's father would take the required precautions. Young Will's cart contained only the items these men needed for the few days it took them to reach Bryan's farm.

Will slowed, looking surprised to catch up to them so quickly. He approached them more sedately. Angus vaulted into the wagon as it stopped, startling the driver. He reached for the second chain and pulled it out, carefully counting the links. There were one hundred.

"This one is good, Sir," he called out to Mr. Dixon.

"Very well," he replied. "Andrew, take your end to where the stob hole is from the previous measurement. We will pick up from there and assume everything is correct."

"Will that be alright, Sir?" asked Liam.

"Aye. The distance we're short equals the amount missing from the chain, so we should be good. And ye paced if off, which matches what we found." He smiled at Angus. "To my mind, it will be fine. There are areas further on which need us to pay closer attention. I want to get to those today."

"Aye, Sir," Angus responded, feeling disappointed in himself. Though Dixon never mentioned it again, the mistake wore on Angus as the work progressed. He remained quiet for the rest of the day.

Every measurement with the other chain proved correct. The chain ended precisely over the last hole whenever they found the earlier mark.

Later, while the men ate their midday biscuits and dried ham, Mr. Mason caught up with them as the heavily laden wagons headed south. There was much merriment amongst the O'Connor clan as Liam's boys danced around him. Taking only a nibble of a biscuit, Maire sat quietly on a rock, watching her family. In this early stage of her pregnancy, she frequently suffered from an upset stomach.

Angus played games stacking pebbles on a large rock with the young boys after eating and wondered what it would be like to be married, to have a family.

Ah, but what prospects do I have? He asked himself. He glanced at Mr. Dixon and Mr. Mason. Angus recalled Charles Mason had two sons back in England, though he had lost his wife in childbirth. However, Mr. Dixon was single, despite being from a wealthy family. It occurred to Angus that if Jeremiah couldn't find a wife, what chance did he have?

His thoughts were interrupted as he overheard Mr. Mason. "The Cresaps, ye say?" Angus stared down at the pair of smooth pebbles in his hand. The feel of them rolling around in his palm was soothing and helped calm him and focus his thoughts as he eavesdropped on their conversation.

"Hmm, I don't know. However, the only people present last night were the Harlans, our team, and the Cresaps," Mr. Dixon speculated. "And Angus counted both chains before putting them in the wagon that evening."

"True, I saw him. And they lingered about until late. A mile difference would be thousands of acres given to Maryland across the length of the line..." Mr. Mason pondered this, then added, "he sure was eager to have us suspect this Finlay Mack of Pennsylvania, though." Mr. Mason smiled. "It seems rather like the pot is calling the kettle black, if ye ask me."

"Aye, that is true. We have this task under control, so ye go ahead as planned, and we shall see ye in a few days at Bryan's. I am confident the measurements are good to this point." As they rose to depart, he added, "Be careful."

Jeremiah paused. Angus wondered why he had added that last bit. *Was he worried?* Everyone hoped there would be no further trouble, but concern spread among the men after the recent events. Ultimately, whichever colony lost ground would not be pleased with their results. There was no hope for it.

"Aye, ye too," Mason replied as he scanned the other man's face.

Mr. Mason mounted his horse as Will helped Maire onto the seat beside him, and Liam lifted his boys into the back. As the larger group pressed on towards Bryan's farm, Angus was more down on himself than ever. Mr. Dixon picked up the chain, and Angus joined him.

"I'm sorry," he said.

"For what?" Jeremiah seemed genuinely surprised. "The chains? I'm just glad ye caught it before we reached this section. We'll need them now. This is the stretch I am most concerned about."

Somewhat relieved, Angus quietly joined Mr. Dixon, often pacing the distances together. They didn't bother measuring with the chains if they matched the previous stob hole. Angus helped with the levels in the hilly terrain, especially in spots where Mr. Dixon felt the measurement needed confirmation.

The countryside was beautiful. The rolling green hills went on for miles, although he had never seen such dense forests. So different, Angus thought, yet in some ways similar to his homeland. He remarked on his observation.

"Aye, 'tis beautiful country here," said Young Will, "and further west, ye can see mountains that reach the sky, with jagged rocks peering above the trees. My pa took me out that way once."

He walked alongside Angus, leading the horse-drawn cart behind him. Mr. Dixon's horse was tied to the back of it for the present. The horse followed passively but was ready should Dixon need to ride ahead.

"That sounds like home to me," Angus told him. "I left Scotland when I was seventeen and moved to London with my uncle. Father Thomas met my mother's brother and thought I could continue my education better with him. Anyway, my uncle invited me to live with them and introduced me to the scientists he worked with, and a few years later, here I am." He paused. "I cared little for London. I missed Scotland the whole time. I'd sure like to see those mountains ye talk about."

Will grinned at him. "I'm sure ye will when ye start measuring west."

"Aye." Angus grinned in return.

The weather remained clear and dry, and they made steady progress. The chain became tangled in the briars three times one day, requiring the men to stop and carefully cut it free. Finally, Mr. Dixon called a halt for the day after completing several miles. Angus coiled the chains while Andrew counted the stobs. Jeremiah mounted his horse, and the three men hopped in the wagon with Young Will and rode to the Freads' place. They were well past the young farmer's home, where they had spent a night on their first journey.

Joseph Freads heard the wagon arriving late in the day as he was mending a fence. He stood, stretching out his stiff back, his hand shielding his eyes from the sun.

Young Will noticed Joseph out in the field and slowed the wagon. "Good day, my friend," he hollered.

"Aye, greetings," replied Joseph, "are looking fer a place to stay? Mr. Mason passed through and said ye might be coming along behind."

"Aye. Do ye mind if we set up camp on yer land again tonight?" Mr. Dixon asked.

"No, 'tis not a problem. But with such a small party, ye are welcome to stay in the stable. Save ye setting up yer tent. My daughter and her children are here at the house just now."

"That's fine, thank ye." As Mr. Dixon's horse moved out of the way, they offered Joseph a ride back to his home.

Young Will took charge of the meal since Fielding, the cook, traveled with Mr. Mason's party. While the men unloaded in the barn, he begged for carrots and potatoes from Mrs. Freads. Taking pity on the young man, she also provided him with a pair of rabbits. Shortly after washing up, the men relaxed and devoured a hearty stew. Later, Joseph joined them.

"Well, ye were part of a conversation I overheard a few days ago," Joseph said, looking at Angus. "Ye and the Indians. I feel I oughta tell ye about it."

"Oh?" asked Angus, wondering, *what next?*

"Aye. I stopped for a beer at Nathaniel's place," he nodded to Young Will, who knew Nathaniel. "Gil Jackson was there, drunk as ever, o' course, rantin' about the death of Rupert. He is blamin' it on the Indians but also mentioned their association with ye."

"Now, wait a minute." Young Will interjected, "they could never be involved, and neither could Angus."

"I know. I know. I don't believe the local Indians were involved." Joseph interrupted, holding up his hand to quiet Will, "I just thought ye ought to know what he told everyone. But, the more Jackson ranted, the more exaggerated his stories became. After a while, it seemed even Simon didn't believe him. I think he wanted to say somethin', but instead, he just left." He turned suddenly to Angus and Jeremiah. "Nathaniel thought I was being ridiculous, said Simon was most likely upset, and he is probably right. The three of them have been friends since childhood. Gil even saved Rupert's life once."

Puzzled about Angus' involvement, though, Dixon glanced at the young man. Angus hung his head and reminded him how the four of them discovered the burned homestead, and Gil and his friends arrived, including Rupert, who was now dead.

"Ah. I remember," said Mr. Dixon softly.

Angus stared down at his feet.

After the others headed into the barn later, Angus stayed outside, staring into the sky. No sign of Orion tonight. Disappointed, he hung his head and joined the others.

CHAPTER II

Before returning to town, Will offered to haul the observatory sections to the cornfield. Angus, Liam, and Andrew would re-assemble it for the next phase of star gazing. Mr. Mason and Mr. Dixon departed with him for Philadelphia to inform the commissioners of their progress. Once confirmed, the point where the Maryland border started would be here on the edge of Mr. Bryan's farm in New Castle County.

Maire stood at the kitchen window, watching the men unload the sections of the observatory from the wagon. She studied Angus, knowing Liam was worried about his friend. Even she had to admit Angus was no longer the innocent youth she met aboard the ship. Something was eating away at him, and her intuition told her it started before he found the body.

"Ah, come and sit yerself down," Martha Bryan told her as she removed the kettle from the fire and poured the steaming water into the ceramic pot to steep. The aroma of the herbs wafted through the air, filling the room. "I am makin' my special tea fer ye. It has a bit of lavender and some mint to help settle yer stomach."

"Ye are too kind," Maire replied.

Reluctantly leaving the window, she sat at the table. Relaxing, she looked around the cozy kitchen with its log beams and large stone fireplace. It stood slightly separated from the main house, also constructed of logs. A covered walkway connected the two buildings. The sun streamed in through the windows hung with yellow and white checkered curtains. Small clay pots of parsley and thyme sat in one window. On a rocking chair in the corner, Maire noticed a sewing basket with an unfinished cap draped over the edge.

Mairi dreamed of moving into a similar home one day. While she thought the Harlans' large stone house was beautiful, Maire felt happier and more at home in this log cabin. It felt lived-in and comfortable. There were signs of the family everywhere she looked. A quilt Martha had stitched hung on the wall next to Alexander's heavy cloak. A cradle sat by the hearth for when their grandchildren visited. The idea of turning a cabin like this into a home delighted Maire.

Martha noticed her looking around. "This building was the original house Alexander's father built. His name was John, and he was the youngest of seven boys. He and a brother decided to emigrate from England as young men. John married a young woman from Lancaster shortly after arriving, and they settled here."

Maire listened intently; this was her story as well, so she especially enjoyed hearing tales of people making a fresh start here.

"I can understand that. I'm the youngest, and most of us are girls. There was nothing left for me. I was truly fortunate to meet Liam, and he was willing to take me with nothin' but my shift." She paused in thought, then continued, "I imagine it was hard for them in the beginning."

"Oh aye, likely 'twas," Martha replied. "As time wore on and the family grew larger, they began buildin' the big house. They chose to keep this, the former cabin, as the kitchen. Set away from the house, there is less risk of fire."

"It would be my favorite room," Maire said, glancing around the cozy space again. Everywhere she looked, she saw signs of Martha's hard work in the gleaming jars of pickled beets and onions on shelves lining the walls and the baskets of cleaning supplies near the wash sink. The salt cellar sat proudly in the center of the table.

The old bedroom had become a storage space on one side of the cabin, which held large barrels filled with oats, wheat, and flour. Other necessities, such as a straw broom, hung on the walls. It was not a grand stone house, but Martha was proud of her home.

"Oh, true, 'tis mine as well. I spend most of my time here." Martha smiled, pleased at the compliment.

Martha rose, poured the tea, and handed a steaming mug to Maire. The two women sat together, chatting about various topics, though, eventually, the subject returned to current events.

"I sure miss havin' young 'uns around the house. I wish my boys would visit more often," Martha said. "Any feelings on what the new babe might be?"

Maire smiled and glanced down at her still-flat stomach. "It is early days yet, but I can't help but feel she's a girl. After those boys, a daughter would be nice."

Martha smiled at her.

"That young man, Angus, do ye know him well?" Martha asked.

"Not too well; we met on the ship." Maire wrapped her hands around the warm cup as she replied. "But I know Liam is worried about him right now."

"I am sure finding a dead body would shake the nerves of the strongest of us."

"True. But a shadow hangs over him now," Maire considered this as she spoke. "I think the lad takes too much upon himself. However, there have been some problems along the way. Liam tells me men are spying on them. And there was a fight with some locals while he was working with the axemen. Liam fears someone is stirring them up."

Martha nodded and agreed. "I suppose that is likely. A lot o' folk are interested in where that border falls."

The wagon was empty. The observatory walls were neatly stacked on the ground in the corner of the field, next to the wooden marker Mr. Dixon had placed when he called an end to the survey. Angus jumped on the wagon and rode with Liam and Andrew toward the house. Once again, he would say farewell—this time to Will and his son. Most of the workmen had departed for home until the surveyors needed them again. When Mason and Dixon returned, their efforts would focus on astronomy again, determining the latitude with the zenith sector.

"Travel safely," Angus said to Will as he gave the man a hearty handshake.

Will grasped his hand. "We will see each other soon, laddie. I'll be back when ye move on again."

Angus watched until Will and the other wagons, driven by his son and George, were out of sight. So many new friends, so many goodbyes. He sincerely hoped he would see them all again. Angus had never had real friends back home. His attention returned now to Liam and Andrew.

"Well, shall we get to it?" he asked.

Both men nodded.

John Loxley, the carpenter, was unavailable this time, as his wife expected to deliver a child any day. But Jeremiah Dixon was confident

Angus could fill in for the carpenter. He assisted Loxley both times they erected the observatory and when it was dismantled and stowed away.

While Dixon expressed confidence in him, somehow, Angus could not help but feel that this was a test. In his mind, he had failed at his tasks lately, and correctly erecting the structure was his final chance to prove himself. Apprehension had filled him ever since the fiasco with the chains. He tried standing a little straighter and convincing himself he could do this.

Liam crossed and placed his hand on his shoulder as if reading his mind. "Ye can do this. Ye've done it afore. Just tell us what ye need."

Andrew nodded in agreement.

Feeling better and knowing he had the support of his good friends, Angus agreed. "Well, let's get to it then." They retrieved the tools they needed from the barn and returned to the site to erect the structure. As they worked, Angus kept thinking about Rupert. What he needed to do was solve the murder. That would put him in good standing.

By late afternoon, the workers had completed the observatory walls. Angus decided it was too late to start on the trusses that held up the canvas roof, so he called it a day, and the men returned to their encampment. While Andrew, Angus, and Fielding shared a tent, Liam and his family slept inside the barn. As before, Angus planned to move into the observatory once it was assembled.

"Have ye decided what ye'll do when the surveyors return?" Angus asked Liam as they walked across the meadow.

"I believe so," he replied, "I enjoy working with ye and the company too, plus earning a bit helps as well. To be honest with ye, I am a wee bit nervous, settin' out on my own. But I owe it to Maire and the boys to find us a piece of land soon. Somewhere we can settle in and call home."

Yet another farewell—and it would be the hardest yet. Angus felt a lump in his throat. Swallowing, he put a smile on his face and said, "Aye, especially with the new babe coming. Ye want to be settled afore then."

Angus heard a horse as they approached the barn. His first thought was that Mr. Mason and Mr. Dixon had returned, but he soon realized it was the clip-clop of a single horse heading away from the farmstead. They had not heard the rider approach while they worked on the observatory. But as the men rounded the corner, Angus spied the rider down the lane. Though he could not identify his face, the man was missing his left arm.

Finlay Mack!

Angus turned to Liam and pointed. "There he is *again*. That is Finlay Mack, the spy." At Liam's glance, Angus added, "What else could he be? He's been following us from the start. I'd love to know what he was doing here. I heard he started that fight among the men last week."

Liam didn't seem so sure. "We never did get to the bottom o' that. I didn't see him, but I heard his name mentioned."

Angus' nerves were frazzled. Would it be rude to ask Mrs. Bryan why that man was here? Or maybe her husband might tell them when he returned from his fields. He wondered about it all afternoon.

The men sat around their small fire outside the barn door that evening. As they sipped the ale, Alexander Bryan joined them. He tossed a log on the fire.

"I hope ye don't mind me joinin' ye. With my sons grown, I miss the company of men about the place." He settled himself on a crate. "Sometimes, 'tis good to hear the news. Other times, 'tis not," he began after settling in with a mug of ale. "Martha ordered some nice woolen fabric at the trading post. Finlay Mack was kind enough to bring it by today on his way toward the Nottingham Road. He told her about a meetin' in Paxton with Reverend John Elder stirrin' up trouble again."

Angus recalled hearing that name before and wondered aloud, "A reverend? What kind of trouble?"

"Aye. Reverend Elder. They call him the Fightin' Parson on account o' him preachin' his sermons with a rifle in his pulpit," spat out Alexander. "That man hates the Indians, claims they ain't true Christians. He feels Pennsylvania would be better off with only Europeans here."

"Ah, yes," Angus nodded as he remembered. "I remember. We heard mention o' him."

"Gets the folk out that way all sorts o' riled up. It would not surprise me to hear he was behind those attacks back in December, where they slaughtered those Conestoga. Sort o' thing he'd urge his men to do. Though he would not take part."

The men sat a moment quietly, remembering the events.

Alexander continued, "Elder claims that the Conestoga secretly provided aid and information to the more hostile tribes during the war. He even wrote to the governor claimin' he had taken care o' the situation himself... since the government had done nothin'."

"I can't see the Indians we've met doin' such things," Liam spoke up, staring into the fire.

"Nay," Andrew responded. "I've known those folks my whole life."

Angus remembered hearing about those raids when they were in Philadelphia. He recalled how his childhood memories had come flooding back, with that gut-wrenching fear of being hated by others re-emerging. Now that he had met the local Indians, he found it difficult to reconcile the stories he had heard about them. He could not envision them scalping anyone. Though he'd heard some tribes did.

Angus' ears perked up. "Wait! Did you say writing to the governor?"

"Aye, why?"

"The last time they met with the commissioners, someone had written to the governor in Philadelphia accusing Mr. Mason of not being fair in his judgments. Fortunately, he keeps that journal. He was able to prove otherwise. But we've been wondering who would do that."

Alexander shrugged. "Any number of people, I suppose."

Eventually, Andrew bid them good night and joined Fielding in the tent. Angus gazed up at the sky. Too cloudy tonight; Orion would have to wait. It had been a week since he last saw the stars of his belt. The tent and his warm bedroll beckoned to him as he stared up at the clouds one last time, and Angus ducked inside.

Angus approached a tiny hut in the woods. On one side was a dirty window. He wiped away enough of the grime to peer inside. There he saw Finlay Mack hand a box to Gil Jackson. Thomas Cresap was sitting at a table laughing as Gil sat down and opened the box, pulling out a broken arrow. Its fletching matched the ones Angus found at the O'Donnell homestead and the one buried in the dead man's chest. Gil held it aloft before passing it on to Cresap, who ripped the feather off the shaft and threw it into the air. Laughing, the three men watched it slowly float down onto the table, landing softly next to the box. Angus didn't realize Cresap had moved until suddenly, a face popped up in the window. They had seen him!

"Angus. Angus, wake up," Fielding gently shook the man as he cried out in his sleep. "Ye are havin' a bad dream."

Angus jerked awake in a cold sweat. It took him several moments to realize he was in the tent with Fielding and Andrew. He peered up at the man with a weak smile, "I am sorry. I must have been dreaming."

"Don't fret. I am fine," the older man said. "Are ye?"

"Aye. It was just so real."

"Do ye want to talk about it? Finding that dead body would give anyone nightmares."

"Nay... nay. I'm fine. Try to get back to sleep," Angus told him.

Both men lay back down, and soon Angus heard Fielding softly snoring again. Wide awake now, he lay there contemplating his dream; the scenes played vividly in his mind. He tried to make sense of it. Angus had utterly forgotten about the box from the ship until it appeared in his dream. What was its significance? He had dismissed it at the time as smuggling, but was it important? And were those three working together? He hardly expected that. Two of them were Pennsylvanians, and Cresap was from Maryland. Angus rolled over, trying to dismiss the dream from his mind.

A cold chill crept up his spine as he realized this was precisely the type of vision his grandmother described to him in his youth. He pushed that notion from his mind. Men didn't have the second sight. Did they? The words of the seer floated into his mind. She told him he would get through if he stayed true to himself. But what did that mean?

Angus tried to comfort himself with her words. It was only a dream, he told himself, though sleep remained elusive until the wee hours of the morning.

Thunder rumbled, and the men woke early to pouring rain. The wind caused the tent sides to flap loudly, but the men remained warm and dry inside. No one wanted to brave the weather. However, nature's call left them little choice. Once up, they made their way toward the shelter of the barn. The trio was quiet as they entered; however, they found the O'Connor family already wide awake.

"The thunder woke the boys," Maire explained. Michael and Patrick sat wide-eyed, curled up next to their mother with a blanket wrapped around them. Patrick, the image of his mother, stuck his thumb in his mouth.

"I have some boiled eggs, bread, and jam," said Fielding. "Will that hold ye while I brew the coffee?" When they nodded, he lit his brazier outside, under the overhang, and out of the wind and rain. A row of apple trees protected that side of the barn. Fielding lit the fire and began setting out the food to break their fast.

"If this keeps up, I imagine we won't get much done on the buildin' today," Andrew pointed out.

The others looked at him. He smiled, chagrined at his rather obvious statement.

Sipping the hot coffee, they discussed what else they could do while they waited out the storm. No one had any suggestions. Until the construction was complete, they could not unpack the instruments—and only Mr. Mason handled the precious zenith sector.

As he sipped, Angus could not shake off the unease his dream had caused. He rose and paced, itching for something to do. "I hope it slows up soon. I want to have this done and ready before Mr. Mason and Mr. Dixon return. They might arrive as early as tomorrow afternoon if the meetings go well," he said.

The door opened. "Morning, all," Alexander greeted them. Having overheard Angus, he agreed. "Aye, 'tis a wet morning, but I believe it will let up by midday."

He gladly accepted the tin cup of fresh coffee Fielding offered, grasping it carefully by the handle.

"Though, 'tis ye I came to see," he moved toward Liam. "The misses and I were talkin' last night, and we both recall a vacant home site less than ten miles southwest o' here. It was built by a young man hopin' to bring his bride out here to settle. She arrived in Philadelphia, took one look around, and booked the next passage to London! Never even saw the cabin he built for her. 'Tis on a nice bit o' land. There is a small but sturdy cabin. And well-built. Far as I know, no one is livin' in it."

Liam's eyes were wide. Maire grasped his arm tightly. Liam asked, "How will we know if it is available?" At the same time, Maire said, "Can we see it?"

Everyone was caught up in the excitement this news caused—even Angus, who had tried not to think about Liam's eventual departure from the team.

"I am goin' to the tradin' post later in the week. I will ask the magistrate while I am there." Alexander crossed his fingers and prayed it would still be empty.

A sense of eagerness filled the air, and they forgot the raging storm. Liam and Maire were excited to see the property at the earliest opportunity. Angus was happy for Liam and Maire but saddened anew at the reminder of his friend's upcoming departure.

The storm had passed by afternoon, and Angus and the others resumed construction. By noon the following day, the observatory was complete, and they were experiencing the first truly beautiful weather in recent days.

Just as they finished, Mr. Mason and Mr. Dixon rode up the lane. Angus was busy spreading straw on the ground inside to absorb the mud from the previous day's rain.

"Nice work," said Mr. Mason as he examined their workmanship. The canvas covering was nice and tight. He even commented on Angus' efforts with the straw. "I was not expecting it to be completed so soon."

"Aye," added Dixon. "Ye did well, lads." He winked at Angus and clapped him on the shoulder.

"I hope all went well with the commissioners," Angus replied. He had impressed them. That was one step in the right direction.

"Well, it went as we expected," Jeremiah answered. "The Pennsylvania commissioners were pleased, as the point is further south than they hoped. The Marylanders were a little less enthusiastic. Regardless, both sides wish we were moving quicker."

"But accuracy cannot be rushed," said Mr. Mason, eager to observe the stars as soon as it grew dark.

Dixon leaned closer to Angus. "I knew ye could do it, Lad."

"Thank ye, Sir." At Dixon's look, he said, "I mean... Jeremiah."

Dixon grinned.

"Oh, just so ye know, Finlay Mack has been seen around here again," Angus told him.

"So, maybe he is spying on us after all?"

"Possibly. And I was talking with Alexander. I think it might be that Reverend Elder writing the letters to the commissioners. He's been known to write to the governor."

Jeremiah glanced at Mason as he entered the observatory. "I suppose I should inform Charles. Thank ye."

Pleased, Angus smiled genuinely for the first time in a week.

Immediately, they began moving the equipment into the observatory while the sky remained clear so the astronomers could resume tracking the stars that night. If they were successful, Angus would be busy with plenty of calculations to compute. He felt good about those; they came easily to him.

As dusk settled in, horses came up the lane. Running Bear, Gray Wolf, and Little Hawk rode toward the house. With another big smile, Angus trotted over to meet the natives, who greeted him warmly.

"I see the horses are fully loaded," Angus said, indicating the pack horses laden with beaver and deer pelts.

"Aye, we'll be heading out in the morning if the weather holds." Running Bear checked the sky. There was not a cloud in sight.

Today, Angus received praise from Mr. Mason and a vote of confidence from Jeremiah, and now his friends were here. Things were looking up.

CHAPTER 12

True to their word, the natives loaded their horses the following morning and prepared to set out on the road again. Mr. Dixon and Angus approached and offered to help.

"Thank ye," answered Running Bear.

"Angus has been telling me about the burned homestead," Jeremiah mused while they sorted through the furs and baskets.

"Oh?" asked Gray Wolf. He glanced at his brother.

"Well, I wanted yer opinion. Angus seems to think there was something off about it."

Little Hawk stepped around her horse. "Aye. We've been wondering about that too. We think someone is trying to sabotage your work and blame us."

Mr. Dixon froze. "So ye agree this survey is stirring up trouble?"

Gray Wolf agreed, "Oh, aye. We just don't know who is behind it."

Angus paled, and after finishing tightening the strap, moved near the surveyor.

"I hoped I was wrong," Angus said to Jeremiah.

"I'd like to talk more about this when ye return," Dixon said. Running Bear nodded in reply. In silence, Jeremiah and Angus watched the natives depart.

April was fickle and brought lousy weather. The observatory sat empty. The weight of the rainwater on the tent had caused it to collapse. Now, the team slept in the barn. Early one morning, a lightning bolt struck a nearby tree, jolting everyone awake with a loud crack—though, as usual, Andrew slept through it.

The following day, the rain continued to drum hard on the roof while the men entertained themselves as best they could, playing cards.

"Ha! And another hand to me." Andrew, the only one fully awake, was enjoying himself immensely. The others groaned and tossed their cards on the table.

Fielding tried desperately to keep his brazier lit, so the robust, hot coffee was always ready. Cunning at negotiations, the cook had bartered for two bags of roasted beans from Mrs. Worth the night they stayed on their property. Black tea was increasingly difficult to obtain after the French and English war. Still, coffee beans smuggled from the East Indies by the Dutch were readily available, and the men preferred that to the tea the natives brewed from dandelions. Mrs. Worth's coffee was the best, and every time Fielding saw her, he tried to get her to reveal her secret for roasting the beans. But he always came away without success.

There were overhangs on two sides of the barn, creating a dry area beneath; however, the capricious wind switched each time the cook set up his brazier under one side, forcing him to move repeatedly.

Angus paced nearby, offering Fielding a hand whenever he relocated. He was anxious and bored, having nothing to occupy his mind. Angus had never enjoyed being idle, and he missed his friends.

"Ah, Lad, give it a rest," Fielding said to Angus. "Ye are wearing a path." The older man winked at him. Angus glanced down at his feet and noticed the slight signs of wear he had created in the hard-packed earth. He nodded at Fielding and wandered near the doorway, staring at the dreary, wet weather. The gray sky matched the slate tiles on the roof of the house. Ominous black clouds in the distance threatened further stormy weather. It would not let up today.

Jeremiah Dixon rose from the card game and joined them, handing his empty mug to Fielding for a refill.

"I guess the cards are not in my favor today," he muttered, "and I believe the storm has settled in for a while." The threesome stood outside, protected by the overhang, watching the trees bend in the wind.

Angus continued to study the leaden sky when the other two stepped inside. The rain pounded on the roof. As he gazed toward the house, he observed Mr. Mason step outside onto the broad porch while a scruffy-looking man came toward the back stairs. The stranger was soaking wet, as if he swam in the river in his clothes. Pools of water formed at the man's feet when he halted before Mr. Mason. He fidgeted with his wet hat and stared at his feet as he spoke. Then Mr. Mason nodded and moments later indicated the other man should follow him to the barn.

As the pair approached, something about the man caused the hairs on Angus' arms to tingle. *Who is he? What does he want with Mr. Mason?*

As they entered, Angus finally got his first glimpse of the man's face and froze. Before him stood the other man from the O'Donnell homestead, this man was also with Gil in Philadelphia those months ago. Angus did not believe in coincidence. *A spy, maybe?*

"Sit yerself down, and we will find dry clothes for ye," Mason said as they entered. Several men offered items of clothing while Maire took the dripping clothes, wringing them out before hanging them up to dry by the warmth of the fire. The men had dug a pit in one corner of the barn and lined it with stones. Though small, the fire at least took the edge off the chill.

Once clad in the borrowed clothing, Mr. Mason introduced the man, "Jeremiah, this is Simon Tanner. He is somewhat down on his luck and hoped we might offer him some work."

"There is no work now, as ye can see," Dixon replied, gesturing to the men lounging about in the barn.

"Aye, I've already told him that," Mason responded and turned back to Simon. "We need to identify the latitude of this point accurately before proceeding. But, the weather needs to improve first for that."

Dixon viewed the man, considering. "Ye look strong enough. We might use ye when we start surveying; I'm just uncertain when that will happen. It might be a week or two. Or longer if this continues." He pointed towards the doorway.

The man nodded. "Thank ye," he edged slightly closer toward the other men.

Simon stepped towards Angus when the barn door swung open suddenly, and the three natives entered. Instead, Simon slipped quietly to the fire and held his hands for warmth.

"Welcome back," Angus heartily greeted his friends, "when ye left the other morning, I thought ye'd be gone longer." As he spoke, his glance slid to Simon, gauging his reaction to the natives. Simon seemed to shrink back.

"Well, that was the plan," answered Running Bear, "but the river is flooding upstream, and the ferry couldn't cross." He gripped Angus' elbow and maneuvered him toward the brazier, which Fielding had once again moved to the far doorway. "I could do with a nice hot cup of coffee," he said in a loud voice, his grip firm on Angus' elbow, urging him along.

"What is Simon Tanner doing here?" he hissed at Angus as they stepped through the opening. As their brother lured Angus outside, Gray Wolf and Little Hawk edged over to the fire to warm their hands.

"He claims he is looking for work," Angus informed Running Bear softly, "but I am not sure I believe that. I think he is spying just like I believe Rupert was spying on our work... though Simon seems genuine enough."

"Hmm, maybe," the tall native responded. "Times are tough here, and he may truly be in need o' work, but I reckon I'd keep an eye on him."

"I wonder if Simon is here to see what we know about Rupert." Angus noticed the flicker in Running Bear's eye.

"Well, if so, I hope he's not in any danger." He paused, sipping his coffee. "As ye know, we have been asking folks if they recognize those arrows. Every tribe uses a unique design to identify itself, so if we can find the tribe that uses this fletching, we can likely find the man who shot this arrow. However, nary a soul recognizes it."

"Oh? What does this mean?"

"I am not rightly sure; we are still asking around. We want to know what happened at the O'Donnell's. They were friends of ours, and they lost everything. And I don't like the idea of our people being blamed." Running Bear gritted his teeth.

The two men stepped back inside. Simon stared at Angus. It was clear to him that Simon was uncomfortable in Gray Wolf and his sister's company. Angus pondered this, then crossed to give Little Hawk a big hug in greeting. While doing so, he kept an eye on Simon, who moved further from the natives. Angus saw Simon was more than uncomfortable. He was downright nervous in their presence.

Angus chatted with Little Hawk for several moments until Mr. Mason noticed Simon was missing, and puzzled, he asked the others where the newcomer had gone. Dixon shrugged as he looked down at the pile of borrowed clothing, neatly folded and laid on the crate before him. The clothing on the line, which was still wet, was missing.

"When this weather subsides a bit, ye oughta come hunting with us," Gray Wolf invited Angus.

"That would be grand," Fielding piped up, overhearing their conversation. "I wouldn't mind a break from snarin' rabbits, and I am sure ye all had yer fill o' fish." Everyone agreed, though no one ever complained about the excellent meals he prepared.

"I would like that very much," Angus grinned.

Little Hawk stepped shyly up to him and held out her hand. In it was a small bit of cloth. "For ye."

Angus took the offered gift, his gaze beaming down at her. He removed the fabric and found a large bear's claw, like those he had seen at the trading post. The sizable claw was set in a silver mounting on a thin strip of leather. Puzzled, his gaze returned to Little Hawk.

"It is a good omen for protection."

He smiled as he slipped the leather thong around his neck. Besides the occasional sweet from his gran, he could not remember anyone ever giving him a gift.

"Thank ye," he replied shyly. He was touched.

"I think ye may need it," she replied and stepped away to chat with Maire, who was always happy for some female companionship.

Alexander Bryan leaped between the puddles as he came out to the barn when the rain slacked off that afternoon. He apologized to Maire and Liam.

"I wasn't able to reach the magistrate to inquire about the homestead. The river crested the top of its banks, and though we were under no real threat here, the ferry could not cross."

"No worries. We can't go in this weather, anyway," Liam replied. While he looked mildly disappointed at the delay, Angus knew he would not venture out in this storm with his family.

"Have a coffee?" Fielding asked.

"Aye, I will. I would recognize the aroma of Mrs. Worth's coffee anywhere." Alexander took a seat with the others around the makeshift table. He told the group that while he understood their eagerness to return to their task, to his experienced eye, this storm would linger for at least a few more days. Dixon dealt another round of cards, and each man tossed his peanuts into the center of the table.

Angus watched them, reclining against a post clasping the bear claw Little Hawk had given him. He wondered why she thought he would need extra protection. His gran had taught him to heed warnings of events yet to happen and had instilled in him a complete faith in such charms. He thought back on the ones his gran made. Few of hers were protection from danger, as far as he knew. Gran filled most of hers with herbs to protect against the illnesses that plagued the community. But she also made lovely-smelling love charms. Later, as an adult, he learned their intended purpose.

Angus joined the natives who remained by the small hearth when everyone returned to their card game. Simon Tanner's brief appearance that morning was a puzzle the natives were discussing in depth.

"I don't believe in coincidences," Angus told them as he sat down. "Gil Jackson seems to show up wherever we are. I don't believe Gil has a very high opinion of the survey."

The others agreed.

"In fact, I think Gil blames your survey for Rupert's death." Gray Wolf added.

"Aye, Joseph Freads said much the same thing," said Angus.

The barn was quiet; the slap of the cards on the table and the soft crackle of the fire were the only sounds. For a long time, no one spoke.

"What was Rupert doing working with us?" Angus eventually asked of no one in particular. "Was he spying too?"

"Spying, *too*?" questioned Little Hawk.

"Aye. While ye were away and we were still at Harlan's, Thomas Cresap came to warn us about Finlay Mack, who he accused of spying for the Pennsylvania commissioners."

Running Bear laughed out loud, momentarily startling the others with his deep voice. After his outburst, he continued quietly. "Well, now, that is funny. Everyone around here knows Cresap is doing the same thing for Maryland."

Angus smiled, remembering Stephen had said the same thing.

"Cresap had his sons with him that evening," Angus told his friends. "The next day, we discovered someone had tampered with the chains we use for the measurements. I know they were both fine when I put them in the wagon. It had to have been the Cresaps."

"Only Maryland would benefit from shifting the line further north," Running Bear observed.

"Aye, that's true."

"Now, that does sound typical of Cresap," Gray Wolf said, considering it a bit. He chuckled to himself. "Sly old dog..."

"Luckily, at that point, we were merely confirming the distances as we returned here, and I caught the mistake early. But I should have rechecked the chain before we started." He held up his hand to stop their protests. "It's my responsibility."

Angus leaned forward on his stool and continued in earnest. "And I believe there is something suspicious with that one-armed man, Finlay Mack, as well. I keep seeing him lurking in the shadows wherever I go, and he shows up at odd times. Is Cresap right? Is he a spy?" He told his friends about the box he had seen the sailors exchange onboard the ship and about seeing that same sailor slipping the box to Finlay Mack in a dark alley in Philadelphia.

"He was at the trading post that day when we were there. I wonder why he keeps appearing wherever we are. I would love to see inside that box."

"Well, I suppose if Cresap is spying for his commissioners, someone is likely informing the Pennsylvanians as well," said Gray Wolf. "Finlay would be a good choice. He knows everyone. And as a trader, no one would think twice about his movements. It would make sense."

"Aye. This border has created so much trouble. Two kings gave the same land to different people, and neither cared that people were already living there. No—don't get me started. I hope ye can sort it out." Running Bear sat back on the wooden crate, stretching his long legs and staring into the flames.

It was growing late, and the card game had broken up. Only the foursome remained.

"But, it still doesn't explain the recent events," Little Hawk mentioned. She had been sitting quietly, her shrewd mind working over this news. "I just can't see Finlay or Cresap having anything to do with Rupert's death."

"Maybe," Running Bear stated. "It's possible."

And with that simple statement, he rose.

"Why?" Angus asked, stopping him.

"I can't quite put my finger on it, but I suspect there is more to Finlay Mack than he lets on. He has a past, that's for sure, and he's mighty secretive about it. I've always suspected he's killed a man afore. But he's been good to us."

"And Cresap has also killed when his land was encroached on," added Gray Wolf.

He turned to leave, his siblings following. Angus lay awake, wondering at this.

The storms continued the next week, and everyone grew exhausted from being idle. Tempers flared now and then after being confined in tight quarters for so long.

When the dark clouds finally left the area, Angus stared hopefully out at the observatory, ready and waiting to track the stars that night.

Keeping their word, the natives invited Angus on a hunting expedition. They would spend the morning in the dense woodlands surrounding the farm. Dixon encouraged him to join them, telling Mr. Mason that Angus needed a distraction. And as there were no calculations ready, the timing was perfect.

Little Hawk opted to stay and forage for early berries with Maire and the boys and skipped off, a child holding each hand.

"Do ye ever use a rifle for hunting?" Angus asked as they left, noticing the bows the brothers carried.

"Sometimes, if food supplies are low and we want to ensure success, we might." Running Bear handed a spare bow to Angus. "But this method shows more respect to the animal who gives his life for us. And it gives them a fair chance. Do ye know how to use one?"

Angus nodded. As a lad, he and his cousins shot bows and arrows for sport but were more likely to fish or snare rabbits.

They ventured further into the woods as Gray Wolf talked about their tribe and explained members accepted Christianity generations ago.

"However, even those folk still believe in the spirituality that flows through all things," he continued. "We see this spiritual world interacting with our physical world daily. We are thankful for what it provides for us. The Great Spirit lives in the world with us. But that is a bit different from the Christian concept of God."

Memories of his father kneeling over a wild boar he killed flashed through Angus' mind.

"When I was five, a wild boar was in the woodlands near the house," he told them. "It had killed some of the sheep. My father killed it. I was more interested in the creature's enormous tusks at the time. But, I remember, he offered a blessing." As he thought about it now, he wondered whether his father had similar beliefs.

Gray Wolf smiled at him. "I was baptized," he said. "But I still practice many of the old ways." He smiled at his twin, who wore a cross next to the bear claw around his neck. Angus had noticed that Gray Wolf did not.

Birds chirped overhead, flitting from branch to branch above them. Small creatures scurried alongside the men as they moved deeper into the forest. A mouse hurried across the path in front of Gray Wolf, who scarcely reacted but calmly allowed the small critter to pass. Angus took a deep breath of the fresh air, which was still slightly tinged with the dampness of the recent rain.

Once deep in the woods, the men ceased talking and moved soundlessly along the thick forest floor. They had been treading softly for a while when Running Bear suddenly held up his hand, motioning them to stop. Angus peered over the native's shoulder and saw the buck nibbling on fresh green leaves. As Angus and Gray Wolf stood silently, Running Bear crept forward a few more paces and slowly drew his bow. Sighting down the long arrow, he released it. The deer dropped to the ground, thrashing, and Running Bear ran to it, the others following. He mumbled a prayer of thanks in his native tongue as he slit the animal's throat. The three friends set about preparing the animal for transport to the farm.

"Well, we won't be eating fish all the time," Gray Wolf joked, recalling Fielding's comment. He turned to Angus as they worked. "I know ye lived in the city afore ye arrived here, but what about afore that? Did ye hunt much?"

Angus shook his head. "Nay, the king forbade hunting deer. I mostly fished or snared rabbits and sometimes caught wild birds." He jumped as the sound of a rifle ricocheted through the trees. The natives exchanged glances, rolled their eyes, and continued their work, visibly dismayed.

"Now, I know you Europeans tend to toss out the bones, but we use them for tools, sewing needles, and such, so we will take them if you don't want them."

Angus countered, saying, "Oh, no, we use the bones for the same things and also for buttons."

Gray Wolf looked up at Angus in surprise. "I've seen many Europeans waste much of the animals they kill. We use every bit."

Angus smiled and held up his hand, stopping the men. "Aye, I understand. I have known ye long enough to notice these things." The brothers apologized, and Angus continued, "besides, it's not much different from the highlands. Though there, we primarily use sheep and cattle we raise for those items."

They continued working relaxed and easy in each other's company. When the animal was trussed up on poles of branches, they set out with their kill to return by an easier path.

Angus was in the lead. He abruptly stopped when he spied a man's foot sticking out from behind a huge rock, creating a bend in the path.

Angus held up his hand in warning and stepped slowly around the rock. Simon Tanner lay on the ground in front of him, his sightless eyes staring at the sky.

"Not again," Angus gasped.

Simon sprawled flat on his back, an arrow protruding from his chest with the same fletching as before. Angus sank to the ground beside the man. He touched him on the shoulder and noticed Simon was still warm.

The others approached as Angus kneeled beside the body. Suddenly, the man's eyes blinked, and his mouth began moving. Startled, the three men jumped.

"He is alive," Angus said to the others. "Go for help!"

The natives remained still. When Angus looked up, Running Bear shook his head.

"I... tried to... come... warn ye," Simon gasped as he breathed his last breath.

CHAPTER 13

"Warn who?" Angus shook him. "About what?"

Frustration filled him when he realized he would not receive an answer. Aggravated, he gave the man another shake in a desperate attempt to wake him. The arrow in Simon's chest moved as Angus looked up at the others.

"It is no use, Angus," Gray Wolf shook his head. "The man is gone."

He gently squeezed Angus's shoulder and helped him to his feet.

"There is nothing ye can do." Gray Wolf looked him in the eye.

"It is the same." Running Bear stared at the arrow.

"Aye, I saw it." Gray Wolf agreed. The brothers exchanged a glance. "We are near Bryan's. Let's take this deer there and send for the sheriff."

"I suppose I oughta stay," Angus told them, "someone should." Gray Wolf hesitated, but Running Bear agreed with Angus, which settled the matter.

Disappointed, Angus was standing guard over a dead body once again. He would miss arriving with the brothers and their kill when they returned. Angus mentally kicked himself for those selfish thoughts. The man before him was dead.

The men lifted the deer, trussed on its poles, and departed, promising to return as soon as possible. Alone with a dead body, Angus waved his fist at it. He picked up a nearby stone and threw it at a tree. *Why is this happening?*

He kneeled next to the body, staring at him, desperately hoping the man would wake.

What did you want to tell me? Why didn't you talk to me that day at the barn?

The arrow sat loosely in Simon's chest. Angus stared at the shaft. He gently touched it, and feeling it move easily, slid it from the hole. His stomach was queasy.

He rocked back on his haunches, puzzling over this. Subconsciously, he reached up and touched the charm Little Hawk had given him. She said he needed protection. He speculated on these native women who seemed to possess the sight as his grandmother did. The old seer warned him of trouble ahead that night he spent at the longhouse, but she told him he would get through it. He clung to those words of hope and to the protection the charm provided.

Be true to myself, she said. I need to solve these murders.

A few hours later, the natives stepped out of the trees. Lost in his thoughts, he had not heard their approach. To Angus, it seemed they had been gone forever. Joining them were Charles Mason and Alexander Bryan. The men found Angus sitting cross-legged on the ground next to Simon's body. He was twirling the arrow between his palms, staring intently at it. He looked up at them as they drew near.

Mr. Mason approached and squatted beside him, resting his hand on the younger man's arm. "Andrew is fetching the sheriff, but we decided to come and sit with ye."

"Thank ye. The deer?" Angus asked. Somehow, this seemed important to him.

"Fielding and Liam have it. Don't worry about that right now," answered Running Bear, taking charge. He looked at the others. "Afore that fool sheriff arrives, does anyone have any thoughts on who he wanted to warn? Or what he wanted to tell them?"

Mason shook his head. "Nay, I don't. I only met him a few days ago when he came for work. He seemed nice enough," he paused. "Though, as I recall, he did disappear rather abruptly."

"I'm curious," said Angus, looking up at the natives. The men turned toward him. "We saw him with Gil Jackson and Rupert Jones at the O'Donnell's homestead. The one we found burned," he explained, turning to Mr. Mason. "But before that, Mr. Dixon and I saw all three of them when we first arrived in Philadelphia. They warned us not to trust Indians. Then Rupert comes to work for us and is killed. Now Simon comes wanting to work with us and is also killed. I suspected both of them, maybe even Gil were spying on our work."

"Spying? Ye believe this is connected to our survey?" asked Mason, turning back to Angus.

He shrugged. "I don't rightly know, Sir. Cresap sure thought Finlay Mack was spying for the Pennsylvanian commissioners. And I have seen that man lurking about ever since we were in Philadelphia."

Mr. Mason nodded. "Yes, Jeremiah shared your concerns with me."

"Do these men work with him? They are Pennsylvanians, after all. And what about that man, Cresap? I'm convinced he spies for Maryland. But I can't find a reason for either side to kill Simon. Or Rupert, for that matter." Angus' words gushed out of him, tumbling over each other as he spoke.

"It does merit consideration," Mason responded. He leaned back, his brows knitted together. "But like ye, I agree it doesn't make much sense. Spying is one thing, and there's been some sabotage. But murder?"

"What about the survey, Sir?" Angus asked. "I hope this won't cause any further delays."

"Well, it looks like the weather will hold. I think Jeremiah and I will still be able to start our observations tonight. This won't interfere with us if that is what ye are worrying about." At Angus' nod, Mr. Mason grinned at him. "We'll need ye to apply that brain of yours to the calculations tomorrow. Leave this to the sheriff." He turned and glanced again at the body.

"Aye, sir," Angus replied, trying to sound hopeful. "Thank ye. That will certainly be an improvement."

Then the sheriff arrived.

A squeaky wheel alerted them to the approaching wagon. Following their previous meeting, Angus stood ready to face the sheriff, whom he did not hold in very high regard. As before, the sheriff was not pleased with being summoned from his afternoon pint.

"Ye again," he muttered as he saw Angus, "and another body." He spied the arrow lying across the dead man's chest. "And I recognize that from afore, too. I think ye need to come along with me for some questionin'."

After barely glancing at the body, the sheriff gestured for Angus to follow him and turned to leave.

"Ye seem to be good at stirrin' things up around here," he grunted over his shoulder at Angus.

Alexander Bryan glanced back and forth between Angus and the sheriff as if trying to reach a decision. The corners of his mouth were drawn down in a frown. Angus noticed the tic at the corner of the man's mouth for the first time.

After a tense moment, Mr. Mason stepped up to the sheriff. Unlike Jeremiah Dixon, Mr. Mason was not an imposing figure, but his authoritative manner forced the sheriff to step back from him.

"I think not," Mr. Mason said. "Angus had nothing to do with the man's death."

Angus looked gratefully at the astronomer.

Running Bear stepped forward, joining the two men. "How could ye believe he was involved with this?"

"I don't need any advice from ye, Indian," the man snarled at him. "Ye can come with me too." The native stood his ground, towering above the short, fat sheriff.

"Now, let's discuss this reasonably, like adults," Mason said. "We called ye here because we found a body. That in no way implies one of us was involved in his death. Angus, tell the sheriff what ye saw, and let's return to work."

Eventually, Alexander Bryan also stepped forward, agreeing with Mason and coming to Angus' defense.

Angus briefly described what happened: they returned from their hunt and discovered the man lying across the path. He even included the man's final words. Angus knew the sheriff was not pleased, still stinging from Charles Mason's snub. Obviously, he considered the matter concluded and wanted to charge Angus with the murders of Simon and Rupert and be done with it. But he noticed the deputy behind him cocked his head and studied the scene.

So, with a grunt indicating his disbelief, the sheriff told his deputy to load up Simon's body. "First, Rupert. And now, Simon." His shoulders sagged.

Then the sheriff recovered. "Ye haven't heard the last o' this, so stick around. If this happens again, I will take ye in with me. No arguments."

He stepped aside to let the cart pass. "These deaths are beginning to ruin my quiet little county," he said to the deputy.

The deputy asked Andrew to help and pulled the wagon closer. The large stone created a bend in the path, barely wide enough for the small horse-drawn cart to fit. In his hand, Simon still clutched the cap he had fiddled with the day he spoke to Mr. Mason at the farm. It dropped to the ground as the men lifted him. As the deputy tried to retrieve the cap, he accidentally let the body slide from his hands. The torso landed awkwardly on its side while Andrew maintained a firm grip on the man's legs. Angus, still standing nearby, spied the blood on the back of the man's hunting shirt when the body twisted and hit the ground.

"Wait! Set him back down." He directed, "no, no, on his side, as ye had him. Look." He pointed at Simon's back. Andrew and the deputy obliged as the rest gathered around, staring at Simon's back.

"What now?" grumbled the sheriff, glaring at Angus as he stepped closer.

The men stood examining the dead man's bloody shirt. There was blood dripping from his back and covering the ground beneath him.

"Judging by this, I'd say Simon was shot with a rifle." Gray Wolf, kneeling closer, pointed at the spot. The other men agreed as they examined Simon's back. There was a perfectly round hole in the middle of his left shoulder blade. "Shot in the back. Clean through, it appears."

Angus squatted next to him. "Hmm. While ye went for the sheriff, I examined the hole in his chest. The arrow was there, so I didn't suspect anything else. But, aye, it was loose."

"And we heard a shot earlier, remember?" added Gray Wolf. Angus nodded.

"Well, that changes things," Mr. Mason said as he rose and indicated Angus and the natives, "they were not carrying rifles. They were hunting, but only with bows."

To the sheriff's dismay, Alexander Bryan confirmed it. The tic was no longer visible.

Mason clasped Angus on the shoulder, saying, "Come along, lad, let's leave these men to their business and get back to camp. Ye alright to get back on yer own, Andrew?"

"Aye, Sir. I know this territory well. Be back shortly."

At the farm, Mrs. Bryan stepped outside and crossed to the men sitting near the barn. "I am beginning to think ye like my port," she teased Angus, handing him the tin cup again.

He managed a weak smile as he looked up at her kind face and sipped the wine. She reminded him a lot of his gran. His heart ached from the loss of her.

Martha poured herself a cup and pulled a stool next to him.

Angus noticed the gray in her hair glistening in the sunlight. "Have ye lived here long?" Angus asked.

"Aye, been here my whole life," she answered. "Why?"

"I was wondering if you knew a couple of people—Finlay Mack and Thomas Cresap."

"I am not well acquainted with Finlay Mack, though he seems a decent person, very helpful. Lives up near Conestoga Village somewhere, I believe. Many folks I know trade with him and tell me his word is good. The Indians could tell ye more about him. They know him better than I do."

Angus wondered about that. No one mentioned knowing him well. But then, he had only recently mentioned Finlay to them by name. The brothers had differing opinions of him, but both agreed that the idea of him spying for the commissioners was a distinct possibility.

"Thomas Cresap, on the other hand," she continued, "him, I know a lot about. I am quite familiar with ol' Thomas. Around the time Alexander and I married, he was stirrin' up a heap o' trouble. If I recall, that was around when they did the other survey in '38. Afore that, people thought the line was further north. Cresap lived on the Susquehanna River, just about opposite Conestoga. He ran a ferry there. One day, some Lancaster deputies boarded to cross, and in the middle of the river, they shoved Cresap off his boat. Well, that sly dog, Thomas, hung onto his boat long enough to cut the line, letting his ferry drift off downriver. Quite a ride for them deputies. Mighty wide, that river." She chuckled to herself, remembering. "That caused quite a stir. I reckon that was the beginnin' o' his fight with the sheriff. 'Twas a different sheriff in those days but cut o' the same cloth."

Encouraged by his interest, she pulled her stool closer and continued to regale him with stories of the man and his running battle with the sheriff and the taxman. "Why, at one point, he even moved German families onto his own land to help increase the number of Marylanders in the area."

"Why?" Angus asked.

"I suppose he thought the sheriff would leave them alone if there were more folk in the area. And more and more were arriving from that part o' Europe at the time."

During their conversation, her husband joined them. "His wife, bless her soul, was tough and often joined in on the fightin'. Can ye believe she shot a deputy in the kneecap?"

"Aye. I heard about that," Angus said, remembering the stories Will told him on their journey out of Philadelphia.

"Both of 'em tough," Bryan continued after a bit. "Though now, the family lives out in Oldtown in the wilderness. So hangin' around in these parts is a bit out o' his usual territory. Ye may be right about him interferin'."

Their stories about a man trying to save his land and provide for his family rang true to Angus and were not so different from the stories he listened to in his youth about folk trying to save their way of life. They only wanted to provide for their families and be left alone. Angus didn't know what to believe.

Thoughts continued to swirl through his mind as he rose from the stool and stretched. Cresap is very outspoken and seems such an obvious person for causing trouble, but murder? Why would he do that? Or what about Finlay Mack? No one seems to have much information on him. Angus decided he needed to talk to Running Bear.

It was all so confusing. Angus wandered around mulling it over, but in the end, his logical brain told him either of them could have done it. Or neither of them. But if not them, then who else?

In the early evening, Angus quietly rose and slipped off to view Orion. The constellation disappeared from view in the spring, only to appear again in October. Angus meandered toward the upper field where viewing might be best.

Oblivious to his surroundings, Angus strolled to the fence as he allowed his gaze to drift across the sky, trying to clear his mind and focus on the stars. Jeremiah explained that because of the earth's rotation, viewing the stars changed—Orion was still there, but as sunset grew later, he wasn't visible during the daylight hours of spring and summer.

Angus took a deep breath, trying to relax and put recent events behind him. *What would the great hunter, Orion, do if he kept finding dead people?* His mind wandered along that path for several moments. Could he be as courageous and strong as he imagined the hunter to be?

He closed his eyes. When he opened them, he saw the stars on the belt. Finding them was easy. Glancing down, Rigel, one of the two stars that comprised his knees, appeared. It was less difficult each time to find its blue-white brightness. And above and between them, he could barely see the soft lights of the nebula that outlined the sword hanging from his belt. Angus grew excited at this discovery. His eyes scanned further upward, and for the first time, he found the red hue of Betelgeuse, the second brightest star in the constellation, which marked the hunter's right shoulder.

And Bellatrix! He saw the blue-white light which formed his left shoulder. Angus held his breath. He noticed the sword at his belt; his club raised high in his right hand, the shield in his left. The stars were all there, precisely as Jeremiah described them. There they were in their full magnificence. Suddenly, the mighty hunter appeared in all its glory, just as he had in Jeremiah's sketches.

Angus' hand reached up again, finding the charm around his neck, and clenched it tightly. He could get through this. The old seer's words echoed in his ears. *Just be true to yerself.* Confidence filled him, and he felt more sure of himself than ever. He stood a little straighter, admiring Orion once more before finally making his way to the observatory and the calculations awaiting him.

CHAPTER 14

Little Hawk slowed as she walked through the meadow. The time alone gave her a chance to relax. Yellow dandelions glistened in the sunshine, still moist from the morning dew, and she made a mental note to grab some on her return. Dandelion tea was her favorite; she had never developed a taste for the English settlers' strong black tea. And Soars with Ravens enjoyed the salve she made from their flowers, which she massaged into her grandmother's aching joints. Her current task, however, was down at the stream where she wanted to gather willow branches. Willow bark tea was the best remedy for pain and was simple to prepare.

There was no hurry; she had plenty of time to enjoy foraging today, and she stood in the middle of the meadow, letting the warm sun wash over her face. Spring was her favorite time of year when everything was fresh.

Then she paused; she felt someone's presence intrude in the silence. The feeling was human, not animal, and whoever it was, they were moving stealthily, as if they did not wish to alert her to their presence. Pretending to be interested in the plants surrounding her, Little Hawk scanned the area as she bent over the blossoms. Despite her finely tuned senses telling her someone was nearby, she saw no one. Her gaze drifted over the hillside opposite as she observed her surroundings.

While she enjoyed foraging and usually took her time, she opted to move more quickly. Little Hawk crossed the meadow toward the stream and rapidly cut several slender branches from the willow trees at the water's edge with her small, sharp knife. These would see them through for a while. She straightened and placed them in her large wicker foraging basket.

As she returned, crossing the meadow, she added some dandelions she had seen earlier. As she continued, her fingers played through the clusters of small white yarrow flowers, and she impulsively collected a handful. It never hurt to be prepared for the winter sicknesses that plagued the tribes in recent generations. The tea she made from the leaves and dried flowers was especially effective against cough and fever.

Moving toward the forest's edge, she spied wild violets peeking through the grasses. She grabbed a bunch to give to Martha Bryan, who enjoyed adding them to the soap she made for her family. Little Hawk smiled as she looked down at the bright purple flowers in the sunlight.

Snap!

Little Hawk heard someone step on a branch. Instantly, she froze. The hair on the back of her neck stood on end, and her arms prickled. Slowly, Little Hawk straightened and turned but saw no one. With her small knife ready in her hand, she decided to return to Bryan's farm, her senses on full alert.

Little Hawk hoisted the leather straps of the heavy basket up onto her shoulders and began her trek. Returning by the road would be safer than the shorter path through the woods, and she relaxed somewhat upon reaching it and spotting several horse-drawn carts heading toward her.

Hitching her basket higher on her shoulders, she breathed a deep sigh of relief.

After a few miles, she reached the intersection of the Newark-Lancaster road, where she was overtaken by Angus and Andrew returning from New London, having collected Martha's supplies and mail for Mr. Mason.

"Well met, my friend." Andrew saw her first as Angus guided the horse around a series of ruts from the previous rains.

"Where are ye headed?" Angus asked. He slowed the cart as they caught up to her.

"Back to Bryan's," she replied. "My horse is there."

Angus stopped the horse. "So are we. Hop on up." Slipping the basket from her shoulders, Little Hawk gave it to Andrew with pleasure and gladly accepted a ride with the men. Andrew jumped into the back with their goods, offering Little Hawk the seat on the single bench next to Angus.

"It looks as if ye have been busy," Angus said, indicating her full basket. With a click of his tongue, the horse headed down the road again.

"Aye, the spring brings out many of the plants I use for medicines. I could spend an entire day wandering the meadows."

"My gran loved foraging as well," Angus replied wistfully. Then, more soberly, he asked, "Did ye, by chance, meet up with Gil Jackson?"

"Nay, why do ye ask?" Little Hawk offered nothing further at first, waiting to hear his answer. But she was curious.

"Up the road a bit, we spied Gil slip from the trees. He searched both directions, then raced across the road. At first, we thought he was looking for someone. It was odd."

"He ran like a scared rabbit scurrying away when he spied us," Andrew spoke up from behind.

"Aye, he sure gave that impression. Honestly, he may not have seen us."

Little Hawk turned in her seat to face him. She was grateful now that she had decided to take the road and had met her friends.

"I wonder," she began. "While I was down by the river, I sensed the presence of someone. Animals are always around, and many watch me while I gather my plants. But this was different."

Angus looked at her, and she continued. "I didn't see anyone, though."

Still guiding the horse through the ruts, Angus shot her another glance. "Would Gil be so bold as to follow ye down the road?"

"Oh, I wouldn't think so," Little Hawk answered. "I'm not sure why he would be watching me, anyway." She thought about it for a while.

"The Jacksons don't think highly of my people," she added after a time. "Haman, Gil's father, died in the recent war. But their dislike of us and our ways goes way back. The old man was a drunk, and people stopped offering him work. He and Gil tried their hand at trapping and trading, but we'd been at it much longer and seeing the condition of his pelts...." She shrugged. "Under Soars with Ravens guidance, we did much better, which didn't sit well with them. Haman refused to work his land to provide for his family that way. Somehow, that was also our fault."

"I am learning so much about this new world," Angus replied. "Though, in some ways, it is not so different from back home. It seems there are always people that don't like others."

"Aye," Little Hawk nodded. "There is plenty of land here for people to start a new life. But some have this idea of their perfect world. And often, that doesn't include those of us who already lived here."

"Aye, I heard Gray Wolf express those same thoughts," Angus said.

Little Hawk knew Gil's opinions about women leading the councils. But that didn't explain whether it was Gil that was watching her. Or why? A shiver ran down her spine. She wanted to talk to her brothers.

Eventually, she shrugged it off and changed the subject. "It looks like ye went to town."

"Aye. We picked up some things for Martha, the post, and some packages for Mr. Mason," Andrew replied.

"And I've got a letter from my cousin, Rose. She had a baby girl back in November. She named her Mary."

Little Hawk congratulated Angus, and the threesome chatted until the lane to the farm came into view. Little Hawk hopped down, grabbed her basket when they stopped, and set off to share her bounty with Martha.

Jeremiah Dixon woke up around midday and stepped out of the house onto the covered back porch. His coffee was too hot to drink, so he sat at the wooden table, watching the buzz of activity. Martha tested the water in the big washtub with her finger, checking that it was hot enough to start the washing. Her husband urged the plow horse through the field on the ridge, turning the rich soil for the spring planting. His sons, who now lived in their own homes on the farm, were helping. It was a domestic and peaceful scene. He leaned back in his chair.

Jeremiah wondered whether he would settle down one day and marry, perhaps have children. He shook his head at the thought. Charles was a father, yet somehow Dixon could not picture that life for himself. His own family life had been far from peaceful. Jeremiah was a younger son of a wealthy mine owner who expected his boys to follow him in the family business. But the young Dixon snuck off and learned the surveying trade in Durham. The dreamer of the family, Jeremiah, often remained out late, gazing at the stars. Once his father discovered this, he disowned him. Living a life of drunken debauchery, full of women, he was hardly considered husband material, especially cut off from the Dixon wealth.

As he sipped, he watched the busy life on the farm. His glance fell on their observatory in the far corner of the field, and he smiled. He enjoyed the work they were doing and the challenge it provided him.

In the bright sunshine, he saw Angus bent over the calculations from the previous night. Their assistant reminded him of himself when he was younger. Usually, Angus toiled over them inside, but today was warm, and there was no breeze to blow the pieces of paper away. Angus was taking full advantage of the lovely day. The complex solutions came so effortlessly to the lad. The sun glinted off Angus' auburn hair, and Jeremiah noticed how red it was in the light. Usually pulled back with a strip of leather, it now curled down over his shoulders.

Angus tugged at a curl as he concentrated. He must have sensed something as Angus looked up and noticed Dixon sitting there, sipping his coffee. He waved and reached across to hold up a package and an envelope. Ah, there was mail. Mug in hand, Dixon walked across the field.

"Morning," Angus greeted him with a smirk as he approached. "I am almost finished here for today. These are for ye." He handed the mail to Dixon.

"Thank ye," he said as he took the items. The letter was dated four months previously.

"John Byrd. He is probably asking how the zenith sector is working." Jeremiah set the letter aside to open the package, which contained a knitted scarf his sister had sent him for Christmas. He smiled at the bright red color.

"This would match my frock coat," he said to Angus. Jeremiah looked down at the drab hunting frock he now wore, which was more suited for their work, "I miss that red coat."

He threw the brightly colored scarf around his neck despite the warmer weather and, with a smile, bowed deeply. Angus laughed as Dixon sat down and read his letter, absorbing the news from London.

"Mr. Byrd sends his regards," he told Angus.

When Dixon finished his letter, Angus handed him the calculations to check over. Angus sat quietly, waiting while Jeremiah studied the figures and watched the workings of the farm as Dixon had been from the porch.

When Dixon finished, Angus asked, "how long do ye expect the survey to continue?"

"Why? Are ye eager to return to England?" he asked, gesturing to his letter, assuming Angus was referring to what he'd been reading.

"Oh, nay, I am finding I like it here very much." He shrugged. "Besides, there is little back there for me."

"I reckon I have little as well. I disobeyed my father by becoming a surveyor—he had intended for me to join my brothers, managing our coal mines. He disowned me, actually. Oh well, enough about that. Once we confirm this is the starting point for the border, we will start moving west. I expect that will involve another year at least. We will know more after we present our findings."

Mr. Dixon rose and picked up the calculations from the table. "I should show these to Charles. He was up and gone when I awoke." He looked up and saw Mr. Mason walk past the house. Jeremiah rose to join him.

Angus was pleased to hear that the work would take that long, as he was in no hurry to return. He had not thought beyond this opportunity and now knew he had no desire to return to his uncle's fancy home in London. But where would he go? Those were thoughts for another day. He needed to focus on the present issues.

Running Bear and Gray Wolf would accompany them as full-time guides through the wilderness. Angus considered that next phase of the expedition with some trepidation, considering the recent events, but he hoped to put the rest of this unpleasantness behind him.

Angus watched Liam splitting logs for the Bryans. Sometimes, he found himself a bit jealous of his friend starting a life here. But then, his mind shifted to concern for his friend as he recalled the murders and the burned homestead.

Will Liam and his family be safe here? He crossed the field to join his friend.

As the day wore on, Angus helped Liam mend fences, and then the pair helped with other tasks on the farm. He was enjoying himself tremendously. His muscles relished the manual labor, but mostly, he delighted in spending time with Liam.

Angus could not remember ever having friends, and though a few cousins tolerated him in his youth, they were never friends. But the people here accepted him; where he came from was unimportant to them.

"This labor is good for me," Liam told him, "I was gettin' a bit soft. I must get used to doing everything once I purchase my land—or at least until my sons are old enough to help."

Angus pointed over at Michael, now six, trying to lift a heavy bucket of water. As Maire bent to help him, Martha rushed to grab the handle instead. Martha stooped slightly to let Michael hold one side of the handle as she lifted the bulk of the weight.

"I've got it. Ye ought not to be doin' this in yer condition," Martha scolded Maire.

"Looks like ye will not have to wait long," Angus laughed as they watched him try to help. "Boy's eager to lend a hand."

Liam smiled. "I just hope he is still as willin' when the time comes."

The magistrate was away in Philadelphia, so Alexander had learned no details concerning the homestead. Rumors abounded of increased Indian activity in the county's western portion, and the magistrate had been summoned to the capitol. No one knew when he would return.

Liam and Angus finished chopping and stacking more wood, then walked to the barn and poured mugs of ale. Angus wiped the perspiration from his brow, swigging back the refreshing brew and enjoying the fine weather. After a few moments of peace, Angus heard the hoofbeats of two horses charging up the lane, coming on hard and fast towards the homestead.

Work on the farm stopped abruptly. Alexander wiped the sweat from his brow as he squinted towards his home with his sons beside him. Andrew rushed out of the barn, hearing the commotion. Dismounting as the horses slowed to a stop, Running Bear and Gray Wolf came running to where Angus and Liam stood.

"Have ye seen our sister?" both men gasped as one.

"Not since she left earlier to meet up with ye at Freads'. But that was hours ago," Angus reported, feeling a knot forming in the pit of his stomach.

Andrew nodded in agreement as he approached.

"She gave me some wild violets when she returned for her horse," Martha confirmed, joining them, "then she mounted up to catch up with ye. But that was afore midday."

Alexander and his sons raced in from the field. "Is there a problem?" he panted.

"Aye, when we left here for Freads' this morning, our sister told us she was going to do a bit of foraging and meet us there," Running Bear said with concern in his eyes.

"But she never showed up. Sometimes she gets carried away gathering her plants, so we made little of it at first. But we expected her to ride up any minute." Gray Wolf was worried as well.

"But her mare just arrived without her," Running Bear gasped.

"We should get a search party going," said Alexander as he took charge, ordering everyone to grab a horse. He began assigning pairs of men to each potential path to the Freads homestead. He pointed to Fielding, the cook, "ye stay here with the women, and if Little Hawk returns, send word to us." He glared at his wife, silencing her demand to come with them. "Someone should stay, just in case Little Hawk comes here. If she fell, she might be injured."

Mairi hugged her boys closer to her.

"We will help too," said Mason and Dixon in the same breath, "just tell us where to ride."

Everyone set about saddling their mounts, and within moments, the men set out in pairs, with each man from the survey party accompanied by a local familiar with the area. Riding along with Gray Wolf, Angus was worried about what could have happened to her. *Did she fall from her horse? Is she lying injured somewhere?*

"She has always been headstrong," Gray Wolf told Angus. "But she can take care of herself. I am sure she is fine, and we will find her."

It sounded more like he was trying to convince himself this would be true. Angus agreed, trying to convince both of them that Gray Wolf was right.

The pair took the shorter path toward Freads' farm. Making their way along, calling her name occasionally, the men scanned the track and the underbrush of the woods surrounding them. Angus' horse broke through the trees into a tiny clearing, and he spotted her basket lying in the taller grass to the side of the path.

"Here," he shouted to Gray Wolf behind him.

Both men slid from their horses. There, in the grass, was not only her upended basket, the contents spewed across the ground, but her foraging knife as well. The grass beyond was torn up, and a patch of earth trampled down, obvious signs of a struggle.

"Look! She tried to fight." Gray Wolf read the signs on the ground. "She was taken. But by who?" he questioned Angus with his dark eyes. He pointed at two footprints near the basket; one set was Little Hawk's, the other much larger. "She would never leave her knife." He stooped and picked it up.

Angus stared at the sight before him. *I should have come with her.* The knot in his stomach clenched tighter, and he shook in anger.

Angus rose after examining the footprints. "We met up with her on the way back from town. She told us about being watched by the river." At the other man's sharp glance, he added, "We saw Gil Jackson in the area."

"Jackson?" Gray Wolf turned to him. He wore a grim expression, and Angus swore the tattoo on his face darkened.

CHAPTER 15

Little Hawk's head felt like it would burst as she slowly regained consciousness. Pain shot through it, and she closed her eyes against the dim light. Her hip felt bruised; she sat on a hard-packed dirt floor sprawled against a rough wooden wall. One wrist throbbed, though nothing seemed broken.

"What happened?" she asked aloud. "Where am I?"

All she could tell was that she was in a small shed of some sort—but one good sniff gave her a clue—sour mash. Someone was distilling whisky nearby.

Slowly, snippets of memory flooded back: of riding to meet her brothers, of being grabbed from behind. Thrashing and fighting someone off. Bouncing on horseback, unable to move... Gil.

"Why?" she had asked as she roused and fought to free herself, attempting to look up at Gil as the horse trotted along the pathway. She lay draped across the horse in front of him. And though she struggled, she was firmly bound by her hands and feet. She tried to slide off, but his grip was tight.

"Don't ye know? Ye are the problem here, and I aim to solve it." He growled at her.

Little Hawk's foggy brain tried to make sense of this as she bounced along on the horse. "What problem?"

"Thinking women can lead, what kind o' man puts up with that? Women makin' decisions. Not in my world. I'll get ye to confess that ye Indians are up to no good."

Little Hawk lost consciousness and did not hear the rest of his rant.

Now in the shed, she struggled to move and realized her hands and feet were still tightly bound. It took a moment to realize there was no gag in her mouth.

"I wonder why?" she said to the empty space.

"Oh." Realization sank in, "Gil knows no one would hear me out here, no matter how loudly I scream."

Dim sunshine filtered in around the edges of the ill-fitting door. It was still daylight, but evening approached. She figured it must be later the same day.

"How was I so stupid?" Distracted by wild onions, Little Hawk had dismounted. And then she'd spied mushrooms under a rotting log. The next thing she remembered was being on Gil's horse.

Her head throbbed, and she decided to ponder this later as she drifted off, slumping against the wall.

Sometime later, she roused again. The light showing around the door was faint; it was growing dark. Lucky for her, Gil had bound her hands in front and not behind her. It was possible to reach her ankles, but loosening the rope was awkward, with her hands tightly bound. The knots were constricting, her hands tied in a position allowing only the use of her fingertips. These were not strong enough; nevertheless, she picked at the bindings strand by strand. Eventually giving up, for the time being, Little Hawk scooted across the dirt floor by bending and straightening her arms and legs and pulling herself along as she tried to reach the door. Pain shot through her head and forced her to stop several times. She could feel the throbbing in her wrist intensifying. The rough floor scraped her hands and knees as her tunic rode up in her efforts, but she kept going and finally reached the door. With great effort, she managed to pull herself to her knees. She leaned on the door, raised her bound hands, and tried to open it, but the latch held firm. It was sturdier than it first appeared.

"Well, I see no escape there," she muttered.

Then, she noticed a single tiny window... which was boarded up. She could never reach it, anyway. In frustration, she leaned against the wall and, glancing down at her red linen tunic, noticed a six-inch tear in the bottom. Despite all she had been through, that rip saddened her, and a tear ran down her cheek. She had to find a way out; she just needed to think. Another tear flowed onto her skirt.

Angus paced back and forth, the thoughts running through his mind making little sense. *Who would take her? It had to be Gil. But why? Was this connected to the deaths of Rupert and Simon?* He shook his head at the idea of that. The murders had more to do with the survey. However, someone had made it look like Indians. And Gil believed it.

The men gathered outside Joseph Freads' barn near Kennett Township in the growing darkness, arguing about the best way to proceed. But no one knew which way to go.

"I know it was Gil Jackson." Angus blurted out and stopped pacing.

Running Bear regarded him. "What about Gil?" He rose and crossed to where Angus stood by the fire.

"We met up with Little Hawk after fetching the post this morning," he told them, "shortly afore that, we saw Jackson come out of the woods. He glanced around like he was looking for someone. But Little Hawk said she hadn't seen him, so I didna think much about it." He looked apologetically at the brothers.

"Aye, Gray Wolf told me what ye said." Running Bear was clenching his fist.

"It was odd," agreed Andrew. "But Little Hawk didn't seem too concerned, so I didn't worry about it either. She chatted with us on the way back to the farm."

Joseph spoke then, "I know he hates yer people, and he suspects they are involved with the deaths of Simon and Rupert. Maybe he took action, and that's why he took Little Hawk. Ye know he blames the natives for his pa's death. Revenge, maybe?"

"True. I guess one could see it that way," said Alexander Bryan.

"Well, after the death of Rupert, I overheard Gil in Nathaniel's place. I told Angus about it, how Gil was carryin' on, rantin' about the sheriff not doing anythin', about the Indians, and the survey. But they were drunk as usual, so I didn't pay no mind." Joseph looked around.

"Aye, Angus mentioned it to me. I can understand where Gil would blame the Indians for their deaths. And maybe he took Little Hawk as revenge." Jeremiah Dixon said. "But, I think the events are separate. Unfortunately, I think our survey is linked to those deaths. Rupert was working for us. And Simon came looking for work." He looked sadly at Charles Mason. "I'm wondering what we got ourselves into."

Mr. Mason shrugged. "Aye, there's a lot more riding on this than first appeared. It seems we have people following along, spying on us at any rate. And there's been sabotage."

"I was with the natives when we met Gil at the O'Donnell place. I don't think he approves of our friendship with the natives, nor them working with us."

"Well, whatever his grief with us, ye weren't part o' that." Gray Wolf said. "It's a bold step for Jackson. But it looks like he's all we have for now."

"So, where do we go from here? What do we do next?" Alexander asked.

"Well, Gray Wolf here is an excellent tracker. It's too late tonight for him to see anything. We should grab supplies and be ready to leave in the morning. We'll see then what Gray Wolf can come up with," suggested Joseph.

"I'll try. The weather has been fine so that any traces will remain visible."

Angus watched his friend's agitated movements as he spoke and knew he did not want to wait. The tall native gave Angus a smile that did not quite reach his eyes. "We will find her. If I know our sister, she's left a trail a blind man can follow."

Little Hawk roused again. It was dark now. As she pieced together more memories, she realized she had lost her knife somewhere along the way. The blow to her head must have been more substantial than she first thought; otherwise, she certainly would have remembered her knife sooner. Without it, she could not cut the ropes from her hands and feet. Her head ached less as she tried to see the binding around her hands. But it was nighttime, and she saw only dark forms against the inky blackness.

It was cold and damp in the shed, and she shivered. Her cloak was in her saddlebag.

Little Hawk picked again with her fingernails at the knot around her ankles to no avail. She raised her hands to her mouth, and despite the strong smell of tar, she tried using her teeth on the rope but quickly gave up that idea. She wondered if she might discover something in the morning to cut through the rope around her wrists, and then she could untie her ankles.

If she were lucky, Gil would get drunk tonight. If possible, she could be gone before he was up and about. She sat in the darkness, running the possibilities through her mind. Little Hawk didn't know how far away he lived but knew she was at Gil's whisky still. He must live nearby. All she had noticed when she roused earlier were some kegs stacked in a corner. If she searched as soon as there was light enough to see, she might free herself before he arrived.

She reached up to her throat and clasped the bear claw she wore for protection. It filled her with a sense of strength.

"Where is my mind?" she blurted out. Little Hawk reached up with her hands and slid the thong over her head. Diligently, she began using the sharp point to pick at the knots in the dark.

As the others prepared for bed back at the farm, Angus excused himself to retrieve his blanket from his saddlebag in the nearby stable. Instead, he quietly moved his horse away from the others and saddled him in preparation, tying him at the far end of the building. During the evening's discussions, Angus had reached a decision. He would go after Little Hawk. And go tonight. He didn't want to wait until morning.

While pacing the floor earlier, he worried about Little Hawk. What would Gil do with her? Would he hurt her? His instincts had been right that morning when she mentioned sensing someone. Angus knew it had been Gil after seeing him cross the road. Even though Little Hawk had said otherwise, Angus firmly believed Gil would have followed her down the road if he and Andrew had not come along. Angus heard that Gil blamed the Indians for the death of his friends. And his father. But where would he take her?

As Angus headed back into the barn with his blanket tucked under his arm, he glanced up at the sky. The waning crescent moon would not provide much light for his journey. It was too late in the season to see Orion, but he felt the hunter's magic flowing through him, urging him on. Angus selected a spot near the door and spread his blanket on the ground, noting where the two natives slept. Gray Wolf and Running Bear were stretched out on blankets near the far doorway that led toward the house. Of anyone, they were the most likely to hear him slip out. He hoped he was far enough away.

Possibilities ran through his mind as he curled up, feigning sleep. He knew Gil lived somewhere between Lancaster and the native village they visited. If he headed northwestwards and bypassed Harlan's farm, he could travel toward the Fleming family trading post on the Brandywine River. From there, Angus remembered the road into Lancaster. He would ride to that point before worrying about where to go next. Though it was not a sound plan, it was a course of action. As he lay there listening to one man, then another snoring, Angus succumbed to exhaustion and drifted off to sleep.

"The town is the other way if they are going for the sheriff. Gil's whisky still is the only thing in that direction. It is common knowledge here, but he thinks no one knows about it."

Little Hawk's voice penetrated Angus' dream. He woke with a start, remembering her words that day at the homestead when Gil walked off in the opposite direction of the town. *Gil's whisky still.* Of course, where else would he go? Especially if he believed no one knew about it, Angus reasoned.

Slipping out silently, he mounted his horse and headed north. The night was darker than he expected. Tree cover overhead blocked the minimal light of the moon, and it wasn't easy to see the narrow path.

"It will be easier to see when we reach the main road," Angus told the horse. And visibility did improve when they reached it only because the trail was broader and fewer trees blocked the light.

Could he find the burned-out O'Donnell homestead? And from there, the still? Angus pictured the scene as he rode, envisioning the direction Gil headed that day. He had to try.

Angus changed his original plan now that he had a destination in mind. Instead, he opted to bypass Lancaster to the south. His brain mentally ticked off how they had traveled months before. He grew bleary-eyed as he rode through the night.

The surrounding area was densely wooded, with only an occasional farmstead set back from the road. Few locals were about this early. However, further along, Angus saw a man with a cart coming toward him.

"Good day, friend," he greeted the man. "Is this the direction to Conestoga?"

The man paused and scratched his head as he curiously looked him over. "Aye. But why would ye be going there?"

Remembering the massacre, Angus thought quickly. "Oh, I'm not heading to the village. I have a friend out that way." That was not exactly a lie. He believed Little Hawk was there.

"Ah," said the man, relaxing. "If ye stay this here road, afore ye get to Lampeter, follow the southbound track along Mill Creek. It'll take ye there. There be a small cabin with a large oak tree in front of it beside yer turn."

Angus thanked the man and continued in the direction he indicated. He spied smoke curling above the trees about an hour later as a small cabin came into view. A large oak stood in front precisely as the man described. The narrow but heavily traveled track veered off to the southwest, just past the cleared land surrounding the home.

As he proceeded, Angus thought a few farmsteads looked familiar as the early morning sky lightened, improving visibility. He remembered traveling along this way before with the siblings. He passed north of the village where the natives were massacred and felt a chill down his spine. Angus knew Charles Mason was curious to visit the site to understand what happened, but Angus had no desire to see the village. Such things were beyond his comprehension, and he believed visiting it would serve no purpose.

That suppressed feeling of being hated by others bubbled again to the surface. Angus shook it off and realized he was near the O'Donnell place. Further on, Angus knew his friend's village was nearby, and part of him felt he should inform her family. But he opted to bypass the trail leading there. To go to the settlement would waste valuable time, and she had been missing too long.

Angus recognized the spot where they noticed the smoke rising from the smoldering homestead. Now he knew he had followed the right track. Taking the northern branch, Angus soon arrived at the site. Surprised, he noted the beginnings of a cabin being constructed. These hardy folk had put losing everything behind them to eke out a living in this wilderness. In that instant, the notion that folks back home had probably rebuilt their lives struck Angus. He speculated as he rode whether anyone back home cared for the cross on the hill for which his former home, Creag na Croise, was named.

No one was at the homestead; the family must live elsewhere while they rebuilt their cabin. Angus pulled his horse to a halt at the point he remembered standing when Gil and his friends appeared. He dismounted and led the horse behind him. It was mid-morning now and much easier to see as he followed the direction the men had gone that day.

"Oh, look, here are hoofprints," he spoke to his horse, pointing to them in the soft earth beneath a tree.

It was not much, but someone traveled this path recently. Reaching the edge of a sizeable clearing, Angus tethered the horse and peered out from the trees. He thought it might be wise to proceed on foot, unsure of what to expect. Angus removed the axe from his saddlebag and shoved the handle through his belt. No one was around, but he spied a small shed just ahead of him. As he approached, he thought it did not appear very well-built or sturdy.

Little Hawk's finely tuned senses heard someone outside. She paused her efforts to pick at her bindings with the bear claw and braced herself for the coming confrontation with Gil. Her attempt at finding something more substantial in the shed to free her hands that morning had been fruitless. The building was empty except for those barrels. She sat up straighter, ready to give him an earful when he entered.

The door creaked as Angus removed the peg from the latch and swung inwards. He peered inside as Little Hawk let out what he could only believe was a curse in her native tongue. He stepped inside, allowing his eyes to adjust to the dim interior.

"Ye? What are ye doing here?" she hissed at him. Little Hawk had expected Gil. It surprised her, and it took a moment for her to realize help had arrived.

"I came to find ye," he answered, surprised at her reaction. He stepped back.

"Do the others have Gil?"

"Others?" He stepped back toward her.

"My brothers, the others that came with ye. Did ye get Gil?"

But she suddenly stiffened before Angus could explain he had come by himself to rescue her. A shadow filled the doorway as she screamed, "Angus! Watch out!"

It was too late. Angus spun—at that exact moment, a large piece of wood caught him hard on the side of his head. Down he dropped, unconscious on the floor.

CHAPTER 16

Gray Wolf squatted and studied the ground as he read the marks in the packed earth. "His horse stood here for some time. I'm sure he saddled him when he came out to get his blanket." He wore a grim expression on his handsome face.

Shaking his head, he rose and stepped to the other men standing outside. Gray Wolf noticed his brother's clenched jaw as he stood rigid, grinding his teeth, his hands on his hips.

"It was stupid of him to leave on his own like this. What could he do during the night?"

"Why didn't he wait? And where did he go?" Running Bear asked.

After much discussion, the men agreed that Andrew and Liam would go with the natives while Mr. Mason and Mr. Dixon returned to Bryan's farm to resume their calculations. The commissioners expected prompt results, and it would not help matters to get further behind. As they prepared to leave, both men admitted they would rather join the search. It would be hard to remain focused on their task while worrying about their young apprentice, but it was for the best that they continued working. Alexander Bryan decided to accompany his guests back home.

Mr. Mason expressed displeasure with the young man's "impulsive" behavior.

"Aye. It was impulsive, but I may have done the same thing when I was younger." Gray Wolf overheard Dixon tell Mr. Mason, compassion in his tone.

Joseph provided supplies for the team headed west, and the two groups parted ways. As they said farewell, everyone wished the trackers good luck finding Little Hawk—and now Angus.

"Where do *ye* think he went?" Gray Wolf asked Liam accusingly.

He assumed Angus had confided in him and confronted him as soon as the others were gone. Suddenly, Gray Wolf realized that part of his anger was because Angus had not confided in *him*.

"I don't know. He didn't tell me anything," Liam replied, holding his ground against the taller man's accusations. "But he was positive last night that we needed to find Gil Jackson. Know anything about him?"

"A good-for-nothing wastrel, if ye ask me," Andrew chimed in as he mounted his horse to leave the farm. Running Bear shrugged and agreed.

Gray Wolf realized Liam was also hurt and angry and apologized, knowing they needed to work together to get his sister back. Liam shook his hand, accepting his apology.

Running Bear said, "I suppose the task now is to figure out where he took her."

"Well, let's see what the trail tells us for a bit afore we jump to conclusions. Now, I looked around where we found Little Hawk's basket. There is evidence of a horse heading north from there." Gray Wolf continued studying the ground. "And this looks as if Angus has done the same. So, let's head that way and see what we find."

They'd only ridden a few miles when Gray Wolf paused and pointed out fresh horse droppings.

"These can't be but a few hours old. No one else would be out at that hour."

The anger on his face turning to concern, Running Bear agreed. But it was unlike Little Hawk not to leave a trail for them to follow, which concerned them both. Soon, a freshly broken branch showed that Angus and his horse had likely been there. Gray Wolf pointed out the hoofprints in the damper muddy areas.

"This is the same horse. See how that one nail in the shoe is bent?" The others peered where he pointed. "Same the marks we saw back at Joseph's."

So far, Angus' trail was easy to follow, but progress was slower than they wished. They bypassed Harlan's farm as Angus had done, following his trail northwest until it intersected the road to Lancaster.

"Well, Liam, I believe ye may have the right of it. He is definitely headed due west now." Running Bear said as they reached the main road and saw the prints continuing in that direction.

"Aye, this part should go quicker. I am sure now Angus is on his way to Gil's," Gray Wolf told the others as he mounted his horse. "Few paths split off, so we'll ride on, checking each track as we pass."

"Aye, that's true enough. Lots o' rivers out this way and few places to ford 'em unless ye know the way," Andrew explained to Liam.

Meanwhile, in the shed, Angus groaned and opened his eyes. A sharp pain shot through his head as the light entered, and he quickly closed them again. Moments later, he opened one eye a slit and looked around. Little Hawk was sitting opposite him. He was bound hand and foot, just as she was. Memories came flooding back. *Gil.*

"How long was I out?" he asked in a hoarse whisper.

"Not long." Her tone was sharp. Even bound, she had somehow crossed her arms over her chest. Her jaw was firmly set.

"I thought I could help." He refrained from adding the words 'to save ye.' Her look spoke volumes, and Angus knew that was not a good idea.

"What were ye thinking?" she hissed at him. "How could ye come by yerself? Why didn't ye bring someone with ye? Did ye even tell anyone where you were headed?" Without taking a breath, the questions gushed out of her, and she continued before he could get a word in, "Men! So, what happens now? Do ye even have a plan?"

Realizing she was right, Angus merely shook his head and said, "I am sorry." He maneuvered himself into a seated position, leaning against the barrels opposite her.

"I dinna think this through," he admitted. "I dinna ken what will happen now.

He looked so pitiful. Little Hawk could not stay angry at him long. "Well, we will figure something out. Got anything sharp on ye?" She held up her bound hands, suggesting something to cut the rope. "I've been picking at it with this, but it's been slow going," She held up the bear claw.

Angus remembered the axe in his belt but noticed its weight was no longer there.

"Gil took your axe," Little Hawk said.

"Nay, everything else is in my saddlebag." Watching Little Hawk work, he pulled his claw from around his neck before asking, "what is going on between ye and Gil? Why does he hate ye and yer brothers so much?"

"It is not us in particular, just that we are not Europeans."

"Aye, I understand that, but this seems different; somehow, his hatred seems more focused on ye," Angus said.

He shifted off a stone in the dirt floor that poked into his thigh.

"It goes a long way back. His pa was let go from his work at the courthouse for drunken behavior. He tried to become a trader but was sloppy in his work and couldn't make a go of it. That man was a loudmouth drunk like his son. He couldn't keep a job and lost his house. Moved out here further west, squatting on land nearby. Then he built this still for his whisky operations." She paused.

"I was a child then. But under Soars with Ravens, our people prospered. Haman couldn't compete with us, so he blamed us for his failures. Us, and the Conestoga. He lumps us all together. Everyone knows his hatred for them, in particular. But we thought it was harmless, all bluster. It seems it continues in his son. Things got better when Running Bear took over as the face of our operations. But my brother does nothing without our grandmother's blessing. Gil doesn't understand this. He wants everyone to be like him."

"Conestoga? Was Gil part of the massacre, then?"

"Gil? I don't know for sure, but I don't think so. He's not much of the church type, but I think he listens to Reverend Elder. And that man preaches good riddance to us all from his pulpit. He claims this land for the Europeans."

"When I was a wee lad, they blamed the clans in Scotland, especially the Catholics, for all the troubles. So that I can understand." Tribes... clans... they were beginning to look a bit alike to him. "But why take ye?" he asked.

"I know Gil hates our people; he has made that clear. But this, taking me? I am not sure. He muttered something about me being part of the problem."

"Your brother tells me this Reverend Elder claims the Conestoga tribe was secretly spying on the English and providing information to the French."

Little Hawk scoffed at this. "That's ridiculous. I think it's more because I am a woman. He doesn't believe women can lead. And he blames their failures on Grandmother."

Angus shifted, and his arm brushed against the canteen hung on a strap across his chest. "Oh, I have water. Would you like some?"

Little Hawk smiled in relief, "Yes, please." She crab crawled toward him as he did the same. He slid the leather strap over his head and down between his linked hands so she could grab it and drink. She took a big swig, swishing it around the inside of her dry mouth.

"There must be something we use that is better than this," he said and nodded at the bear claw. Now that his eyes had adjusted to the dim interior, he scanned the room for something of use. Inside the small structure, he saw only the barrels.

"I couldn't find much either," she said as she watched him look around.

Shifting again on the hard ground, Angus remembered the stone cutting into his thigh near the barrels. He maneuvered his way back and found the jagged edge. *Will it be sharp enough?* He swung his bound legs around for a better angle on the stone. Thus positioned, he slid his wrists back and forth across the sharp edge, trying to slice through the rope binding them. Fortunately, the stone was firmly lodged in the earthen floor. The rope was strong, but he observed a few loose strands. He realized loosening them this way would take hours, but he was encouraged by doing something.

"It might take me a time to be free to help ye," he said.

"I'll find another, thank ye," she replied.

Angus, feeling chastised, watched Little Hawk look around for another sharp edge. She slid near the barrels to a corner previously in the shadows. The tip of a broken rock was just visible. Little Hawk set to work, scraping the dirt around it until she exposed a sharper edge beneath the soil.

The pair chatted about their childhoods and their families as they worked. This distraction helped pass the time and keep their minds off their weary muscles.

It took a long time before Angus was close to breaking free. His muscles ached by this point, but he worked harder, moving his hands back and forth to slice through the stout rope. Suddenly, his ears perked up. It was merely a whisper of a sound, but it differed from the woodland noises he had grown accustomed to, and he glanced at Little Hawk. She nodded; she had heard it, too. It was too soft, too stealthy to be Gil. The hairs on the back of Angus' neck stood on end.

Little Hawk motioned for him to be silent; she mouthed, "my brothers." They both hoped it was them slipping up to the shed to check if they were inside. Angus needed no warning. He stopped his work and fidgeted silently with his hands. He thought he might snap the rope with one good jerk, but he was afraid of making a sound, so he continued to pick silently at the loose strands. The captives held their breath.

There it was again. The pair looked at each other and nodded. Someone was definitely sneaking around out there. Soft footsteps slowly approached the shed. A shadow fell across the cracks around the edge of the door as it slowly creaked open, a shadow filling the opening.

In one sharp snap, Angus broke the remaining strands of the rope, freeing his hands. With them free now, he reached down and untied the rope around his ankles. Just as the door opened, Angus leaped to his feet and landed upright. Though not fully recovered after being hit on the head, he swayed dizzily.

Reeling, struggling to maintain balance after rising so quickly, Angus spun to see who entered and readied himself to attack. Unable to see in the blinding sunlight, Angus knew anyone sneaking would be a threat. He was ready.

Angus lunged as the figure stepped inside, catching the man in the midsection. Both men grunted, and Angus began swinging. He swore that he was not going down without a fight this time.

Little Hawk screamed, "Angus, no!"

Angus swung hard and fast at the man, but he was still wobbly on his feet, and the man reacted quickly, ducking under Angus' fists and hooking a strong arm around his chest. The man held him firmly against his body. The movement had the dual effect of keeping Angus upright and pinning him tightly.

"Hold on there, laddie," the voice said. The man spoke with a Scottish accent reminiscent of home. As he pressed back to continue the fight, Angus realized the man had only one arm.

Finlay Mack.

"What are ye doin' here?" he sputtered. "What do ye want?"

"I figured the two of ye needed some help," Finlay spoke in Angus' ear. "Can I trust ye not to swing at me if I release ye to free Little Hawk?"

"Aye. But can I trust ye?" Angus fired back.

"Aye, lad. I suppose that is a chance ye'll just have to take." Finlay let go of Angus and crossed to Little Hawk.

"Are ye alright, lass?" he asked her as he untied her wrists and then, kneeling, untied her ankles. "I heard someone in the tavern in Lancaster last night sayin' they saw ye ridin' with Gil Jackson on his horse. I knew that couldna be true. So, I decided to find where he took ye when it was light. I followed his tracks which led me here, o' course." He smiled wryly at the last statement. "All along the ride, I hoped to find ye safe, though I expected ye to be alone."

She rose to her feet. "Thank ye, Finlay. The help is much appreciated." She turned to Angus. When he said nothing, she continued. "I was unaware of anything after he hit me on the head. He tied me across his lap, and I woke up here."

"I figured he might come here. He still thinks no one knows about this place. Gets away with his illegal operations by supplying that sheriff with whisky. But then I saw a horse in the clearing." He turned toward Angus. "I've moved it to the other side. Figured Gil might notice it where it was."

Angus stood staring at the man. Up close, he seemed familiar. There were strands of red still visible in his graying hair. His eyes were a piercing green. Angus dismissed it as having seen him lurking about so often. Maybe Finlay was not so bad. Little Hawk seemed to trust him.

"Thank ye," he whispered grudgingly. Then, clearing his throat, he repeated his thanks.

"Not a problem, lad. But ye ought to get out o' here afore Jackson returns."

The trio walked out of the shed. Once outside, Angus breathed deeply and allowed his eyes to adjust to the bright sunlight, grateful for his freedom. When he turned to thank Finlay once more, the man was gone, disappeared into thin air.

CHAPTER 17

Angus spun, looking for the man, but no one was there. Where had Finlay gone?

"Ye can't just disappear into thin air!" Angus sputtered. Walking briskly, he searched behind the small shed.

Little Hawk glanced around. The sun was sinking lower in the sky.

"Forget about him," she said, walking from the shed. "Nothing surprises me anymore, it seems. We need to get out o' here." She took a few steps toward the clearing before turning. Angus was not following her. "Come on! We must go."

Little Hawk stood, her hands on her hips, glaring at him.

Angus took one last look and followed her to the clearing where he had left his horse. Little Hawk was right; they ought to go before Gil returned. However, Angus privately hoped Gil would appear. He was ready for a fight. Gil would have difficulty sneaking up on him out in the open. He furtively scanned the area, hopeful of catching sight of the man. His hands curled into fists at his sides.

Entering the stand of trees separating the still and the clearing, something on the ground caught Angus' eye. A feather. Not just any feather but a perfect match to the ones they collected at the burned homestead and the murder scenes.

He stopped, frozen in place. "Little Hawk, look at this."

Turning and retracing her steps, she asked, "What is it now?" Little Hawk crossed her arms over her chest as she stopped in front of him. "We need to get out of here. Now."

"That," he pointed at the ground.

Spying the feather, she bent over it, her frustration melting. "It matches the others."

"Aye," Angus nodded. "It does." He squatted next to her and picked it up, inspecting it closely. "Finlay."

Little Hawk rose, her hands again on her hips. "Why do ye say that? The man just rescued ye. How could ye believe he is responsible for all of this?"

"Well, he didn't take *ye*, but he was here," Angus protested. "And he moved my horse, which puts him in this exact location. The feather is here. He must have dropped it. I suspected Finlay was up to something. This is proof." He stood. "On top of that, he just disappeared."

Little Hawk gestured impatiently at him. "Ye could say the same for Gil. The feather was found on his land," she stated firmly. "We need to go."

Glancing around one last time, Angus noticed several other feathers and picked one up before following her again toward the clearing.

"I've seen Finlay everywhere I have been since I arrived." He paused when she turned to look at him in disbelief. "I know he's involved with what I saw on the ship. I saw that same person give Finlay the box in a dark alley. Something is up with that man."

"That may be true, but ye make too much of it," she replied as they entered the clearing. "Finlay is a friend. He has been there for my people. And he just saved us!" She raised her hand before he could protest further. "I understand ye believe he is a spy for Pennsylvania and keeping an eye on your survey. I can accept that, though that is as far as I go," she stated firmly. After a moment, she added, "Finlay helped us keep our land when Europeans tried to force us out. I find it hard to believe he would be behind the death of those men."

As she spoke, they crossed the clearing to where Angus' horse stood, nibbling on the grass on the far side. Seeing them, it gave a soft nicker, startling a group of birds nestled in the tall grass—wild turkeys. Little Hawk and Angus froze as they recognized the turkeys' feathers—the same feathers Angus now held in his hand.

"Angus, look at those!" Little Hawk exclaimed. "They are the same birds!" She turned toward him, her dark eyes wide in surprise.

Angus noticed them, too. "What does this mean?"

"I've never seen their like afore." She taunted him, "still believe it's Finlay?"

Angus shrugged and wondered if he was wrong about the man. Suddenly, they heard Gil shout. He had returned and noticed they were gone. As one, they sprinted for the horse, mounted up, and galloped away.

As he wandered along the path from his cabin, Gil suddenly spied the open door of the shed and swore in outrage, cursing at the opening. He rushed to it and looked inside, dreading what he would find. The space was empty. The ropes lay on the floor inside.

How did they escape? He made sure they were securely bound. Where were they now? For the first time, he questioned how Angus had gotten there. He must have had a horse nearby. As these thoughts ran through his mind, Gil heard a single horse speeding away, rustling through the trees.

Gil cursed. Why hadn't he looked for it? He never even considered they might escape. He glanced down and saw the peg from the hasp lying at his feet, confirming his suspicions. They didn't break out; someone helped them. But by who? No one knew about this place.

But that was just one horse. Where were the others? Or were there others? There must have been. Gil ran his fingers through his dirty brown hair in frustration. He wanted to find the sheriff and ply him with whisky in case he needed help.

They rode hard, Little Hawk clinging to Angus, and in less than an hour on the road east, the pair met up with the search party heading toward the still, having worked out Angus' plan. There was much shouting in excitement as they approached.

"Ye found her!" hollered Running Bear, reining in his horse and sliding to the ground before the animal stopped.

Excitement filled the air when the men saw she was safe. Gray Wolf slid his sister down from behind Angus, swirling her in a circle. Running Bear encircled them both in his arms in a giant bear hug.

Liam and Andrew slid from their horses and ran to Angus, clapping him on the back. Little Hawk was tired and thirsty but otherwise unharmed. Angus had succeeded.

Honest as ever, however, Angus would not take credit for the rescue. He admitted he had acted rashly and not given it proper thought.

"Gil got the better o' me. It was Finlay who came to our rescue."

"Finlay?" asked Liam. "What was he doin' there?"

"How on earth did Gil get the better o' *ye*?" Ye are half again that drunk's height," Andrew exclaimed. Blushing, Angus looked away.

Little Hawk and a much chagrined Angus filled them in on the recent events as they swigged down the water. After refilling their canteens in the nearby stream, they gobbled the food Joseph provided for the tracking party.

"We'll not return tonight." Gray Wolf pointed at the setting sun. "We ought to find a safer place to camp; somewhere farther away would suit us better." Everyone agreed.

The natives were familiar with the area, and Gray Wolf knew an ideal spot beneath a rocky outcrop along the river. While Little Hawk rode in front of Running Bear, chatting happily with her brothers, Angus sensed a definite chill in the air. He knew they had not forgiven him for his escapade. *Some hero I turned out to be.*

As dusk descended, the party made camp in a secluded area along the river. Andrew slipped down to the water and returned shortly with four nice, fat fish. He fried these and supplemented them with Joseph's remaining nuts and fruit. There was some ale left to share.

"I owe ye each an apology," Angus said as he stared into the fire. "It was stupid o' me to take off alone. I didna want to wait until morning. We knew Gil had taken her, and I thought I could save her. I feel terrible about the way I treated ye." He looked at each of them in turn.

"I admit I was angry," said Running Bear. "I still believe what ye did was wrong, but my sister is safe, so I won't complain."

"Ye could've told me," Liam said softly. "I woulda helped ye."

Angus looked at his friend and hung his head. "Aye, I know. And I thought about it." He looked back up at him. "Truly, I did, but I decided it was too risky, and ye with the new babe coming, well..." Angus held out his hand. "Still friends?"

"Of course." Liam shook the offered hand and punched his friend on the shoulder.

After a while, Liam spoke up. "I still don't understand why Finlay was there. Him coming to yer rescue and all... well, it just doesn't make sense to me."

Angus agreed. "How did he know where we were? Finlay claimed he heard about it in the tavern. I didn't believe him at first, but then again, he moved my horse to safety and helped us escape. So, I just don't know."

Mentioning escape reminded him of the feathers in his pouch. He reached for his bag.

"Look what we discovered near the shed."

He pulled three striped feathers from his pouch and held them up for everyone to see.

Running Bear recognized them immediately. "Those are the same as the others. What were they doing there?"

Little Hawk shrugged. "We discovered turkeys with these same feathers in that clearing. I have never seen wild turkeys like those."

"These are the same feathers we found at the O'Donnell's," Gray Wolf pointed out as he snatched one from Angus. "Since the turkeys were at his still, does it mean Gil was involved in burning their cabin?"

"Didn't you say he was there, Angus?" asked Liam.

"Aye, he was," Angus answered him. At his reply, they all began speaking at once. Angus stood and gestured for them to settle down. "Aye, we saw him, alright. I don't know if he burned their cabin, but now I suspect he did. However, he was with his friends. Simon and Rupert were there too, remember? They are both dead, and these match the feathers I found with both bodies."

"Hmm... does that mean Gil is next?" Running Bear asked of no one in particular as he stared into the fire. "Is someone setting him up?"

"I still think Finlay is involved somehow," Liam spoke up. "He's always following our movements on the survey."

Once again, Little Hawk came to the man's defense. "I'm sorry, I don't see it that way. If following the survey is your theory, ye could argue the same for Thomas Cresap simply because he wants to ensure the border goes *his* way. And he follows ye too."

Andrew interjected, "but people have been killed over that border."

"Aye. And Cresap's been involved," said Gray Wolf. "His hands ain't clean either."

Angus had to admit that blaming Finlay was beginning to seem a bit farfetched, but he wasn't ready to let it go. "I don't trust Finley or Cresap, but I suppose they are just spying on us in their own best interests. Though, mind ye, I believe Cresap and his sons messed with our measuring chains. But we don't know who stole the harness. Or who is writing those letters? Or even who started that fight with the men?"

"But that has nothing to do with taking Little Hawk. *That* was Gil Jackson. He had it in for us afore his pa was killed," Running Bear said. He rose and stretched. "We're getting nowhere, arguing in circles. Let's get some sleep. We ought to stop by the village in the morning on our way east to let Grandmother and the others know our sister is safe, as the news will have reached the village."

"And who knows, we may get some breakfast out of it," added Gray Wolf with a grin.

After the others retired, Angus remained by the fire, staring at the clear night sky. While he knew it was too late to view Orion, he felt the hunter's presence again. He curled up in his bedroll, suddenly filled with a warmth that did not come from the fire's dying embers.

He spent his life solving puzzles. Surely he could work this out, too.

While Angus stared at the sky in the forest miles away, Charles Mason and Jeremiah Dixon were also staring at the stars in their observatory. The weather was chillier than the previous evenings, and the wind howled—however, the sky was crystal clear, and the stars glowed brilliantly. Jeremiah rose from his stool and paced around inside the tiny enclosure. He stepped outside and checked the transit before entering again.

Charles Mason, lying positioned under the telescope, scolded him. "Do ye mind? I can't work with ye lumbering about."

"Oh, sorry," the other man replied and sat. "It's just I can't stand not knowing what is happening. Where is our lad? Is he safe? Did he find Little Hawk?"

"Ye've asked those same questions a hundred times," Mr. Mason replied, looking up at him from where he lay on the ground. "I have no answer for ye. Just wait. Be patient. We ought to hear something tomorrow, I would imagine."

Dixon tried to focus on his work with great effort, but patience had never been his strong suit. Dixon poured himself into the work, and soon the familiar routine overtook his concerns about Angus.

A while later, soft footsteps approached, and there was a gentle tap on the door. Mr. Mason looked at Jeremiah, who rose to open it. Maire, wrapped in a warm cloak, peered up at him.

"Come in, lass," Jeremiah held the door for her. "Get yerself out of the night air. Now, what can we do for ye? How can we help?"

He towered above her as she entered. His smile was kind, not at all intimidating. His gentle blue eyes peered at her in concern.

"I don't mean to be a bother," she said. "I saw yer lantern lit. Would it be alright if I sat with ye fer a spell?"

"Worried about Liam?"

"Aye. And Angus, too," she answered. Mason rolled onto his side and gestured to the stool. She gratefully took a seat. "I'm a bit antsy tonight, and I just felt ye both might understand."

"Aw, don't worry yerself. Jeremiah here can't settle tonight either," Mr. Mason teased. Dixon rolled his eyes and made a face at his friend.

"If Angus is correct about Gil, the way I figure, he is probably near Lancaster, even as far as the Susquehanna River. Late tomorrow is the earliest we would hear anything, but more likely the following day." Mason smiled at her as he tried to reassure her.

"Tea?" Dixon asked Maire as he reached for the kettle on the brazier.

CHAPTER 18

The sharp ears of the natives in the woods near the gate ensured the villagers were aware of their arrival well before they entered. It seemed to Angus the entire village was there to greet them. All the Raven Clan were there, jostling and bumping into each other in their excitement. Little Hawk and her brothers hurried to dismount and greet their family. A little girl squealed as Gray Wolf scooped her up. A slender woman in a green woolen dress caught Little Hawk and held her. The smell of wood smoke filled the air.

Amidst the excitement, Angus and the others were more hesitant. This was their first visit to such a village for Liam and Andrew. However, this anxiety was short-lived as a petite older woman with long gray braids soon approached them. She wore an intricately beaded leather vest over a bright yellow woolen dress and buckskin leggings. There was a sense of authority about her.

"Soars with Ravens," said Little Hawk reverently, "these are my friends. Ye have met Angus. This is Andrew, and this is Liam." She gestured to each in turn, then, turning to the men, continued, "This is Soars with Ravens, the mother of my mother and our matriarch."

Uneasy at how to respond, Liam offered a slight bow of deference. Seeing this, Andrew copied his actions. The older woman smiled and stepped closer, her hand outstretched. Stepping forward, Angus took the offered hand first and shook it.

"Good day to ye, ma'am," he said. "I'm pleased to see ye again."

Soars with Ravens replied, "Welcome to all."

The ice was now broken, and everyone relaxed. Little Hawk was safe, and most of the people returned to their tasks, always keeping an eye on the strangers.

It was evening and growing dark when Angus came before, so he took this opportunity to study the buzz of everyday activities throughout the village. Two women worked on a deer hide stretched across a frame. The scent of urine wafted toward him as they beat on it. Next to the end of a longhouse, three more women tended herbs in a garden. Angus recognized rosemary, mint, and sage. Three young girls were grinding grain in a hollowed-out stone. Stretching beyond the village were fields of corn where several men worked. An older man returned to sharpening his knife on a whetstone. The woman in green returned to the two small girls and examined their work on a simple beading pattern on a sash attached to a piece of wood. Small baskets placed near them overflowed with beads, shells, and bone, as well as amber, ivory, and horn. Angus saw similar beadwork for sale at the trading post, and these intricate patterns also brightened several women's vests. Natives busily attended to their daily tasks wherever he looked, though many snuck surreptitious glances at the three men.

Little Hawk greeted her grandmother with a warm hug after introducing the men. The older woman approached Liam and reached out to touch his bright red hair.

"That one," she pointed at Angus' darker auburn locks, "does not have your bright color." Liam blushed as red as his hair. He froze as she reached out, his eyes wide, allowing her to run her fingers through his soft shoulder-length locks. "Very nice," she told him. Angus grinned at his friend.

The woman in green left the girls and returned. One youngster followed and showed Angus a sash she was decorating with brightly colored porcupine quills. He noted the quality of her work despite her young age. Since Soars with Ravens had accepted the strangers, it was acceptable for the others to approach them now. Little Hawk introduced the men to her mother, Gray Dove, as the woman drew near. Angus recognized her as the woman who caught Little Hawk as she leaped down from her horse.

"Welcome," she said. She gracefully offered her hand, a shy gentleness spilling from her in place of the direct frankness of her mother's handshake. She gestured at a man hurrying toward them, "and this is the father of my children, Beaver."

The man approaching was darkly tanned. He wiped his work-roughened hands on his thighs before extending one to shake each man's hand. That morning, he had been working hard, hollowing out a birch-bark canoe. The aroma of wood smoke clung to him. He hugged his daughter, muttering softly to her in their language. His eyes glistened as he wrapped his arms around her.

Little Hawk explained, "My father's name roughly translates to He who Builds, but the Europeans prefer to call him Beaver—and my father likes it."

"I must thank ye for returning our daughter," he said to the men. They each smiled at Angus, who blushed deeply. "Glad to meet ye. We were away last time ye visited, but ye left quite an impression on the village." Puzzled, the men looked at Angus. Beaver smiled as he explained, "we rarely get Europeans coming to visit."

Beaver stepped back as the matriarch stepped forward with Clever Otter.

"I must warn ye," the seer said. "The sheriff's deputies arrived last night and were looking for ye, Angus. They claim ye attacked Gil Jackson." At their protests, she hushed them. "I believe ye. I know it's not true. I'm just warning ye what is being said. That man will bring ye trouble, so beware."

Clever Otter smiled and nodded at Angus. At that moment, he understood her message. He would get through this. Angus returned the smile.

Running Bear, who had joined the group after feeding the horses, replied, "I figured he would try something. I'm betting Gil went straight to the sheriff with a whisky and a story. We stopped here to let ye know our sister is safe and unharmed. But we oughta continue back to Kennett Township. I think she will be safer there."

"And we need to let Mr. Mason and Mr. Dixon know everyone is safe," Angus said. He smiled at Liam and added, "Maire and the boys, too. And I must return to work."

"I'd like some food afore we are on our way," interjected Gray Wolf. Everyone chuckled; his ravenous appetite was well known.

Gray Dove shook her head at her son with his long, lean build, "I don't know where he puts it," she laughed.

"I think we can provide ye something afore ye go," Soars with Ravens smiled and gestured to a woman nearby who nodded and disappeared into the longhouse.

She reappeared shortly, assisted by two others, and set bowls of food on the long tables. Dried corn from the previous autumn was rehydrated, boiled with herbs, and served with dried deer meat and thick slices of brown bread. On the table were bowls of fresh berries and nuts. As the men ate, the conversation inevitably turned to current events; all were anxious to hear the latest news. The villagers seemed to agree that Thomas Cresap and Finlay Mack were likely candidates for the troubles on the survey, but opinions were mixed over the murders.

"I agree with ye—Gil ain't keen on us, never was—is that why he took our girl? Was it revenge?" an older native with a scar down his face wondered aloud. Little Hawk introduced him as Restless One.

"He and his sons were trapping out west and got caught up in the recent war," she explained.

"Aye. I was there when Haman Jackson died. That was Gil's pa," he explained.

Angus leaned in to listen to the older man's soft voice.

"Gil likes to think of his pa as a war hero, but in truth, he shot himself in the leg in a fight when he was drunk. His leg went bad, and there was nothin' anyone could do. Most people know the truth of this, but Gil won't accept it."

The natives nodded. Restless One continued. "The old man blamed it on us; we were huntin' in the area. They charged at us, firing. Haman slipped and shot himself in the leg in the confusion. A fight ensued, and we were outnumbered. That is how I got this scar." He gestured to his face. "Anyway, they took us to their camp. Haman tried to claim we shot him, but we weren't carrying pistols. The men expected me to heal his leg. But, I have little knowledge of medicine and could do nothing. When they moved on, they let us go."

Angus sat quietly, absorbing this information. No matter how he looked at it, none of it made sense. He wanted to blame Finlay. But Cresap and his sons were equally suspect. And Gil? Once again, the men discussed what they knew but couldn't come to any new conclusions.

Suddenly, the natives at the table sat up straighter, interrupting his thoughts. Angus heard hooves pounding on the hard-packed ground outside the palisade a moment later. Horses charged in fast but slowed before continuing into the village, escorted by the natives on watch. Everyone around Angus relaxed a bit as Thomas Cresap and his sons came into view. While he was known locally in Pennsylvania as the Maryland Monster, he had no issues with the natives—nor did they with him. His problems had always been with the taxmen and law enforcement along the contested border.

As he had never entered the village, Cresap remained seated on his horse until Soars with Ravens gestured to them. The men dismounted and headed toward where she stood, allowing them to approach. Thomas offered her a silver pendant in greeting.

"I come in friendship," he told her. "It is these men I wish to see." He pointed at Angus in particular. Feeling all eyes on him, Angus rose and strode toward them.

"Aye?"

The older man shuffled his feet a bit. "I came when I heard ye were in the area. It'd save me a long trip if ye would kindly take this letter to Mr. Mason and Mr. Dixon. Umm, tell them I am sorry for interfering with yer measurin'. My sons had too much drink at John Harlan's that night, and I am afraid they took my jokin' seriously. They messed up yer chains."

As he played awkwardly with his cap in his hands, he gestured to his sons, who stared at the ground and held out the missing links.

Angus was unsure what to say. The three men appeared so pitiful he could not help but feel sorry for them. On the other hand, he appreciated that the older gentleman was not in the habit of apologizing. Angus smiled as he took the letter.

"No problem. We caught the errors early on as we re-measured the distance. But thank ye for returning these." He took the links from his sons and stepped closer to the older man, saying, "I don't believe we met last time. The name is Angus McKay. I remember ye at Harlan's that night." He held out his hand.

"Thomas Cresap." He shook Angus' hand. "My sons, Daniel and Michael. My older boy Thomas is at our trading post." He paused before continuing. "I suppose ye know I been keepin' an eye on yer work." Angus nodded as the older man chuckled a bit. "Now, mind ye, I would still prefer the line to be a bit more northerly, but it seems ye ain't choosin' sides and are doin' the measurin' fairly."

Angus smiled down at the small, wiry man before him.

"Thank ye. We are trying to do our best. We signed a paper afore we left London that we would not take sides during the project. And Mr. Mason is nothing if not thorough in his work. Ye can trust him. I'd be happy to deliver the letter."

Little Hawk stood and gestured to the Cresaps, indicating space on the benches around the table. "Please, join us."

Thanking her, Thomas took the seat next to her, opposite Angus. His sons found places at the end of the table. After filling his plate, Thomas turned to Little Hawk.

"I heard what happened. I am glad to see ye home safe." He said to her gruffly, acknowledging her hospitality.

"And I am glad to be here." She smiled back.

"It bothered me to hear of it, o' course, but I can't say I was surprised," he told her.

"What do ye mean?" asked Angus, listening to their conversation.

"We were just talking about that. Many of us would put Gil at the attack on the Conestoga last year," Gray Wolf said.

"Oh, aye, he was there," Thomas replied. "Or he was braggin' later on that he was. Ye can never tell with him."

"We heard him braggin' in the tavern that he was doing it all for his pa," added Daniel Cresap from the end of the table. "Though he's drunk so often, ye can't always tell when he is braggin' or 'tis true. He gets carried away sometimes."

"Aye, especially with the drink in him. He talked about ye too," said his brother, Michael, indicating Angus. "Well, unless there are other tall redheads on the survey."

"What's this?" asked Angus.

Michael stole a glance at his father. "We were drinking in Nathaniel's place one night, a while back. Yeah... must o' been just after the fire at the O'Donnell's. After a few pints, Gil began rantin' about how Indians were burnin' innocent folks' properties. I sat there, sipping my drink, not payin' him no mind, as he always rants about the Indians. But then, he started talkin' about the survey, and my ears perked up, as that is of interest to us." He stole another glance down the table at his father.

Daniel finished the story when his brother paused. "He claimed he saw ye at the O'Donnell homestead, and ye must be involved, so how could they trust ye to do the survey?"

"Anyway," Michael continued, "his friend, Rupert, leaned toward him and said somethin' I didn't catch. And Gil punched him in the face right there in front o' everybody. Clean knocked him out... Anyway, the whole place erupted into a brawl. Rupert roused after a bit, looked about, and staggered off. We helped Nathaniel clear everybody out and cleaned up the mess." His brother nodded.

Angus and Little Hawk exchanged a look. This was getting interesting.

Michael's tale was cut off as those around him suddenly leaped to their feet. Angus realized something was happening near the entrance. A native on guard approached, leading a horse. The horse was blowing and dripping sweat as if ridden hard. The others at the table ran towards them, knocking over several benches.

Mounted unsteadily on his horse was Finlay Mack, blood covering the front of his hunting shirt and running down his one arm. As they watched, he swooned and tumbled from the horse, hitting the hard-packed earth with a thud, sending a cloud of dust.

"No!" Angus shouted. Another body. He stood rooted to the spot, unable to move as everyone rushed forward.

"Stand back!" Soars with Ravens commanded in a loud voice. Everyone stopped where they were. She approached with Gray Dove and Little Hawk. As she kneeled next to him, Finlay groaned and tried to move. His mouth tried to form words in an effort to speak, a pitiful attempt to tell her something.

"Steady," she told him softly. "We need to get him inside."

Beaver hurried off and returned moments later with a long stout piece of wood

"Slide him onto it gently," she instructed as four men carefully slid the wooden plank beneath him. "It looks as if he has lost a lot of blood."

The men slowly lifted their load as Soars with Ravens gestured to her daughter and granddaughter to follow. They were the healers. If anyone could save him, it was these three women.

Angus stood shaking, frozen to the spot, horrified at the sight of Finlay. But at least he was still alive. Finlay stretched his hand out to Angus as they carried him past, and a single feather drifted to the ground. Then, as Angus bent to pick it up, Finlay lost consciousness.

Angus stared after the party as they entered the longhouse, sending silent prayers for the health of the man he so recently believed was the instigator of the trouble. Angus paced back and forth.

Running Bear, who helped carry the wounded man inside, stepped out of the longhouse and approached him.

"He was shot," he told Angus. "But it appears the bullet went through his shoulder and straight out with little internal damage. Soars with Ravens is worried about the loss of blood. My mother will do what she can to clean the wound and ease his pain."

"Thank ye," Angus replied. "I dinnae think I could bear another death."

He crossed to the fire and sat on a stump, his elbows on his knees, his head in his hands. Liam and Andrew joined him, plopping down on either side of their friend. They sat with him in silence.

CHAPTER 19

"I don't know... maybe I misjudged the man," said Andrew eventually. "Early on, I suspected him, but now..." he trailed off.

"Aye, me too," Liam said quietly.

"I realize now that he played no part in the murders," Angus said as he raised his head. "But this is the key."

He held up the feather Finlay dropped, rolling it between his fingers.

"Finlay is telling me Gil shot him," Angus said, finding it difficult to believe. Logic was what he was good at; could he work this out?

"Though we've had trouble during the survey occasionally, it plays no part in the murders after all," Angus reasoned. He paused, trying desperately to remember all the details. "First, I found Rupert's body with an arrow in his chest. He was working for us. That sheriff seemed mighty determined to blame it on the Indians, but the fletching wasn't one that anyone recognized. It was one of these turkey feathers."

He sat for several moments, staring into the fire. Liam and Andrew sat quietly by, giving him time to focus.

"And then there was Simon. He wanted to work with us. I thought they were spies." He stared at the feather he twirled between his fingers. "His final words before he died were that he wanted to warn me about something. He, too, had an arrow in his chest."

Again he paused, his mind clicking away as if adding up numbers.

Running Bear joined them. He nodded at Andrew as he pulled up a seat.

"Ye were there too. Remember? He was shot with a rifle, not an arrow."

Andrew nodded. "Aye. I remember ye said the arrow moved when ye touched the body, and then it fell out," he said. "And we saw the hole in his back when the deputy dropped him."

At this, Angus stopped twirling the feather and looked intently at Andrew. His eyes widened, and he leaped to his feet. He removed his pouch from his shoulder and began taking items out of it, placing them on the stump. Bits of string, a small knife, scraps of paper, two smooth round pebbles, and several distinctly marked feathers spilled out. Finally, he pulled out a scrap of oily fabric from the bottom.

Holding it aloft, he stated firmly, "Rupert was shot with a rifle too!"

The other men looked puzzled, but no one examined that first body.

"I found this rifle patch not far from the body, but as I thought they shot Rupert with an arrow, I didna make much of it. Don't know why I kept it. As I think back, that arrow was loose, too. It moved when I touched it. Something nagged at me at the time, but I didna pay attention."

He peered at Andrew and watched a glimmer of understanding light up the man's eyes.

"Aye. Just like Simon. And remember? Alexander told the sheriff he heard men hunting in the woods." Angus was dead calm now. "So did we." He looked at Gray Wolf.

"It's difficult to accept." Angus shook his head. He looked at Running Bear as Gray Wolf joined them. " We first saw this fletching at the O'Donnell homestead after the fire."

"Aye. And ye believe he is trying to blame all of this on us?" Gray Wolf rose, pondering the idea. He looked at his brother as understanding dawned on them.

"Aye, I do believe he is attempting to blame ye. Foolishly, I've been connecting it to the survey, as a lot is riding on where that border falls. I've been trying to blame it on one side or the other... Cresap or Mack."

Angus had their attention now. He watched the truth dawn on each of the men.

"But it was Gil Jackson."

The men all began speaking at once.

"Aye, he feels he has motive..." began Running Bear. Gray Wolf agreed.

"I don't know," Beaver said as he joined them. "A couple o' years back, Gil saved Rupert's life when he fell in the river. He tells that tale to anyone who will listen." He paused, taking a breath. "I suppose that kept Rupert doin' his bidding."

"Rupert and Simon... they were his friends," Liam said in astonishment. "I cannot fathom that."

Their statements tumbled over each other.

"Aye, that is the sticky bit," Angus picked up on Liam's and Beaver's comments. "We know he blames the Indians for his father's death. Rupert and Simon were shot with rifles and arrows placed in the hole to disguise it." He resumed pacing. "Ye know that sheriff never examined the bodies. He just assumed Indians were responsible. But we saw that fletching at the fire. Gil was there, making sure to blame the Indians. I don't believe his being there at the same time was a coincidence. That was what Finlay told me when he handed me this." He gestured with the feather. "He saw those turkeys too and understood their significance."

"I see where ye are headed, but killing one's friends is hard to swallow," Andrew dropped on the stump, gazing up at Angus as he spoke. "I mean, he saved Rupert's life...."

"I think that is why it was so difficult for me to accept," Angus continued. "I believed Rupert and Simon were spying *for* Gil. But actually, I think he thought they'd turned on him. Ye heard what Cresap's son told us about Rupert and their disagreement in the tavern. That matches what Joseph told us he saw with Simon. Gil's friends disagreed with him."

Angus, too, sat back down. "Did he feel as if they turned on him? And was it enough to kill them?" He rose and resumed pacing.

Around the fire, the men discussed it among themselves. No one noticed a deputy had arrived. He stood behind them, listening intently to the conversation. Now he stepped forward.

"Pardon me. I came when I heard about Finlay. I didn't mean to listen, but I couldn't help overhearin' ye talkin'. Ye might be onto somethin'... I dunno," he said.

Angus rose. "Aye. I recognize ye. Ye brought the cart with the sheriff."

The deputy held out his hand. "John McDonald, I'm a deputy here in these parts."

Angus shook his hand. "Angus MacKay. I'm working on the survey." The deputy nodded, and Angus gestured for him to join them.

"Simon Tanner was a good friend o' mine. He told me he needed to tell me somethin' extremely important, somethin' I wouldn't believe, but he said he had to put somethin' right first. He needed a day or two. We were to meet, but he never showed up. He was dead." The deputy's eyes watered, and he bit his lip.

"And his last words to ye were that he came to warn ye," Gray Wolf said to Angus.

Deputy McDonald cocked an eyebrow at him. "What did he say?"

"Nothing, only that he came to warn me. He died before he could say anything else. Was that the real reason he came seeking work? So he could work up the courage to tell me something?" Angus wondered aloud. "That day at the barn, he showed up in the rain but snuck out pretty quickly when ye arrived," he said to Gray Wolf and then looked at Running Bear. Both men nodded. They remembered.

John McDonald listened as they went through the events with him. Pieces of the puzzle dropped into place.

"Gil was aware the sheriff hated the Indians and was also working with Reverend Elder to clear the lands for the settlers. He would be only too happy to blame the Indians," said the deputy. "The sheriff's idea of a perfect world does not include them."

While killing one's friends seemed inconceivable to many of the men, they eventually accepted the facts. Gil must have thought his friends had turned on him. He made no bones about blaming the Indians for his woes, especially since he blamed them for his father's death. Folks often heard him vowing to avenge his pa. If Rupert, or Simon, planned to tell the authorities, it merited consideration.

"Well, I see nothin' for it but to arrest Gil. Or, at least, bring him in for questioning," the deputy said eventually. "I'm willin' to bring him in, though gettin' the sheriff on board will be the issue. I don't expect Gil to admit to anything. However, I do have some questions I would like to have answered, at least for my friend Simon's sake." Angus saw his concern and understood the sheriff would not listen to the others. McDonald would need to get his answers before that man arrived.

The deputy suddenly turned to Angus. "Would ye care to be in on this?"

"Aye, I would." He grinned.

A few miles north of the village, Gil entered the church, seeking sanctuary with Reverend Elder. As he sat in the pew next to him, Gil related the events and explained how Finlay Mack interfered in his plans after that surveyor attempted to rescue the Indian. He told him how he had taken care of Mack when he spied him in the clearing and figured out who freed them from the shed.

"I can convince the sheriff to believe me over the rest of them. If only Mack had not interfered. He has a good reputation among the locals." The list of bodies was growing longer. Would the sheriff believe Gil or Mack? The reverend wondered.

Gil concluded, saying, "the safest place for me is with like-minded folk like yerself. Ye understand."

After listening to his tale, John Elder sighed, frowning. "What do ye want from me?"

"I am workin' on avengin' my pa," Gil told him. "Everythin' will point to them Indians. I made sure o' that. That should also help ye with your plans to clear 'em off our lands. We can work together, ye and me. Now with Finlay out o' the picture, it's my word against them Indians, and we know who the sheriff will believe." He nodded to himself in satisfaction and crossed his arms over his chest. "A beautiful partnership."

"Aye, I can offer ye sanctuary for a bit here in the church," Reverend Elder said, stalling for time. He sat with Gil, considering this news for a while. He had his own agenda, and Gil was not part of his plans. It was true; everything would certainly be easier with Finlay Mack out of his way. He'd been a thorn in his side all along. Mack always sided with the Indians, while Reverend Elder worked hard to free these lands for the settlers. In fact, he recently sent another notice to the governor informing him the Indians were acting up again. The fact that his band of boys out of Paxton were the ones causing trouble was omitted from the letter, and things were progressing well. The last thing Reverend Elder needed was for some drunk to turn vigilante.

Inspiration suddenly hit. "But you can't avenge your pa by hidin' here in the church. Let's see what happens when you find the sheriff. He'll know what to do." Reverend Elder crossed his fingers that this would buy him time to figure out how to handle this situation. Fortunately, Gil accepted it—he relaxed, a smile on his face.

After a few moments, Gil rose to his feet. "Yeah, ye are right about that, Reverend. What am I doing, hiding here in the church? I am a man of action. I owe it to my pa to continue the fight, to avenge his death. But I can't do that, sitting in yer church." He looked at Reverend Elder, who was watching him cautiously.

Gil slipped out of the pew. "Ye got yer mission, Reverend. I got mine."

He started down the aisle toward the door, muttering, "I'll give Sheriff a whisky so I can get ahead of any stories reaching his ears. News travels like lightning here."

He opened the door, not noticing the smile on the minister's face as he remained seated in the pew.

Gil's horse was grazing in the late morning sunshine right where he had left it, and all seemed quiet. Gil glanced back at the minister and waved. Then he skipped down the stairs, a smile on his face.

Gil strolled across to mount his horse, still smiling, until Deputy McDonald stepped from the shadow of the nearby trees. Along with Angus and two deputies, Gil was surrounded.

Inside the church, peering from behind the curtain, Reverend Elder watched it all transpire and smiled. He couldn't believe what was happening. The fact there were Indians there, too, pleased him. He couldn't have planned it better if he'd tried. The minister would be sure to mention that in his next letter to the governor. *Now, how should I tell the story?*

Two deputies met Deputy McDonald's party as they left the native village and had mentioned seeing Gil enter the church earlier. Upon hearing this news, the men raced straight there. McDonald filled the deputies in on the events as they rode.

As the circle tightened, Gil spun around and looked wide-eyed at the men in each direction. Angus was sure he was looking for a way out. He'd better keep a close eye on him.

"Gil Jackson, I think ye ought to come with me. I have some questions I want to ask ye," the deputy told him as he neared his horse. The lawmen left no opening for escape, and beyond them were Angus, Andrew, Liam, Running Bear, Gray Wolf, and a few other men from the native village. Escape was not an option.

"I ain't goin' with ye." Gil looked at the men surrounding him. His shoulders twitched.

"Aye. I believe ye will," answered McDonald. He gestured at the other deputies. "I suggest ye mount that horse and come with us willingly." The deputies closed the circle.

Angus watched Gil assess the situation. Gil looked at each man, his expression grim. Though his lip curled in a half-smile as he studied Angus, clearly, he did not consider him much of a threat. Eventually, Gil backed down and reached toward his horse. At that moment, Andrew moved to speak to Liam, opening a gap between the men. That slight movement caught Gil's attention, and before the deputies tightened their circle, Gil bolted past his horse.

Even before hearing McDonald shout, Angus was in motion, racing into the opening Andrew created. Gil tried to beat Angus and ran toward freedom, but Angus raced into the fleeing man's path and planted his feet. He braced and swung at Gil, catching the man sharply in the jaw and dropping him to the ground.

"That's for hitting me afore," he said, scowling at him as the others ran toward them.

Cheers erupted from Liam and Andrew as Gil dropped hard to the dirt. Angus rubbed his knuckles and smiled. That felt good.

Clutching his head, Gil half-crawled trying to get away. Angus grabbed him by the back of his hunting shirt and dragged him to his feet, where he flung him at the boots of the approaching John McDonald.

"And that's for Little Hawk."

To Gil's humiliation, Running Bear grabbed him from the ground and dragged him to the horse. With Gray Wolf's help, he hoisted him across the saddle. Angus held him firmly while McDonald bound his hands and led the party slowly to the jailhouse, keeping a tight grip on the horse's reins. Bound firmly and with a deputy riding on either side, flight was no longer possible.

The jail sat on the edge of town, a low squat building of sturdy logs with small, shuttered windows. Most of the time, the sheriff used it as his office. Prisoners were only held here until their trial, so they fortified a tiny cubicle and barred the windows.

"It's our good fortune Sheriff Brown is not here. Ye can sit out here," John McDonald took charge, instructing the others to wait in a small anteroom with benches lining one wall. Motioning Angus to follow, he escorted Gil into the inner office. McDonald removed the ropes from Gil's wrists as he indicated the chair on the far side of the desk. Gil couldn't get past it or the men in the outer room. The deputy told Angus he planned to handle matters by the book but did not completely close the door. And with Angus in the room, he had witnesses if there were any discrepancies later.

"I told ye, I ain't answerin' nothin' til Sheriff Brown is here," Gil shouted again at McDonald's persistent questioning. He winced as he rubbed his jaw, which was already turning purple and beginning to swell. A smile flitted across Angus' face, and seeing this, Gil dropped his hand into his lap.

Angus lounged against the wall as he twirled a feather between his fingers. The deputy kept at Gil, asking again, "what do ye make of these feathers?" He laid one on the table.

Gil swallowed. "Nuthin'. Just some old turkey feathers. Why?" The deputy laid another beside it. When Jackson said nothing further, McDonald picked up a feather.

"Ye know, we've only found these at places connected to ye. The O'Donnell's homestead, ye were there... The body of Rupert Jones... The body of Simon Tanner... On your own property... and now Finlay Mack." McDonald counted each item waving the feather as he spoke. He noticed Gil winced at the mention of Rupert and Simon.

"Right, Angus? Did I get them all?" At his nod, the deputy turned back to Gil. "How do you explain that?"

"What is he doin' here? And where is the sheriff?" Gil repeated. He glared at the deputy and shouted, "ye oughta be talkin' to them Indians. They are the ones causing all this trouble. They killed my pa."

"Nay, they didn't," said McDonald softly. He looked at Gil, his eyes full of sympathy at his loss. "I was sorry to hear about yer pa. But the militia report shows that his death was accidental. I know the surgeon that wrote it. He had no reason to lie. Yer pa accidentally shot himself in the leg, and it went bad. They couldn't save him. Sheriff Brown received the report a few months back."

"No. Not true." Gil shook his head stubbornly. "He'd have told me."

The deputy motioned for Angus to hand him some papers from the shelf above the desk. Angus gave him the document, and McDonald slowly slid it across the table, holding his breath.

Gil sat in his chair, refusing to look at the papers. The deputy sat quietly, waiting for Gil to say something. His chair was uncomfortable, but he did not shift in his seat. Gil continued staring at his feet, not moving, though his eyes kept drifting to the document. MacDonald knew the men were straining their ears to hear in the outer chamber.

Gil wanted to scream at the man but held himself in check.

He'd had heard that story before but refused to believe it. Now, he was confronted with the report, the government seal visible on it. He winced as he regarded the papers. That seal with its bright red wax screamed at him.

Suddenly, Gil sat up straighter in the chair. He glanced at Angus, who leaned calmly against the wall, giving nothing away. "Nay. 'Tis a lie. It's a forgery. That can't be true," he insisted.

He raised his head high and glared in defiance at McDonald across the desk before reaching out and knocking the pages to the floor.

McDonald merely nodded at the document on the floor, saying, "Aye. 'Tis true." He maintained eye contact. "I could read it to ye if ye prefer," he offered softly.

Gil was taken aback by the offer. Angus took his cue and squatted down to collect the scattered papers.

At this, Gil sat up straighter in his chair. "Nay, I can do it myself," he declared. Gil snatched the document from Angus' hands and scanned it slowly. Gil really needed the sheriff to show up now so he could ask him if it was true. That way, that redhead and McDonald need never know he couldn't read.

"Where's the sheriff?" He demanded again as he tossed the papers to the desk.

"I don't know," answered the other man, sitting back in his chair. "Big county. Could be anywhere."

Realizing this was going nowhere, Gil sulked back down into his seat, staring at his hands in his lap. He picked at the ragged edge of his fingernail, trying to buy time for the sheriff to arrive. He prayed he would come through the door soon. The minutes ticked by as the men waited in silence.

McDonald once again began twirling the feather between his fingers. Gil roused himself. Looking away from the papers, he pointed at the arrow.

"See, ye have the proof in your hand," he spat at the deputy. "*That* belonged to an Indian."

"Nay, this isn't used by any local tribes. They each have their own identifying pattern." McDonald paused a moment. "These are not wild birds, but a rare species." He held out the arrow, a glimmer in his eye. Angus saw the unspoken 'got him.'

Angus twirled the arrow he held.

Gil shifted in his seat. How was he supposed to know tribes had different fletchings? Or that these turkeys were special? And now this document? It wasn't his day. He ran a hand across his sore jaw and crumpled.

"What have I done?" He said softly, staring down at his hands in his lap. The men outside barely heard this confession.

"What *have* ye done?" the deputy asked quietly when Gil did not continue.

No one made a sound, waiting for a response. Gil brought one hand up and began gnawing on a dirty fingernail. McDonald crossed his fingers under the desk and waited. Angus leaned against the wall as the clock loudly ticked off the minutes.

Gil finally gave up. By this time, the sheriff was probably well into his third pint. He would not come.

"I had to avenge my pa," Gil paused and took several deep breaths. "We were gonna burn some homesteads and use the arrows to make people believe it was the Indians."

CHAPTER 20

The outer door exploded open, slamming into the wall behind it—and in burst Sheriff Brown, scowling. He had heard McDonald had arrested Gil Jackson outside the church from a neighbor, but no one knew why. Finding those men in his outer office only made things worse.

"What in the hell is happening here?" he thundered. He frowned, seeing the men sitting there, and glowered at each of them. "And ye? What are ye doing here?" He glared at the natives. "Get out!" He stormed off into the inner room without waiting to ensure they left. They remained seated.

"McDonald, I demand to know what is going on here," Sheriff Brown thundered.

"Based on the information I received, I brought Gil in here to talk to him a bit and ask him a few questions," the deputy answered calmly, meeting his boss' icy glare. Eventually, Brown looked away.

The sheriff glanced at Angus.

"What is he doin' here?"

"I asked him," McDonald replied.

"Well, I *un*ask him. Get out."

Angus stood firm, crossing his arms over his chest, still holding the arrow.

The realization help had arrived stirred Gil into action. He needed to deny the admission he had made. Or had he actually admitted to anything? He had only moments to devise a plan. Gil snatched the papers and waved them at the sheriff. He needed answers before he said anything further.

"Is this true?" Gil asked.

Though the sheriff did not answer, Gil saw the truth in his eyes. Sheriff Brown grabbed the report from his hands and threw it back on the shelf. With his hands on his hips, the sheriff scowled at his deputy, but McDonald only sat up straighter in his chair, meeting the man's gaze and holding it.

The truth dawning on him, Gil slumped in his chair. It was over. He and his father had bribed the sheriff to keep him on their side. And they got away with a lot. The whisky operation in the woods was only the beginning; their smuggling business grew more successful each day. Sheriff Brown, who once turned a blind eye to their activities, was a major part of their operations now. But Gil understood he could not bribe him this time. He'd gone a step too far, even for that man. Gil resigned himself to his fate.

"It's no matter now, Archie," Gil looked briefly up at the sheriff. "John here is right. I have done some terrible things." He removed the cap he still wore on his head and began running it through his hands.

The sheriff paused behind his deputy and gave Gil a slight shake of his head before resuming his pacing. Gil understood the message. He was on his own now.

Angus relaxed and leaned against the wall, his arms falling to his sides.

"Maybe now we'll get some answers," Running Bear muttered. Outside the door, the listeners let out sighs of relief. Though Gil had spoken softly, they heard him. The others nodded in silence. No one wanted to remind the sheriff or his deputy they remained there.

However, John McDonald was fully aware of their presence and was pleased the sheriff had left the door wide open when he barged into the room. Even though Angus was present, he wanted other witnesses; the more, the better. Though Gil had not specified what terrible things he'd done, McDonald was sure Gil was close to making a full confession. His chief fear now was interference from his boss. They might never learn the truth if the sheriff got in the way. He would have to tread carefully. McDonald was surprised he did not smell alcohol on him, so there was a chance the sheriff was reasonably sober. Usually, he reeked of the stuff. Sheriff Brown huffed and sputtered as he stormed about the room.

John McDonald sat patiently waiting and ignored him. He gave Gil a few moments to pull himself together before saying quietly, "I am listening if ye want to talk about it."

Gil turned from the glaring sheriff and gazed at the deputy's kind expression.

Gil swallowed hard and then took a deep breath. "What do ye want to know?"

McDonald calmly replied, "ye were about to tell me something. Feel like talking about it?" As they waited for Gil to respond, the sheriff glared at his deputy. Angus stood quietly.

"I did it. I took that Indian. I thought she would confess to being involved with my pa's death."

The deputy saw Angus clench his fists at his sides.

The sheriff started to say something, but McDonald cut him off. "I see. Now ye know they had nothing to do with it. Anything else?"

"I thought Rupert and Simon were my friends... I even saved Rupert's life. But when it came down to it, I couldn't trust 'em. I got them to help me with burnin' that homestead. I convinced 'em I wanted to get back at the Indians for the death o' my pa. Oh, they were plenty willin' at first. Rupert mentioned that the O'Donnells were away, so we decided to burn their place first. They could rebuild it. Nobody would be hurt, and we could blame the Indians. We figured the sheriff would believe us."

He glanced uneasily at the man. "It'd be so easy, and Reverend Elder would approve, too. But after *he* showed up," he pointed at Angus, "Rupert got nervous and told me he would tell him what we did since he'd seen us there. I couldn't let him do that. I had to stop him. He wouldn't listen to me."

"Nay, ye didn't... not Rupert?" the sheriff asked in dismay.

Gil looked defiantly at the sheriff. "Aye, I did. And later, when Simon also worked it out, he turned on me and ran off to tell *him*." Again, he pointed at Angus. "If they'd come to ye, Archie, we'd have been good. But I guess they both knew that."

He glanced again at the sheriff, pleading this time. The sheriff turned his back.

Gil gulped. "I couldn't let that happen, either. There were so many feathers on the property. It was easy to make the arrows to use when we burned the homestead. Oh, why don't those Indians use a rifle like normal people? I jabbed the arrows in, so it looked like the Indians had killed them. How was I to know there was something different about those fletchings?"

"But, ye shot Simon in the back!" the Sheriff sputtered.

"Yeah, he was gonna tell. He wouldn't listen to me and turned to leave." Gil paused for a bit to catch his breath. Then he turned to Angus, "though I was worried he might have told ye already." Angus shook his head. "I was afraid ye knew when ye come lookin' fer that girl. I figured ye knew it all. Otherwise, how did ye know where she was?"

"The pieces fit," Angus said. "It was the only explanation that made sense."

The sheriff took charge. "Gil, I am afraid I am goin' to have to hold ye on the charges of the murders and settin' that fire." Gil rose unsteadily to his feet as Sheriff Brown added, "oh, and I guess for takin' that girl too."

Angus said, "let's hope we don't have to add Finlay Mack to the charges."

As he asked, the sheriff's head bounced back and forth between Gil and McDonald. "Ye mean...?"

The deputy nodded. "He was also attacked. He's at the village right now with Soars with Ravens; they're trying to save him."

While they finished, Angus joined his friends in the lobby. The men sat in stunned silence. It was over. After putting Gil in the cell, McDonald came out as well. Angus was impressed by the man's analytical mind.

"I suppose ye heard it all," he said as he wiped his brow. They nodded. "Thank ye," he told Angus and shook his hand. "We got it from here." The men filed out, some quiet, some talking among themselves. No one could believe what they had just heard. In a somber mood, they mounted their horses and headed back to the native village.

In his youth, Angus had heard stories of clan members turning on each other, though he felt removed from it as a child. He shook his head to clear his mind.

In the village, everyone was relieved to hear the news. Fortunately, it was resolved, with no one being falsely blamed for the incidents. Angus counted that as a good thing.

"How is Finlay?" he asked Little Hawk as she emerged from the longhouse.

"He will make it," she said, "but it will take time afore he fully recovers. He lost a lot o' blood. He sleeps most o' the time, but that is what he needs. Ye can go in if ye want. Just don't upset him."

Chastised, Angus left her and slipped through the hide flap covering the doorway. He paused as his eyes adjusted to the dimly lit interior. Then he crossed to the cot by the fire and sat on the small stool beside it. The aroma of the pungent herbs used to ease his pain and help him sleep filled the air. He studied the man's gaunt face. Finlay's eyes were closed, his skin deathly pale. His long fingers stood out white against the dark green blanket.

"We got him," Angus said, unsure whether the man heard him. "Thank ye for the feather."

"Yer welcome," Finlay replied in a hoarse whisper, though he didn't open his eyes. "Now, ye go work on that border." His lips curled upwards slightly in a smile.

"Aye, ye are right. I ought to get back." He placed a hand gently on the man's good shoulder. "Ye get better soon, alright?"

Angus watched the man's uneven breathing before rising slowly to find Andrew and Liam. If they left soon, they could ride for a few hours, grab some sleep, and return to work the following afternoon. Angus hugged Running Bear and Gray Wolf, bidding them farewell until they returned to guide them through the wilderness heading west.

He gave Little Hawk a tighter hug. "Thank ye," he said, nodding toward the longhouse where Finlay slept. She smiled back at him.

Jeremiah was pacing as he had each day back at Bryan's farm, all ears listening for horses approaching. To his great delight, the three men finally rode up the lane. Jeremiah spread the news, and everyone hurried from all directions to greet them. Liam's sons, Michael and Patrick, climbed all over their father. The initial excitement over, everyone demanded to hear the story, all speaking at once amidst much confusion.

"Did ye find Little Hawk?" each asked.

"Aye. And solved the murders."

"Angus figured it out."

"It was Gil Jackson all along."

"What?" The Bryans said in unison. After bringing out pitchers of ale to celebrate, Martha eagerly joined in as they grabbed mugs and sat around the table. The excitement eventually subsided, and the story unfolded of Angus' escapades to rescue Little Hawk and his eventual capture. He was much chagrined, but this was short-lived as they related the tale of how Angus figured out who committed the crimes. And he became the hero again.

"That's our boy!" said Jeremiah Dixon while he and Mason clapped each other on the shoulder.

"Well, I'll be damned," said Alexander when the tale finished. "I'd never have expected that. It's hard to believe..."

Maire sat next to Liam, his arm around her shoulders. Both boys bounced on his lap.

"By the way, I have some news for the two o' ye. I was waitin' until ye returned, Liam. I saw the magistrate. He says we can do a good deal on that homestead if yer interested. It's still available."

The O'Connor family jumped up and hugged each other. They nearly knocked Alexander down in excitement as the entire family hugged him, too. Martha stood by, smiling.

Angus looked at Mr. Mason, who smiled back at him. "Aye, lad, ye are free to go with them, though I'd like it if ye would take one last look at the calculations afore ye depart. We are off to New Castle to meet with the commissioners. We hope they sign off on this location to start the border, and we can head west."

"Aye. I'd be happy to look them over for ye," Angus replied.

Early the following day, Mason and Dixon left for their meeting. His calculations were finished, and Angus joined the O'Connor family to see the abandoned homestead. Young Michael rode in front of him on his horse, pointing out everything they passed. Maire and wee Patrick rode in the cart with Alexander and Martha Bryan. It was a lively group and a beautiful May day. Angus was content, riding along next to Liam, chatting amiably.

Soon, the party reached the homestead. Liam was enchanted. The property was overgrown. However, clearing the long, thick grass would require minimal effort. Altogether, it comprised several acres, most of which were relatively flat. The original owner cleared the trees and stacked the wood neatly in a lean-to at one corner of the cabin. Liam was pleased to see a foundation for a barn and a fenced paddock. Angus walked around; this was perfect for his friend. Maire and Liam stood holding hands and gazed at the site. They grinned at each other.

The house was sturdily built of logs with a broad stone chimney. Flanking the heavy door were wide windows to allow plenty of light inside. A covered porch ran the length of the front. Maire skipped off with Martha to look inside. Liam grabbed Angus' arm, dragging him off to explore the land. Afterward, they joined the women inside.

A massive stone fireplace dominated one wall. A sizeable cast-iron pot sat on the hearth below the metal crane that held it over the fire. There were two rooms plus a loft over one end of the main room. When Michael and Patrick were older, they could sleep there. In the meantime, the family had plenty of room in the smaller bedroom. The loft held plenty of space for storage, as well. A wooden table, four chairs, and an oak hutch had been left behind. All the family required to move in was a bed. Martha had offered a wooden cradle for the baby when it came. Her youngest grandchild recently outgrew it.

Maire wandered about the space, telling Martha how she would create a lovely, comfortable home for her family. She smiled at Liam when he lifted her and swung her about in a circle. Angus laughed as she squealed.

"Will it do for ye, lass?" Liam asked.

"Oh, aye, it'll be grand," she said, grinning at her husband. "When can we move in?"

"I don't imagine it will take long, just some paperwork. Then, it needs cleaning, though I know my Martha will be dying to help ye with that." Alexander winked at Martha, who nodded. He put his arm around his wife. "And she has been putting aside some of her stores for ye to help ye get started."

"Thank ye!" Maire gave Martha a big hug.

"Ah, lass, it's the least I can do." Martha blushed.

Happily, Maire swept off the porch with the broom she found in the corner as Martha unpacked the lunch she had brought. While Maire worked, Liam, Angus, and Alexander studied a handful of the dark, rich soil. It would do, they decided.

Soon, they were sitting on the clean porch, enjoying bread, smoked ham, cheese, nuts, and berries and swigging down ale while listening to the birds chirping overhead. The two boys ran in circles, barely eating anything. Liam chatted cheerfully with Angus and Alexander about what he would do first.

"I want to finish the barn for sheep, a couple of pigs, and maybe a milk cow. But, first, I must clear the land and plant the grain. I need to start now!"

All too soon, they had to go so they could return before dark. The couple would accompany Alexander to the magistrate the following day and arrange the purchase. While he was happy for his friends, Angus realized he would miss them terribly. Liam had been at his side since they sailed out of London all those months ago. Though he would be busy with work, he hoped to visit as often as possible.

Mr. Mason and Mr. Dixon returned from their meetings to report that the point marking the northern boundary of Maryland had been accepted. However, instead of heading west to identify the colony's long border, the commissioners had decided a previously surveyed border between Maryland and the lower three counties of Pennsylvania needed to be confirmed. This was their next priority. That additional task was not in the original agreement. Mr. Mason and Mr. Dixon were not pleased with the change of plans, even though additional funds had been allocated for the task. But for Angus, it meant being close to Liam and his family for a few extra months.

Two weeks later, Angus and Andrew dismantled the observatory. When they finished, Mr. Mason and Mr. Dixon drove an oak post into the ground at the point where the zenith sector stood. On one side of it, someone had carved the word 'west.' This marker identified the starting point of their survey, the place they would return to when they continued.

While stacking the observatory sections in the wagon, the pair heard horses arrive and hurried back to the house. Four horses slowly approached the farm. Leading the group was Running Bear, followed by Little Hawk, who rode alongside Finlay Mack. Gray Wolf brought up the rear. The ride had taken its toll on Finlay, who appeared weak and unsteady on his horse. Angus grabbed the reins when they reached the house and led Finlay's horse to the porch, helping him dismount onto the raised planks. Martha spied them coming up the lane and brought out lemonade and shortbread.

Once they exchanged greetings and the latest news, Little Hawk lured the others away, leaving Angus alone with Finlay. Angus was curious why she did this until Finlay reached into his pouch and pulled out a small box. Angus felt the hair on the back of his neck stiffen.

"What is this?" Angus asked slowly.

"I paid a man to return to my home in Scotland and retrieve this. It belonged to my family for many generations," he said softly. "As I grew older, it seemed important that it stay in the family. I believed I was the only one left and the only person who knew where it was hidden," Finlay paused. It was the longest sentence he had spoken in a while. Angus waited while he caught his breath. "That ride took more out o' me than I thought." He took a deep breath. Reaching out his hand, he pushed the box across the table. "Open it."

Angus pulled the box closer as he said, "I don't understand." He was afraid to see what was inside.

Finlay smiled at him. "Just open it."

The box was made of dark wood and slightly larger than his hand. Intricate knotwork had been delicately carved into the top. The box was smooth and well-worn. Once opened, he folded back the soft blue velvet covering, revealing a sizeable, ancient-looking brooch set with gemstones in shades of red. The brooch reminded Angus of the type used on a nobleman's cloak. It was cross-shaped and beautifully made, but what struck him most was the design in the middle, which showed a hand holding a dagger with the Latin words *Manu Forti* encircling it. These were the coat of arms of Clan MacKay. Angus translated the familiar motto 'with a firm hand.'

Though forced from the family estate as a child, Angus recognized the emblem from a few items his gran kept, including the ring belonging to his grandfather. It was Angus' most cherished possession, but fearful of losing it in this unknown world, Angus had left the ring behind with his uncle in London. But this brooch? *Was this a' chrois dhearg?* His gran told him tales as a child of the Red Cross of the Templars. The clan was to hold this token for safekeeping until the order was restored. He had believed her stories were only a myth.

"I don't understand. Who? How?" he stammered. He gazed at Finlay, struck again by how familiar he seemed.

"My true surname is MacKay."

Angus sat stunned. He could not believe it and started to protest, but suddenly his mind clicked. "My pa's brother..." Fragmented memories came to Angus, a laughing young man, placing him on a giant black horse. The same man laughed, chasing him through the garden as he played with the man's large white dog.

Finlay nodded, "Aye, one and the same. My pa, that's yer grandda, and Alasdair, yer pa... gosh, ye look so much like him... they marched off to the battle to join the others up on the moor. I was almost eighteen, but I was left at home. I couldna stand it. I felt I was brave enough to go with them. Eileen and I handfasted, then I snuck off with some of the other younger MacKays to join our glorious mission. Or so we thought. The soldiers ambushed us not far from home."

He paused. After composing himself, he continued, "That's how I lost the arm. They killed some of us. I was taken prisoner with a few others and held for seven years. I was terrified to tell them who I was, so I gave my name as Mack, which has stuck with me ever since."

"Why did ye not come home when ye were free?"

"I was going to. I planned on it and dreamed about it every night of those seven years. But after I was released, I was walking home when I met up with others who told me that Pa and Alasdair were killed in the battle and the clan scattered. None knew where the rest of ye were and presumed ye were dead." Once again, he paused for a deep breath. He reached out toward Angus. "In prison, I heard yer Mam died, as well as wee Fiona, but no one knew what happened to ye and my mam."

Angus sat, fingering the brooch gently. He didn't know what to say.

"I knew that was hidden and wanted to retrieve it. I didn't want it to fall into anyone else's hands. But they almost captured me again when I tried. So I ran, and well, I just kept on runnin'. I ended up here and tried to forget."

Finlay sat a moment watching Angus, who knew that disbelief showed on his face. He was full of questions.

"I made a life here, and I won't deny it has been a good one. I have two boys and a daughter. But it is all catching me up now, and I recently wanted to try again to save the family's heritage somehow. So I paid a man to retrieve this. Then ye showed up, on the same ship, no less. Ah, Lad, it did my heart good to see ye. The brooch should be yours now." When Angus protested, he continued, "it would have gone to yer pa."

"So that's why ye been following me around?"

Finlay lowered his eyes. "It started when the commissioners paid me to follow the survey to ensure ye determined the border fairly. But then I got a good look at ye. I didn't know what to do, but I couldn't stay away after that, trying to work up the courage. I wanted to tell ye that day at the whisky still, but there was no time."

"I need time to think," Angus choked out as he rose from the table.

Finlay said, "I understand. It's a lot to put on ye. It was a shock to me when I saw ye and recognized ye as the ghost of my brother."

Angus was overwhelmed with emotion. He was making a name for himself. He had new friends who accepted him as he was. And now, he had family on his father's side and his mother's brother in London. Finlay's revelation would need time to sink in; there was much to absorb.

Angus wandered toward the fence and leaned against the gate, staring out at the darkening sky, looking at, but not truly seeing, the stars. He smiled. Life was good. He heard soft footsteps behind him but did not turn.

"Looking for Orion?" Dixon asked as he approached Angus.

"Nay." He turned to look at him, a fleeting smile on his face. "I've no need of him now."

DID YOU ENJOY THE STORY?

If you enjoyed the story, I kindly ask you to please leave a review at the point of purchase.
To follow my random history blog, please follow me and join my mailing list on the website for information on the continuation of Angus' story.

https://www.carolamorosi.com

BOOKS BY THE AUTHOR

The MacKay Mysteries:

Death on the Line

Secret of the Old Tower

Sign of Nine Stripes.

AUTHORS NOTES

As a history enthusiast, I enjoy visiting historical sites and wondering 'what if...' as I make up stories in my head. While some events and people in this story were real, all depictions of them and additional events are purely fictional, stemming from my random wonderings.

Many of the events in the story occurred:

Between 1763-1768, Charles Mason and Jeremiah Dixon surveyed the border between the colonies of Maryland and Pennsylvania using the latest technology. While writing this tale, I used Charles Mason's journal to move the plot along, my Maguffin as it were, an event of no intrinsic value to the mystery, which serves as a device to move the action forward and provide a reason for the characters to be there. I have incorporated a few of Charles Mason's comments, such as his pleasure at seeing the eclipse.

The slaughter of the Conestoga occurred shortly after their arrival, and Charles Mason recorded the incident in his journal. This is significant, as his journal consists primarily of their observations of the stars and calculations associated with them. There are few of his thoughts included. Following the timeframe of my story, in 1765, Charles Mason did visit the site in an attempt to understand what he describes as "a horrid and inhumane murder perpetrated last winter."

Several of the people mentioned lived during this time. However, many are merely names mentioned in Mason's journal, so their characterizations are purely mine.

The actions of Thomas Cresap before my story, however, are documented. He did fight for his land, which he believed was in Maryland. He was thrown off his ferry by the Pennsylvanian deputies and cut the line, sending them floating downriver instead. In 1736, Thomas and his men fortified his cabin and shot at the deputies through slots in the windows. He and his sons were actively involved in the French & Indian War. His sons and my ancestors later served together in the American Revolution in the Maryland Militia.

The Paxon Boys, guided by Reverend John Elder, known as the Fighting Parson, were real people, as were their attacks on the natives and the slaughter of the Conestoga. Reverend Elder often wrote to the Governor about clearing the lands for the Europeans.

The Harlan family became good friends of Mason and Dixon, who visited them often when there was a lull in the survey. The Stargazer's Stone still stands on the property.

Alexander Bryan (whose wife is not named in the journal) found his property dubbed the 'point marked west' in their survey. Joseph Freads was one of many who hosted the men as they passed, though no further information was given.

While many today find the word Indian offensive, it was used in all primary source material I read. In my author's voice, I have used the term native. However, in the characters' speech, they use the term Indian, as they would have at the time. The term Native American did not exist then and did not seem appropriate to use in their words.

Information specifically on the Susquehannock natives is challenging to find. Once a powerful tribe stretching up through the eastern woodlands from Virginia to New York, by this time, they had amalgamated into the Iroquois nation, and it is difficult to separate information that is uniquely theirs. What is known is that they were one of the early tribes to work with the incoming Europeans, and early primary source materials exist from those 17th-century colonists. This decision may have brought about their downfall. These first-hand documents describe them as tall and warlike. Additionally, numerous references are found to Christianity, though this may not be in the form we know it today. I have tried to incorporate what I could find without adding too much detail.

While Angus MacKay is fictional, his story and Finlay Mack's represent that of many Scottish immigrants to the colonies in the years following the Battle of Culloden.

MEET THE AUTHOR

Author-Amateur Historian-Traveler-Celtic Enthusiast

History permeates almost everything Carol enjoys, whether travel or volunteer work. Just ask her family! She enjoys gardening, especially learning about plants from the past and their culinary and medicinal uses.

Today, Carol and her husband, Dave, call Germany home, and she spends her time practicing German on their two cats and Widgit, the History Hound, who often joins them on their escapades.

Over the years, she has put her passion for history to good use as a volunteer and an interpreter spanning different periods from the Romans to the Middle Ages to the Revolutionary War, most recently as a member of the 7th Virginia Regiment.

Recently, Carol achieved a lifelong dream of participating in an archaeological dig when she joined the Melite Civitas Romana Project on the island of Malta. During their tenure in Italy, Carol took part in the Pompeii Food & Drink Study, exploring the eating and drinking habits of the residents in 79 AD. While living on the Eastern Shore of Virginia,

Carol volunteered as a docent conducting tours at Ker Place, a colonial home constructed in 1799.

Printed in Great Britain
by Amazon

18330881R00148